GBH

ALSO BY TED LEWIS

Get Carter
Jack Carter's Law
Jack Carter and the Mafia Pigeon

GBH

Ted Lewis

Published by
Soho Press, Inc.
853 Broadway
New York, NY 10003

Library of Congress Cataloging-in-Publication Data

Lewis, Ted, 1940–1982.
[Grievous bodily harm]
GBH / Ted Lewis.

1. Criminals—England—London—Fiction. I. Title.
PR6062.E955G74 2015
823'.914—dc23 2014033183

ISBN 978-1-61695-550-2
PB ISBN 978-1-61695-646-2
eISBN 978-1-61695-551-9

Printed in the United States of America

10 9 8 7 6 5 4 3 2 1

G.B.H.

1861. Section 18. Offences Against the Person Act:

"Whosoever shall unlawfully and maliciously by any means whatsoever wound or cause any Grievous Bodily Harm to any person . . . with intent . . . to do some . . . Grievous Bodily Harm to any person, or with intent to resist or prevent the lawful apprehension or detaining of any person . . . shall be liable to 'imprisonment only' . . . for life."

Amended 1967, Section 10 (2), Schedule 3.

GBH

THE SEA

A DRY LIGHT WIND ripples softly across the coastal plain, murmuring round the bungalow's corners, bound for the sand-dunes and the shuddering brittle grass.

From the bed, I stare through the window and watch some shreds of cloud pass luminously across the face of the moon. The clouds move on and the moon is solitary once more, its brilliance sharply defining the bedroom's details. A mile away, the sea is subdued as it tumbles on to the flat, hard beach. I look at my watch. It is a quarter to three.

I pick up the handgun off the bedside table and get up off the bed and walk from the bedroom into the large bare L-shaped hall. The moonlight casts the shadow of the open staircase leading to the loft, deep black on the plain linoleum floor. The floor feels unexpectedly warm beneath my bare feet. I walk towards the front door, my approach causing the moonlight to ripple beyond the frosted glass.

I draw back the bolt, unlock the door and open it slightly, quietly. The warm night wind hesitates in the doorway for a moment, then laps over my naked body. For a few moments I remain motionless, then I slowly pull the door until it's fully open. Then I listen.

There is only the soft noise from the shore and the night rustlings from the gorse and the copses and from the hedgeless water meadows that stretch away as far as the horizon. I step forward on to the tiled steps. I look to my left. Three miles away the lights of the gas terminal are brilliantly clear in the night's stillness, like a city centre without any suburbs.

I go back into the bungalow and lock and bolt the door behind me.

In the large lounge, the curtainless windows make it unnecessary for me to switch on the light. I climb the open-tread steps and walk over to the drinks and pour myself a brandy and ginger. I put the gun down on the piano and in the darkness I light a cigarette.

THE SMOKE

SAMMY OPENED THE DOOR, which surprised me, even though he was expecting me. Sammy goes through life as if he's always expecting both barrels. That being so, I'd expected his old lady. And even when he'd clocked it was me and not a different urban gorilla, his squitty little eyes swivelled this way and that, trying to fathom the Hammersmith darkness beyond the relatively large shapes of Jean and myself. What he expected to be backing us up I do not know.

Sammy stepped back and held the door open and Jean and I removed our shadows from the tatty Georgian columns and entered the yellow light that did not do a lot for Sammy's undecorated hall. Nor, when it came down to it, for Sammy's complexion.

"I got rid of Margaret and the kids," he said. "The place is clear."

"That's right, Sammy," I said. As if it wouldn't have been.

Sammy backed along the wall beyond the foot of the staircase, stopped his slithering against the first door on the left.

"I'm here," he said.

"Thanks," I said to him.

Jean looked at me, signalling her opinion of Sammy with an icy smile, and walked through the doorway. I began to follow her, but my progress was arrested more by the expression in Sammy's eyes than by anything of a more physical nature.

"Mr. Fowler," said Sammy, "I got to tell you. I don't like none of this. No way do I like none of it."

I looked at him.

"I just wanted to tell you that," he said, wishing he wasn't having to endorse what he had already said.

"Why?" I asked, and maintained the look and the longer I maintained it the less inclined Sammy was to reply. Relenting I said to him, "You don't have to stay. You can piss off down the boozer. Tell Harry for you to use my slate. Or then again, you can clear off upstairs and watch the match on TV."

"Oh, no. I wouldn't be able to turn the volume loud enough."

"In that case," I said to him, "it's down to the boozer, isn't it?"

A short silence. Then Sammy said, "Yeah. That's what I'll do, Mr. Fowler. I'll nick off down there and take advantage of your kind offer."

As if he'd come to that conclusion all by himself.

"Good," I told him.

I walked through the door and into the room.

Jean was standing by the bay window, lighting a cigarette. The drawn curtains were hidden behind the blankets which had been hung from the curtain's rufflettes. Also as per instructions, the carpet had been turned right back, and on the bare boards in the centre of the room an upright chair stood on its own. Facing the chair was a cheap divan. Next to the divan was a folding card table and on this table was a bottle of scotch, a bottle of vodka, some tonics, some ginger ales, and some glasses. Also on this table stood a table lamp, providing the room's illumination, the central light socket being, for the moment, otherwise engaged. On the floor, next to the folding table, was an aluminium bucket full of water. Next to the bucket, on the floor, was the other equipment.

I clocked all this, and then I looked at Jean, only to find that she was already looking at me. Our gazes, though apparently blank, transmitted our mutual feelings.

In the doorway, Sammy appeared, putting on his overcoat.

"Well," he said, "I'll be on my way then."

We both looked at him.

"I think everything's like what you said."

"Looks like it, Sammy."

"Right then, I'll be off, then."

He paused for a moment, like an amateur dramatic waiting to be cued off stage. Then he disappeared, and there was the sound of the front door closing.

After he'd gone, Jean said, "You think Mickey'll be on time?"

"I'd say so. He put the collar on Arthur at quarter to seven."

Jean looked at her watch. The ash broke from her cigarette and fell to the floor. "I think I'll have a drink while I'm waiting," she said.

I turned to the card table and poured vodka for Jean and scotch for myself. I carried her drink over to her and while I was handing it to her the doorbell rang. Jean didn't look at me as she took the glass from me.

I went out of the room and opened the front door. Immediately in front of me stood Arthur Philips, age early forties, hairstyle late fifties. His open-neck shirt was terylene and the suit Burton modern. Behind Arthur stood Mickey Brice, the yellow light pinpointed in his dark glasses like the eyes of Morlocks.

"Hello, Arthur," I said.

"Mr. Fowler, look—"

"In a minute or two," I told him. "Come inside first."

Behind him, Mickey began to move forward, and when Mickey does that—if you're in front of him—you have no option but to move forward as well, which is what Arthur Philips did. I turned away and Arthur followed me along the hall and into the room. Mickey closed the door behind us all.

"Hello, Jean," Arthur said.

"Arthur," Jean replied.

I stood next to the card table.

"Like a drink, Arthur?"

"Yeah, George. Yeah. I'll have a scotch."

I poured him a scotch.

"Anything with it?"

"No, thanks. As it comes."

I handed him his drink.

"Thanks."

He knocked off half of it in one go.

"Want to sit down, Arthur?"

Now Arthur was no longer able to avoid looking at the solitary chair.

"Look, Mr. Fowler, I shouldn't be here at all. Not at all. There's nothing I can tell you."

Mickey Brice went over to the chair and shifted it a couple of inches, underlining the point of my request to Arthur. Arthur knocked off the remainder of his scotch and went and sat down. Mickey Brice remained standing behind the chair. From his new vantage point, Arthur now had a better view of the accessories that lay beside the aluminum bucket.

"Why don't you start by giving us what you can?" I said, refilling his glass.

Again, Arthur swallowed the first half.

"You know what I can tell you."

"Why not tell us again?"

Jean walked over to the card table and topped herself up. Arthur breathed in deeply.

"Well. Of course, I know all about the job, I mean. There was Lenny White, Tommy Coleman, Maurice Hutton, Billy McClean. So the job goes right. Well, it would, with them on it, wouldn't it? And the finance, well, it had to come from you, with that pedigree, right? Your law knows that, and the Heroes, they know it, too. They know who to collar, but of course they can't, it being Sellotaped up, as always is."

Arthur punctuated his monologue with another belt of scotch.

"But the Heroes pull in Tommy Coleman anyway, and it's not just for show because they roll out two witnesses contradicting the time and location of Tommy's fairy tale. So he's still down there and him and the Heroes are still talking to each other."

"Which leads us to suppose?"

"Well, whoever the convener is, it's got to be one of the workers. Somebody what knows what the rest of the community knows."

"That's right. So why should one of the workers want to speak out against the union?"

Nothing from Arthur except silence.

"Arthur?"

"Well, one of the Heroes could go to one of the workers in the way they sometimes do, and say to the worker, look, I know you weren't on that job, but it was your *kind* of job, and you know who was on it, and if I wanted to, I could fit you up for being on the job you weren't on, so how about it?"

There was no response from any of us. Arthur broke the silence by downing the remains of his drink.

"Give Arthur another one, Mickey," I said.

Mickey took the glass from Arthur's hand and as he walked to the card table he brushed against the wires that hung down from the central light socket. They swayed towards Arthur. He leant away from them as though they were poisonous snakes about to strike. Which, in a manner of speaking, they were.

Mickey gave Arthur his glass back.

"Well, that's what you told Mickey previously," I said. "Which is fair enough, because I said you could do that. But now I'd like to hear a different story."

"I can't tell you anything else," Arthur said, looking into my face. "Honest."

"You haven't got a different story?"

Arthur shook his head.

"Pity."

I went over to the drinks and poured myself another one. The silence in the room was terrific. I splashed ginger ale on top of the whisky.

"Take your pants off, Arthur."

"Mr. Fowler," Arthur said, "I'm straight up. Honest I am."

"Do it for him," I told Mickey.

"Listen—"

Mickey cut Arthur's sentence short by going to work on him. When I turned round from the table Arthur's trousers and underpants were round his knees. Mickey took the glass from Arthur's hand and put it back on the card table and then he picked up the short strands of rope from next to the bucket and tied Arthur's ankles to the chair legs and his arms behind the chair back. After he'd done that Mickey moved the bucket a little closer to where Arthur was, causing a few drops of water to jump over the bucket's rim and slop down on to the bare floorboards. Then Mickey taped Arthur's mouth shut with some gauze and plaster.

"We'll give it a go with the gag a couple of times, Arthur," said Mickey Brice. "You'll scream, and you'll want us to take it off so we'll be able to hear you scream and tell Mr. Fowler what he wants to know. But we won't do that at first. Like I say, we'll give it a couple or three goes so you can get used to it."

Mickey took his gloves from his pocket and put them on, then gathered the dangling wires to him, taking hold of them not quite at their naked ends. I was suddenly conscious of Jean's perfume as she moved very quietly to stand by my side. Now the games were over.

THE SEA

EVEN JEAN DOESN'T KNOW about the bungalow.

Didn't know.

It's been in existence for seven years. Nobody in the area knows who it belongs to. Not even the builder, nor the agent I went through. Of course there was a name on the cheques they got, nice cheques that encouraged them to comply with my specifications and furnishings and deadlines. I've only been here four times since it was built, which in a way is a pity; it's really very nice indeed. And when I'm not in residence, the arrangement is that the agent takes care of its maintenance. When I am, a phone call tells him not to, and another phone call reactivates him when I've gone.

In the specifications the safe was naturally of extreme importance, as was the cellar. Over the phone the agent once asked jokingly, when he was informed of the cellar's specifications, if I knew something about the state of détente the President of the United States didn't. I didn't mind him having his little joke. But I did tell him that I considered the amount of money he was being paid entitled me to the rights in his material. After that he maintained a seriousness appropriate to the business in hand.

From the outside, the place doesn't look much, what you can see of it beyond the remains of the copse. There are two bedrooms. The lounge runs the whole length of the house, the side that faces east, looking over the lumpy flatness of the gorse and the mild ripples of the sand dunes beyond and the unseen lapping of the sea made distant by the enormous expanse of unmarked sand that stretches a quarter of a mile from the dunes before it is troubled by the sea's first overlap. All this seen and unseen is witnessed through a window of dimensions similar to the one in the Penthouse. Only the aspects are different.

When you walk into the lounge, this window is to your left, but its sill, if you are of average height, about a foot above your eye level. But then when you cross the room's first space and climb the broad open-tread staircase to the room's second, broader level, the base of the window is level with the welts of your shoes, if you're wearing any. Academic, really. After the builders had gone home, myself apart, only the agent and the agent's man had ever set foot in the place.

Now, from this new elevation, you would be able to glimpse, beneath the soaring eastern light, the sea, made narrow by the preceding breadth of flatness of gorse and beach. And having gained the room's higher level, at the room's far end, you would be faced by brickwork, wall to wall, ceiling to floor and, in this wall, a small open fireplace, aluminium trimmed. The only other break in this wall's deliberate monotony is a four-foot-by-three-foot painting by Allan Jones and a narrow cupboard door beyond which is a trolley that supports two movie projectors, a sixteen-millimetre and an eight-millimetre. Ranged close to this wall, almost huddled around the fireplace in deference to the impression of coldness caused by the room's lengthy perspectives, is most of the room's limited furniture, low and comfortable. The wall on the right of the room is covered by a shelving unit, which extends from the brick wall to the edge of the drop down into the room's lower level. Apart from a couple of hundred books which, despite the central heating, provide the room's only impression of concentrated warmth, this shelving also supports the drinks supply, the TV and the stereo unit with all its records and tapes. Just in front of this shelving unit is a jet-black grand piano parked almost at the brink of the drop into the lower level and directly beneath the room's raised level is the bungalow's garage, at present housing an unostentatious Marina.

On the brick wall, close to where it converges with the shelving unit, is a small panel of switches, one of which operates the movie screen that slides down from the ceiling if you want it to.

At the moment, I don't want it to.

I climb the open-tread stairs and go over to where the drinks are and pour myself a scotch and look at Jean's photograph, which I'd forced myself to take from my briefcase and place on the piano a couple of days before.

Up until now, I've avoided looking at it, just as I'd put off taking it out of the briefcase.

The photograph is one I'd taken a few years ago, on our honeymoon, the first time she'd seen the villa in Minorca. She'd been standing by the edge of the pool naked, poised for diving in, and I'd called her name, causing her to turn, but she had already too much momentum from the intended dive and I'd snapped the shutter just as she was going into the point of no return between the edge of the pool and the water. Her laugh is frozen in the warmth of the Spanish sunlight.

I take a drink of my scotch and then stop looking at the picture and walk over to the window and look at sunshine of a different kind as the March wind blusters across the broadness of the sky and the sea beneath.

THE SMOKE

IN THE LIFT UP to the Penthouse, Jean was quiet and tense. She held on to me as if I provided some kind of stabilising quality, as though I was supporting her against some form of vertigo. Although there was no longer any need to discuss what Arthur had told us, the course of action cut and dried and needing only implementation, the silence was not for lack of subject matter; in fact just the opposite. Perhaps the expression of our mutual thoughts could not be achieved fully by mere conversation.

The lift stopped, the doors slid softly apart and we stepped out on to the private landing. Below, very faintly, the sounds of the club murmured upwards like the sound of very well-oiled, precision-engineered machinery. Jean still clung on to my arm as we crossed the landing.

Gerry Hatch rose from the landing's only piece of furniture, a sand-coloured hide armchair. He left the copy of *The Ring* behind him on the dimpled seat.

"Mr. Fowler," he said. "Mrs. Fowler."

He took out his own set of keys and unlocked the double doors that opened directly on to the main room of the Penthouse. He closed them behind us and went back to wait for Ernie Hildreth, the night shift.

I stood just inside the doorway and took off my overcoat. Jean had halted at the top of the steps that led down into the sunken central area of the room, her coat still draped round her shoulders, a negative silhouette against the blackness of the picture window that composed the entire wall opposite her, a window that always seemed a carpark's length away. Lights decorated the rain-speckled glass like paint splashes on an abstract. I joined her at the top of the steps and draped my overcoat over the retaining rail. On the low glass table in the centre of the sunken area, Harold had left salad and a choice of rare beef or chicken, and also champagne.

"You all right?" I asked.

Jean didn't answer. Instead she walked down the steps and sat down in the deepness of one of the long hide sofas that were fitted flush to the area's sides. She sat crouched forward a little as if she had stomach ache, or was cold. The coat was still draped round her shoulders and she stared at the food on the table in front of her.

I walked down the steps and took the champagne from the bucket, flipped the cork and poured some of it into the glasses.

"Your very good health," I said to her.

No response.

"Or should I say to our continuing good health, in view of information received?"

Instead of picking up her glass and drinking, Jean tore one of the legs off the chicken, studying it for a moment before beginning to eat.

I drank my champagne and poured some more. Then I walked over to the phone and lifted the receiver.

"What are you doing?" Jean said.

"Calling Collins. Why?"

"Do it later."

"You what?"

Jean put the chicken leg down on the table, stood up and walked over to me. Her coat was still round her shoulders and her lips shone with grease from the chicken. She put her hand between my legs.

"Now," she said.

"I don't want to miss him."

Her grip tightened on me.

"No. Do it to me now."

She was still chewing and a sliver of chicken spilled from the corner of her mouth but neither stopped her from kissing me and putting her arms round my neck and bending her legs so that her dead weight began to overbalance me and tug me down to the floor. I fell on top of her and her legs closed tightly together and then began to slither against me frantically in expectant ecstasy. Her hands almost ripped my zip apart.

"Do it now," she said. "For Christ's sake."

THE SEA

I COME TO THE end of the lane that leads through the gorse to the sand dunes. Then the lane becomes a concrete path that the Ministry of Defence has laid to give access between the dunes to the beach beyond. I automatically read again the sign that warns that if the red flag is flying so is the RAF, strafing the shells of old tanks and army lorries that are dotted around on the beach's vastness. Today the flag is not being flown.

I walk between the dunes, over the slight hillock made by the concrete path, then I descend the mild gradient and now the dunes are behind me and beyond there is only the sea and the beach.

About half a mile to my left one of the rocket-blasted tanks squats like a fly on the edge of a table. I begin to walk across the flat sand towards it. Here there are no ripples in the sand left by the sea's retreat; they don't even begin until a couple of hundred yards from where I am, approximately where the carcass of an old transporter stands, the only object to give scale against the low line made by the joining of the sea and the sky.

As I walk towards the tank, I walk alongside the undisturbed footprints of my journey of the previous day, and the day before that, and as I walk the thoughts I have are the ones that also remain from the previous journeys, and will continue to haunt me.

One of my interests was office equipment. I'd got four shops, and a couple of warehouses. Not one inch of the business smelt. Not one filing cabinet, not one fifty-pence piece. If anybody working in that particular branch of the business had walked in carrying a box of bent carbon paper, he'd have been out on his arse and his cards slung out into the street after him one and a half seconds later. I had two or three businesses like that one.

It was in the London Bridge branch I met Jean. She was one of the workers. Harris was leaving. Paul Edmonds was in charge of the overall business and he promoted Jean and not only because her promotion was strictly in order. It didn't do him any good though because in due course I met Jean and after that he walked around with pennies in his eyes so nobody'd tell me he'd even looked at her.

Of course, it's not like they'd have you believe in the programmes on the box. You don't go down to the nearest watering hole after you've made your first million and tell the first clippie you set eyes on how you got it. Nor do you talk before you make it . . . otherwise you don't. Witness all those sad stories you read about in the newspapers where they were dead unlucky not to hang on to their wages for more than five minutes between stretches.

When I met her, Jean was living in Orpington. She had a house there. The divorce was under way and the house was to be part of the settlement. At the time he was in California wearing flowered shirts and rediscovering his misspent youth in singles bars. He'd said he wanted to be free. He'd played the field before, of course, but that wasn't the same as freedom. They'd married too young, he'd said. When I met her, when we got to talking that way, she told me that she'd never get over him, not ever. They'd loved each other so much it hadn't seemed possible it could have happened, she told me.

Well, that was all right. I wasn't in any particular hurry. She was thirty-three, and time was on my side, not hers. I took her out, the way bosses take out their employees, not giving her the Kilburn Rush. Other more highly paid employees of mine could satisfy my transitory urges, and on office time. As it happened it was three months before I discovered her hair was not its natural colour, and it was two years before she discovered who I was. That was a week before we got married and by that time it didn't matter any more. There had been other difficulties, though.

THE SMOKE

COLLINS CAME ROUND A couple of hours later and he didn't like it. But how could he do the other thing?

He sat down on the sofa, his fat backside causing ripples of contained displacement on the hide's surface. I poured him some of the champagne that was left, then I sat down on the sofa opposite and looked at him. He was as neat and well dressed as ever.

We both drank.

"How's Jean?" Collins asked.

"Fuck that," I replied.

Collins drank some more champagne.

"Why didn't you get in touch before?" I said. "Before all that shit started going down at the station?"

"It was difficult. There was nothing I could do without drawing attention to our relationship."

"Don't do a number on me, Dennis. Everybody down there knows what our relationship is. That's what you're there for."

"That's the point. After Arthur spoke to Farlow they just stood around waiting to see what I'd do. Collar Terry or phone you. They were running a book on it. Whatever they *know,* I had to collar Terry so that justice was seen to be done. Otherwise it would have given Farlow the opportunity to talk to the Commissioner."

I had a few thoughts about Farlow.

"Ever thought about squaring Farlow with us?"

Collins shook his head.

"I don't trust him."

"We could offer him more than the Shepherdsons do."

"He wouldn't. It's a matter of principle. Besides . . ."

"Besides?"

"If he worked for you, either you or him or the both of you might conclude that I was superfluous."

"How could I ever arrive at that conclusion, Dennis? If I ever gave you to the papers you wouldn't leave me out of your memoirs just for old times' sake."

I poured some more champagne.

"When was Farlow expecting Arthur to write it all down and have it Morocco-bound?"

"I don't know. The good thing for us was that they had me fetch Terry in before he got the statements from Arthur and the other two. He was so excited he came before he got his trousers off."

I drank some champagne.

"How is Arthur?" said Collins.

"Well, there didn't seem any point in hanging about."

"And the other two?"

I looked at my watch.

"They should have gone missing about now."

"Mickey?"

I nodded.

"That's all right, then."

He took a sip of his champagne and eyed the food.

"Well," he said, "as you plucked me away from mine, what about some of yours?"

"Dig in."

Collins picked up my unused plate and began to unload some of the beef on to it.

"Even so, Dennis," I said. "I'm still not happy about the time element."

"I told you," he said, excavating some stuff from the salad bowl, "there wasn't an awful lot I could do."

THE SEA

THE TANK, LIKE IN dreams, doesn't seem to get any closer. As the morning has lengthened the wind has dropped, its absence somehow seeming to lengthen the perspectives.

Consider a man like me and love. A butcher loves. He slits an animal's throat and dismembers it and washes the blood from his skin and goes home and goes to bed with his wife and makes her cry out in passion. The man who made it necessary to rebuild Hiroshima loved and was loved back, and I don't necessarily mean the pilot or the man who activated the bomb doors. Whoever left the bomb at the Abercorn rooms would comfort his child if it came into the house with a grazed knee. Everybody loves. Everybody considers things, considers themselves. And I considered why it came to be that Jean should be the one, as opposed to anyone else. And like everyone else, I could compile a list of things that added up to my obsession, and as with everyone else, it just remained a list; the final total defied the simple process of addition.

Her husband couldn't have timed his return from California any better. A couple of days after we'd made love for the first time. For a week I didn't see her; I waited for her to get in touch with me. When she did, she suggested we have lunch together; it was going to be one of those meetings.

We met in Al Caninos. For some reason, it was a place she liked.

She told me that everything was going to work out. What I had to understand was that he'd had to do what he'd done. It was wrong and he'd regretted it almost as soon as he'd gone. Now he was back and he'd been to see his old firm. They could still use salesmen of his calibre. There was no longer any need to progress with the divorce. There would be no more playing around, no recurrence of the freedom urge; home was now where his heart would be.

"Well," I said, "what can I say? That's the way things go. There's nothing I can do. Other than to wish you all you wish yourself." She thanked me for being so understanding. Few men would have the grace to be like that, she said.

THE SMOKE

MICKEY DIDN'T COME IN to see me before ten o'clock. He never did. Not even in a situation like this, when he had yet to report the success or otherwise of locating Wally Carpenter and Michael Butcher and getting rid of their bodies along with the one that used to belong to Arthur Philips. There was no need for Mickey to phone me in the middle of the night. That's how much I trusted him, and he knew it. A matter of delegation.

By the time he'd arrived both Jean and myself had bathed and breakfasted and she had gone through into the office to do a weekly check on various returns. I was sitting at the Swedish glass-topped desk with my back to the window, drinking coffee and reading the *Express*'s report on the match between QPR and Spurs. There wasn't a great deal of doubt about it; Spurs were going to go down, whichever way you looked at it.

During breakfast Jean and I hadn't spoken much. The topics had been restricted to pass the toast and more coffee. But there would be time to talk after the day's business had been attended to.

"Well, Mickey?" I asked.

"Clockwork," he said, pouring coffee into the extra cup I'd made ready for him.

He drank and sat down on the opposite side of the window.

"Although," he said, "it was lucky for us it all went down so quickly."

"That's what Collins said," I said.

"They were all arse about front. The arrangements came second. Beyond me, really."

"Where were they?"

"At what Carpenter used to laughingly call his *pied-à-terre* in Brighton. I really believe he'd convinced himself there was only him knew about it."

"How did it go?" I asked, out of interest.

"I phoned him up. An anonymous well-wisher. Then I waited in Wally's motor. They came out on rollerskates. Then I sat up and told Wally where to drive to. After that I drove back to town and put the bodies with Arthur's. When I'd done that I drove the motor round to Cliff Wray's."

That meant that the car would have been done over from plates to bodywork and by now it would be nice and shiny and on sale on the forecourt of a particular Ealing garage. I didn't insult Mickey by asking him whether the bodies would also be recoverable.

"Thanks, Mickey."

Mickey just made a vague gesture with his hand, causing his identity bracelet to jingle slightly. If you ever got close enough to read it, all that was inscribed on the metal was the single word, KISMET. It wasn't there just because he'd enjoyed the movie.

He clocked the *Express*'s back page and swivelled the paper round on the glass surface so he could read the result of the match.

"Jesus!" he said.

"Well, there you go. You could see it coming last season."

"They should never have elbowed Billy Nick. He was a governor."

"Well . . ."

Mickey studied the paper a little longer, then swivelled it back so that the print was again readable from my position. Then, for a little while, the sky beyond the window behind me appeared to occupy his attention.

"What is it?" I asked him.

He focused his eyes on the edge of the desk, and began to run his thumbs along it.

"I was thinking," he said.

I waited.

"Last night," he said. "You never been there before. What I mean is, not since a couple of months since I joined the firm."

I waited some more.

"And Mrs. Fowler. I know how you and her, you know, sort of come to joint decisions, in many things."

I smiled.

"No need to worry about that, Mickey," I said to him. "You should know by now, anything like that, it's just not on, is it? I mean, you're a major shareholder. That, if nothing else, proves my confidence in you."

Mickey sniffed.

"Well, I shouldn't have mentioned it, really," he said.

"Well, there was no need to."

"No."

Mickey sniffed again, then stood up.

"Anyway," he said. "I'm on my way over to see Maurice Ford. Just a check. Anything you want me to say to him?"

"Not that I can think of. Of course, any unforeseen eventualities, it's up to you what you say to him."

"Right," said Mickey. "I'll be off then."

He tapped the edge of the table once with his knuckles, then walked around the sunken area and opened the doors and closed them behind him.

I looked at the newspaper in front of me. The photographs showed Stan Bowles thrusting his fist up into the air as he turned away from the goal seconds after he'd scored the clincher.

A very clever fellow, Mickey was.

THE SEA

THE TANK ISN'T GETTING any closer.

I didn't go to the funeral. As I said to her later, it would have seemed like an intrusion into her private grief.

Afterwards, of course, she'd had to admit, those months between his return and his final farewell, so to speak, those months had been a strain. It hadn't been the same, whatever she'd told herself. Oddly, she said, a lot of the strain came from him, trying to show her how sincere he was in his declarations. She should have realised, of course, *why* he'd tried to impress her. Ironic, she said. She wouldn't have found out if it hadn't been for the crash. Who the girl was, the police had never been able to discover. Both bodies had been burnt beyond recognition, but you would have thought *someone* would have come forward, somewhere, to report a girl of her age gone missing. She hadn't been from his head office, or from any of the branches. She could have been from one of the firms he called at, but, as Jean said, if she had been, *someone* would have connected the two of them some time. The only evidence of her existence, apart from her remains, came from the publican who ran the pub near his head office, where he often used to drop in for a drink. All the publican could say was that on that particular night, the night of the crash, Jean's husband had been having a quiet drink at the bar when this girl had come in, on her own . . . nothing unusual in that these days. The two of them had got talking. Nothing unusual in that, either. The publican did hear something, when they left, about could he drop her anywhere? Jean had been particularly cynical about that bit: he'd been so careful, even in a place they never went together.

Nobody could really explain the accident. Well, a dozen witnesses, they see a dozen different things; some of them said the car behaved as though a tire had blown, which was impossible to check, the state the motor was in; but they all agreed he must have been doing seventy-plus when he crossed the central reservation. Amazing how, in the resulting pile-up, he'd only taken another two with him, along with the girl.

Regarding that, Jean had been particularly bitter; the other innocent deaths, as much as anything, contributed to his memory becoming more to her than just the literal ashes he had become already.

I'd told her, look, you mustn't dwell on things like that. An accident's an accident. They happen every day.

THE SMOKE

AFTER MICKEY'D GONE, I went through into the office.

Jean was leaning back in the chair behind her desk. Some of the books lay open in front of her. The grey Soho daylight diffused her thoughtfulness. My entrance did nothing to break her present preoccupation.

I sat down by the window.

"You haven't had your coffee yet," I said.

She shook her head.

"You want me to give Gerry a buzz?"

She shook her head again.

"The mail order," she said.

"What about it?"

"Well, at present, there are eighty-four agents."

Which was right: throughout the country, there were these offices, at present numbering eighty-four, run by an agent each with a phone and a typewriter and an addressing machine and nothing else but wall-to-wall brown envelopes. And of course, the merchandise, that being the Blues. This side of the business, being of its particular nature, meant a lot of changing of offices, even with what we paid the law, but apart from that, the overheads were very low. You won't believe how much that side of the business takes. It takes over £1,200,000 a year. I told you you wouldn't believe me. Nobody does, not even the agents, who have no idea how many other agents there are. Except for the law, of course, who in a way are like an extra agent with their ten percent. They know. That's why they ask for so much. If you still don't believe it, look at it this way: each agent has a list of around one thousand clients. They renew a movie once a month, sometimes more than one movie, at our competitive part-exchange rates of £10 a go. The agents do this renewal for them automatically. You can work out your own arithmetic.

This was just one of our businesses.

What Jean did was to check the books. There were other employees who did them, but Jean checked them. She was good at it. The only other area of the business over which she was in direct control was quality control of the girls, and not the ones you can get for a hundred quid a go. She looked after the expensive ones.

Other business matters were attended to by Mickey and myself.

I lit a cigarette and nodded in assent to the number of offices we had.

"Yes," she said, because it hadn't been a question.

I waited.

"And none of them have closed recently," she said.

Another non-question. I waited again.

"In that case I can't make a great deal of sense out of these figures," she said. "Of course, they add up. But compared to the figures for the previous three-month period, they don't."

"McDermott told me he'd had to do a bit of juggling in the Coventry area; we had to set up a couple of new addresses."

"I'm not talking about that kind of thing. Come and look at this."

I got up and stood next to her and leant over the desk. Jean pushed two books side by side. I looked at one set of figures, and then at the other. Then I looked at them again.

I didn't say anything.

"You see what I mean," she said.

THE SEA

I CLIMB THE TANK and sit on top of the turret which has been fused forever to the rest of the metal by the pounding of the rockets. The surrounding flatness causes my present position to seem doubly elevated and the sea takes on a greater illusion of depth.

I light a cigarette and then I withdraw the hip flask from the pocket of my anorak, take a long pull, and wait till it hits. Then I take another drink and set the flask down on the rim of the turret. The blackened cannon points out to sea in metallic parody of Millais's *The Boyhood of Raleigh*.

Of course, in many ways, Jean would have been an ideal choice to look after the business, if I'd been looking for a partner and not only a wife. As I'd been looking for neither, her business sense had been an additional bonus. But I could never have considered her as either until I'd discovered what her reaction was to the real nature of myself and of my occupations.

For a long time, I held off. A long long time. Even in the normal way of things, I stayed away from her for six weeks after the tragedy.

And after that, when things had taken the course I'd known they would, it had been a very gradual process; after all, before the snowball could begin to gain momentum, I had to find out as much about her as she was going to know about me.

But I'd never expected her to assume the mantle I'd gradually extended to her in quite the way that she did. People are a constant surprise; everything conceivable is in them, but very few people know of the possibilities beneath the surface they assume to be themselves, even fewer have the courage to dismiss their former selves as a mere cocoon. Later in our married life, she'd told me that there had come a point at which anything I'd casually hinted at had not only been expected but eagerly looked forward to. And when the barricades were finally down, each new aspect of the view into my world opened up new insights into herself, her reactions tipping and tilting horizons never even considered before. She was like an instant alcoholic with a life pass to a distillery. Literally, after her husband's death, she became a new woman.

THE SMOKE

"IT LOOKS LIKE A case of overconfidence," said Jean.

I stood by the window and lit another cigarette.

"I'm going to have to go right back," she said, looking at the books. "This didn't start yesterday."

I didn't answer. If there was anything I hated, it was something like this. You paid them more than they could ever hope for, and it still wasn't enough.

"How long will it take?"

"God knows," she said.

"There's no point in saying anything to Mickey yet."

"No."

Through the window I watched a jet as it dawdled across the sky.

"Anyway," I said, "I'm going over to the Steering Wheel."

"Do you think that's a good idea?"

"I think it's a very good idea."

I went out of the office, poured myself a drink, carried it through to my dressing room and began to change into one of the suits that had just been sent over from Rome. While I was doing that Jean came into the room and in the mirrored walls I watched from about forty-eight different angles as she took off her slacks and sweater. Then I watched her progress as she walked over to me and leant against me and put her arms round my waist and dug her fingernails into my stomach. When she spoke it was no longer in the businesslike tone she'd used in the office.

"What happened to Arthur?" she said.

I turned to face her. Now her hands slid up to my shoulder-blades and the nails dug in again as her hands trailed slowly back down my spine.

"Mickey's seen to him."

The nails dug deeper and she pressed herself even closer. Her eyes were intense but at the same time her eyelids drooped, hooded like a goshawk's. I knew what she wanted to say to me, what she wanted to express, but to put it into words would be to reveal her feelings too nakedly. I knew the feeling well; it's like when you have your finger on the trigger and as you breathe in to squeeze, you hold the breath as if to freeze the second before firing, before the final act of commitment. But, in any case, I knew exactly how she felt; her body was telling me, and my own body was recognising the signals with ease, because it was reacting in exactly the same way. The Steering Wheel could wait.

THE SEA

I DROP MY CIGARETTE into the well of the turret and take another pull at the flask. I look at my watch. It's a quarter past eight. By the time I walk back to the bungalow and drive the Marina into Mablethorpe the parts of the town that are open out of season will be open. I have a final pull at the flask, put it back in my pocket, jump down from the tank and begin to add another line of footprints in the sand to keep the others company.

As I walk I light another cigarette and the image of Mickey Brice comes into my mind, not as I saw him the second before he died, but at Ling House, Courtenay's place, a few miles out of Newmarket. It wasn't only the races we'd gone there for.

As long as someone like myself is successful and safe enough to be respectable, like a firm star or a singer or a footballer, there will always be people like Courtenay. He liked to associate with people at the height of their particular profession. Not having a profession himself, just a title and a few thousand acres and houses in and out of London and a fortune he needed help in spending, Courtenay liked collections of those who'd had to work for their glittering prizes under his various roofs. Of course, he chose his house guests very carefully. Even with all his money, he felt the indiscreet could lead to costs far beyond mere financial ones.

Even so the entertainments Courtenay provided for his guests had gained a guarded reputation among the select; to be invited to a Courtenay weekend was both an honour and a challenge to the sexuality of the people behind the personalities.

Myself, I didn't go all that often. It was coals to Newcastle. Mickey was quite a regular visitor, though. He and Courtenay got on extremely well, being the way they were. I didn't mind. Whatever Mickey did in his own time was his own business.

When I got the invitation for this particular weekend, I accepted. I'd known Jean for just over a year. It had seemed a suitable occasion to demonstrate that what was indulged in by people in private was not unique, and was often publicly demonstrated in the best of circles. And as Mickey was going as well, his presence and participation would perhaps ease her from one concept to another.

This particular weekend, Courtenay had a large square of coconut matting on the floor of what he smilingly referred to as his Games Room. Silk cushions big enough to accommodate three or four people at a time had been placed around the matting, providing another distinctly more comfortable square. Around eleven in the evening, everyone combined as an audience on the cushions. Courtenay's bearers kept everyone supplied with what they were drinking or whatever else they were on. From the official guest list, only Mickey was absent from the cushioned audience, albeit temporarily. The lights were already dim, but when the main event began they were switched off completely and only a central spotlight provided illumination.

Then Mickey reappeared, accompanied by another man equally well-built, and a very beautiful girl of twenty-three. I can be precise as to that, as she was one of mine. All three of them were almost naked. The other man carried some short slim lengths of nylon rope. He dropped them on the corner of the matting as he stepped onto it.

The idea was for Mickey to take on the other two in a bout

of wrestling, and although all-in, not of the variety transmitted on Saturday afternoons. For one thing, submission in this little charade had a different meaning; if Mickey emerged dominant, he dictated the kind of submission the other two were to submit to. But before that, he had to be able to have tied them up in order to proceed; and vice versa, if Mickey was the loser. For a lot of the audience, of course, the journey would be just as exciting as the arrival. It certainly had been for Jean. Propped next to her on the cushion, I could feel her body transmit the heat the contest generated as the trio writhed on the matting, the two trying to overcome the one and vice versa, all playing it very much for real, until Mickey decided it was he who was going to submit; he wouldn't have unless he wanted to. The ropes securing his hands behind his back were finally knotted and the other two went to work on him.

Then, after it was over, Mickey was released, and the trio were refreshed with champagne before the next event. For this a female member of the audience was to be invited to join, this time with Mickey against the other man. As I'd seen it all before I knew how the plot would work out. This time Mickey would win, and then whoever the girl was, she would help Mickey do to the other man what he had done to Mickey, and after that, unexpectedly, the girl who had previously supported the now subdued competitor would enter the act and attack the participant from the audience with a single mindedness which could only induce a desperate struggle in the audience participant, who invariably lost. In this part of the performance Mickey and the other man took no part.

This was the part that Courtenay enjoyed best and which excited the audience most; the request for the audience participant was just that, a request. An invitation. Who would have the bottle to take part? Who would submit to this kind of sexuality in front of an audience of household names? Would it be one of the names themselves? And who would survive the unexpected and total humiliation of the final act of the entertainment provided and then for the rest of the weekend maintain the cool of her usual exterior? This, to the guests, was also a great turn-on. I remember on this occasion catching a glance of Courtenay, Messalina-like in his expectancy, a lady from history whom he resembled not only in the manner of his sexual tastes.

I also remember receiving Jean's emotions at this particular point; it was the female member of the trio who touted the audience for its participant of another status, like a conjuror's assistant. Perhaps every woman in the audience felt the same, but Jean expressed their collective mixed feelings in the way that she did absolutely nothing at all, was absolutely still, hardly breathing. And when, finally, a girl rose from the cushions, there was no great expulsion of breath from her, nor from the rest of the women in the audience, no joint expression of relief. It was as if, now the possibility of choice had been removed, their feelings were a mixture of expectancy and regret.

Later, in our bed, Jean had said as much to me. What had been strongest in her mind had been the publicness of knowing a lot of the people in there.

And if the participants had been unknown, and there had been no audience, I'd asked her?

She hadn't answered my question with words.

THE SMOKE

WHEN I GOT TO the Steering Wheel, only Johnny Sheperdson was there. The other four were elsewhere for the moment. Naturally I got the full treatment from the management, just as the Shepherdsons would have got at one of my places. The only thing they didn't do before I passed through into the main part of the club was to press my trousers for me.

Johnny was sitting in the deep red leather booth where they always sat, his artificial leg straight and rigid beneath the table. There was no one else in the place. On the table in front of him was a mix of Bucks Fizz. He was pouring some of it into a tall glass as I approached the booth. He was the youngest of the five of them by quite a few years. I made him around twenty-seven or -eight. If he hadn't been family they'd have concreted him up years ago. In my opinion he drank too much.

The staff had arrived with the additional glass by the time I got to the booth.

"George," Johhny said as I sat down. The staff filled the other tall glass for me and retired.

I drank some Bucks Fizz.

"Cheers," I said.

I looked round the club. The cleaners had just about finished. Upstairs I could hear the muffled sound of a Hoover.

The place was very tastefully done out. Knowing the Shepherdsons, I always wondered why.

"Up and about with the larks," Johnny said.

"Yes," I said. "I've done my day's work."

"Neat."

I lit a cigarette.

"Your brothers in?"

"No," he said.

I didn't say anything.

"Which means they're out, doesn't it?" he said.

I nodded.

Then with my right hand I took hold of the front of his shirt and pulled very hard so that the side of his head crashed on to the table top. I brought my clenched fist down on the other side of his head like someone rubber-stamping an envelope. In the process of doing this Johnny's head knocked over the jug of Bucks Fizz. When I'd hit him again, I pushed him upwards and backwards into the red leather. I looked at him a long time, until he was convinced that retaliation would not be a good thing. After that I let him go.

Two third-division heavies began to steam towards us but Johnny gave them a look that turned them round. They should never have set off in the first place.

"Now," I said to him, "as your brothers are out, and not in, I'd like you to tell them this: as even they'll already have guessed, Arthur Philips and Wally Carpenter and Michael Butcher no longer walk among us. Just tell your brothers that the four of them, and you, are still able to perambulate among those who are more or less alive because just at present I have no intention of starting 1973 all over again. Not that I wouldn't win, of course. But because if it were to start all over again, Farlow would no doubt be brought into it and eventually brought down and he wouldn't be selective about what he said, would he? And then nobody'd win, would they? Would they, Johnny? Eh?"

Johnny didn't say anything.

"No," I said to him.

I took a drink from my tall glass. Bucks Fizz continued to dribble from the jug and eventually onto the carpet.

"Do you know what I really hate about you and your big brothers?" I said to him.

He didn't ask me.

"You're crude," I told him. "You're all so fucking crude. That's what I hate about you most of all."

I drank the remains of my drink and stood up.

Then I took hold of the handle of the draining jug and stood it right way up on the table.

"For a lad of your age," I said to him, "you drink far too much of this sort of stuff."

Then I walked away from him, across the thick carpeting, and out of the club.

THE SEA

MABLETHORPE IS A STREET that leads to a promenade and a funfair. The place is dominated by a gas holder and a ferris wheel, when it's in season. When you drive into the town limits and into the street, you can see the promenade and the ferris wheel at the end of the flat straight street. The gas holder is slightly to your right, as you enter. The biggest building in town is a new supermarket built to cream off the summer caravan self-caterers. That's Mablethorpe. People come here for their holidays.

But at the moment it's like a gold town after the lode's dried up. There are a half-dozen pubs. Four of them don't open their saloon bars in the winter. All the gift shops and the arcades and the fish bars and the bingo parlours are shut up at the moment. If they could run to a pier that'd be shut up as well. Instead of a pier they have a huge visible sewage pipe that stretches out to sea, trying to hide behind one of the breakwaters. Whether or not that's closed for the winter as well I've no idea.

Oh no, I tell a lie. One of the arcades does open, the one on the corner where the street meets the promenade. It opens Friday nights and all day Saturdays, when, as if by magic, handfuls of people appear and wander about not spending any money.

As I drive my motor to the end of the street there are no other cars going in either direction. There are a few parked on either side of the road, but nothing that's actually moving.

I park my car on the promenade. As promenades go, I suppose you could say it's all right. The only trouble, though, is that from the promenade you can't actually see the sea. They've had to build this huge barrow-like mound that runs the whole mile length of the front to act as a barrier against the high tides. It was built after the east-coast floods of '52. They've tried to make it nice, a couple of bits of concrete here and there, but it still remains a kind of marine Hadrian's Wall, higher than the sea-front buildings, keeping the merry holiday-makers from gaining the beach or viewing the sea willy-nilly.

There is at least one gap through, and that is directly opposite the end of the street. This gap is bordered on one side by toilets and the other by the funfair, both of which are closed. I thought you ought to know that. The gap itself is a thirty-foot-wide strip of concrete, a ramp that rises seawards in modest imitation of the defensive mound, so that even through this gap you still cannot see the sea until you've walked to the top of the ramp, along which, parallel to the sea, is a string of half a dozen bollards, from promenade level, black against the huge sky. From the top of this ramp you have the impression that the sea is actually higher than from where you've just risen up.

Here, the sea is only a quarter of a mile out.

I park my motor at the foot of the ramp on the whitewash that says NO PARKING. Out of season it's all right to do that, you see. Otherwise it would be against the law.

Because I've got a lot of time to kill, I get out of the car and walk up to the top of the rise and look at this different stretch of flatness. The sewage pipe glints blackly in the sunlight, like some giant turd being forced out into the sea.

An eight-foot-wide path, a mini-promenade, skirts the seaward base of the mound. Fifty yards to my left, it runs past a squat pill-box kind of a building that calls itself the Dunes Theatre. It has a stage, but that's where the resemblance ends. The frontage is all glass, facing seawards so that in season the boozers can watch their offspring dance back and forth along the sewage pipe and dive into the waves as they break past the pipe's length on their way to the beach.

As I've said, inside the theatre, there is a stage. There is no regular seating, just folding plywood chairs. In summer, the kids who aren't playing on the beach run about in this auditorium and knock the chairs over. The adult entertainment they have in the evenings is wrestling or amateur nights or local Country and Western. The bar is in the auditorium which suits one and all during the day's different periods. The Dunes is never totally closed out of season. Sometimes it's open a couple of days a week, for no particular reason other than perhaps to air it, but the days are never consistent. An old puff called Howard, who's seen better days—wardrobe in summer shows at Yarmouth, stuff like that—he looks after the bar on its random openings. Summer is better for him; for three months he has authority to hire and fire and give his minions hell.

From where I'm standing I can't tell whether it's going to be open or closed. The glass frontage just reflects the placid movement of the distant sea. In any case, it's academic; it's not yet opening time. I turn around and from my relatively high vantage point I look back down the street as it stretches back to infinity between the paintwork of the arcades and the rest of the frontages, colours peculiar to seaside resorts, colours which are brilliant but somehow never quite primary. There is a little more activity on the street now; somebody is crossing the road.

I turn towards the deserted funfair and begin to climb the broad concrete steps.

Most of the movable equipment has been shifted out until the summer calls it back again. The base of the ferris wheel is still there, but no wheel. The superstructure of the speedway still stands but the track and the multicoloured cutouts that the track supports are gone. The helter-skelter is nowhere to be seen. The lorry that supports the crazy house stands unveiled for what it is. The permanent shows and sideshows are shuttered and form three blank sides of the funfair's square; the fourth boundary is the length of concrete steps I'm presently climbing.

When I get to the top I wander across the funfair's miniature wasteland until I come to the speedway and then I sit down on a section of its wooden steps, facing the direction I've just walked from. The mound is about the same level as the step on which I'm sitting, central to my point of view. I can see the squareness of the Dunes on the mound's eastern side, and on its other side the endlessness of the promenade as it stretches past the diminishing frontages on its way to the trailer park. The hugeness of the sky diminishes everything. The foursquare shell of the dodgem car ride looks like a gutted matchbox against the sky's breadth.

Someone of pensionable age rises up from the unseen steps, preceded by a dog not too far off state benefit itself. It doesn't so much sniff the ground; it's more as if it can't be bothered to raise its head any higher. When the old bird gains the fairground's flatness, she stops for a while to get a refill of air. I look at her. How old is she, seventy, seventy-five? I probably couldn't even tell if I was closer to her. Has she spent all her years here? Is there an incontinent old man waiting on one of the ramp seats for her? Or is she on her own, waiting to join her partner in the grave?

I take out my flask and try not to think of the way Jean looked when I last saw her.

THE SMOKE

AFTER I'D BEEN TO the Steering Wheel I drove back into the West End. I wasn't hungry so I dropped into Lulu's for a couple of drinks. The minute I set foot inside, I wished I hadn't. There was the usual mix of journalists from weekly political magazines, TV personalities, publishers, idiots, and advertising men in Levi suits. I thought perhaps Toby might be there, but he wasn't. A girl from a current affairs programme pretended not to know who I was and showed out in the hope of getting God knows what, but I was polite to her and took her phone number, and said I'd give her a ring, probably Thursday. She knew I didn't mean it and when I was leaving I noticed her former companion, a front man for the show, sending her up for having a go. She told him to fuck off which made him smile even more.

I walked from Lulu's to Leicester Square and went to a movie showing at the Cinecenta. The movie, instead of being about sex and violence, being British made, was about sex and laughs. It was typical of the English attitude towards sex; if the sex was surrounded by humour the punter could absolve his guilt by telling himself he'd gone to see a comedy.

The movie was about as arousing as *Salad Days* and as funny as a Sunday afternooon in Scunthorpe. But it would make a modest fortune in proportion to its capital outlay. So as I'd got a bit of money in it myself I didn't go and invoke the Trade Description Act to the manager afterwards.

When I got back to the Penthouse, Jean was still in the office.

"Whoever's creaming it, they're being very clever," she said. "Because I'm buggered if I can see where. If it wasn't for the last three months . . ."

"Where is it happening?"

She shook her head.

"How?"

"Only an accountant could tell us that."

I lit a cigarette.

"Well, we can't ask Douglas because we can't eliminate the possibility it might be him."

Jean shook her head again.

"If it was him we wouldn't know this much. Besides . . ."

"Yes, I know," I said. "Douglas wants to be able to collect his pension."

I sat down in the chair by the window.

"Eighty-four agents," I said. "I mean, we know they all skim a certain amount but we already allow for that. Then there's twenty collectors. Which we also allow for. Then the four who collect from them."

"Who we also allow for."

"And finally Douglas."

There was a silence.

"So what do you suggest?" Jean said.

"I suggest we get in another accountant. He won't need to know anything but the figures. If he can tell us how, maybe we'll be closer to where."

"And if we're not closer?"

"There's over a hundred people involved. Let's hope they're not all at it."

I stood up.

"Let's go through and have a drink."

Jean put the ledger in the desk drawer and locked it.

"The Bertegas are coming at seven thirty."

"What's Harold doing?"

"I told him to do the same as last time. They seemed to like it. He'll be serving for eight thirty."

In the lounge, I made us a couple of drinks. Jean didn't sit down.

"I feel all wound up," she sighed.

"Take your time getting ready," I said to her. "Have a long soak. You'll be fine by the time they get here."

Jean took a sip of her drink and then walked down into the sunken area and flopped down opposite me.

"Remember the first time you met the Bertegas?" I asked her.

She gave me a level stare.

"I remember."

The Bertegas had been another stage in my introducing Jean to every aspect of my set-up and of my makeup—and eventually to her own. The Bertegas lived variously around the world, but their main bases were in Zürich and Rio. Bertega was one of those compact self-sufficient Latins who even if he just stood before you in his jockey shorts, his presence would transmit money and power and ruthlessness and an excellence of taste peculiar to the manner in which a man like Bertega would acquire it. His wife, Christina, was a case in point. She came from the kind of Brazilian aristocracy that was more English than the English, more arrogant; the hotter the climate the colder the steel. It was impossible to put an age on her. When she was sixty, she'd never look older than forty. She knew all about how Bertega kept her in the manner to which the generations of her family had become accustomed. Like all true aristocrats, she felt it despicable to discuss or consider the process by which the wealth to which she was naturally entitled accrued. The only morality was that the wealth should arrive at its proper destination. Everything else was of no consequence; any other questions that might be raised were surprising only in that they should be raised at all. If there was any slight embarrassment involved, perhaps it was that Bertega had had to work to establish the foundations of the sources of his wealth instead of getting out of his pram and taking over from a previous generation. But Bertega's own natural aristocratic strength had overcome any misgivings she might have had. He was a powerful man in every sense of the word, and although it would be impossible for Christina ever to betray it, by even the tiniest of public gestures, there was probably an element of the gutter in the aristocratic bedroom which accounted for the un-public power he exercised over her.

Of course for Bertega, as for me, it was no longer necessary to represent his own operations personally, but there were some things that could be discussed only between him and myself.

In one aspect of his business Bertega was particularly specialised, an aspect in which there were probably no more than fifty or sixty clients for his wares throughout the world. I knew of only one in the British Isles, and I supplied him with what Bertega supplied me.

Up to the first time she met the Bertegas, Jean had seen some of the Blues, the high-class ones, not the ones that went out on the mailing lists. The sixteen-millimetre ones, professionally shot, with soundtracks and plots that added to the eroticism instead of merely providing an excuse. The directors and the participants in these movies were extremely well paid, so that, for instance, the flagellation scenes were as convincing as those in *Two Years Before the Mast*; there were no silent-movie histrionics in these productions.

But Bertega, he specialised in the real thing.

It is impossible to satiate the voyeur; he soon becomes

bored by the prospects of what two people do in bed together. As experience enlarges his optical appetite, other elements have to be added in order to generate a new excitement: rape, violence, humiliation. So that in the end it is not the sexual act itself that the voyeur is interested in witnessing; he needs a continuation of innovatory corruptions and humiliations to provide temporary satisfaction. And because the satisfaction *is* temporary, although the search itself corrupts completely, the search for corruption is never completed. This is where Mary Whitehouse and myself are in total agreement; the process itself is corrupting: that is why she is in her business and I am in mine.

There has always been an area of voyeurism, existing either actively or lying dormant, in everyone; an area in which the victims of disaster and resultant mutilations draw from the minds of others the desire to see, not just to imagine, the sections that are always edited out of the newsreels of motorway pile-ups or plane crashes or massacres or of public executions. There has long been an underground and highly lucrative business in films and tapes of atrocities or accidents.

Bertega's material contained atrocities, but they were no accidents.

That was why the list of clients was so tiny, and the prices so astronomical. Even in this world, there were few people who were inclined and could afford to pay and whom Bertega could afford to trust. Of course, in Genghis Khan's day, or in the era of the Inquisition, such entertainment came cheap. Again, just an economic point: not one single item that came from Bertega came for less than £100,000, and that was rock bottom. Ironic. Both he and I could have someone topped for real and in safety for a mere £1000; commit the same thing to film and you were talking about a whole new price bracket.

On the night that I introduced Bertega and his wife to Jean we dined in the Penthouse and Bertega and I exchanged stories about events in our common businesses and discussed the current world economic situation. Bertega said that at last the seeds that he and friends of his had sown in the Italian unions years ago were coming to fruition and they were being split wide open. The resulting greater rate of inflation that would exist for a while could be absorbed in the long term, after stability had been seen somehow miraculously to return. He told me that he'd entertained a member of the Communist high command at his house outside Turin and he'd told Bertega that the Party appreciated the way that the political shake-up that would follow the union business would suit the Party very well indeed.

As far as Christina and Jean were concerned, well, if Christina were ever to be extended an invitation to dinner for four at Buck House, she would make a point of first consulting her engagement book before accepting; in other words, Christina concealed her patronage in the manner of the natural aristocrat.

After dinner we sat around for a while and then Bertega joined me at the drinks and told me about the new piece of merchandise he had with him. Naturally he hadn't brought it into the country himself; he'd had the taxi stop for a few moments between here and Claridges and taken delivery of it from the proprietor of a newsagent's that provided newspapers from all over the world for Soho's cosmopolitan population. This was never mentioned, of course. Bertega would almost certainly realise that as a matter of course one of my employees would be able to tell me exactly how many times he went to the bathroom during his brief stay.

Fine, I said when he mentioned the goods. We'd all go through into the projection theatre. When I said all, Bertega glanced at Jean, who was out of earshot, talking to Christina. The film, he explained, was what one would expect. It happened to be a record of the period of captivity of the daughter of an Italian industrialist. The two-million-pound ransom had been paid. The girl had not been returned to her family. Bertega glanced at Jean again. You understand, he said to me.

I put my hand on his shoulder. My old friend, I told him, if my judgement could not be trusted, then whose could?

That was good enough for him, he said. We all went through into the theatre.

THE SEA

IN MABLETHORPE, THEY OPEN at ten o'clock, in the season or out of it.

My occasional trips into town are not influenced by this fact alone, because I constantly have with me whatever I need. It's just that the act of driving into the town and of going from place to place gives me the illusion that the hours are actually passing by, not just standing still like the timeless void in which my mind stands motionless.

I walk down the concrete ramp and cross the promenade and continue away from the sea along the broad street to the single-storey arcade. The emptiness more than ever continues to give the impression of the Western town that waited for Frank Miller to get off the train and meet up with his brothers.

I stop off at the newsagent's on my way to the South Hotel. In summer you couldn't see the newspapers for postcards, buckets, spades and other seasonal ephemera. Now the counter that faces you on entering is covered only with sets of newspapers. I buy the *Mirror* and the *Telegraph* and while I'm waiting I notice, as I always do, a set of about a half a dozen copies of *The Stage*. I know two members of the community whose lives wouldn't be the same without it, one of them Howard from the Dunes, but in a place like this, who else would be in the market for that kind of paper?

The South Hotel is a hotel in name only. In Mablethorpe,

there are no hotels, only boarding houses. The South faces north. That's the kind of place Mablethorpe is. But the South looks like a hotel, at least. The gas holder apart, it's the town's tallest building, all three storeys of it. Like everything else in the town, only part of it is used. The whole town is just the sum of parts of its buildings. Unsurprisingly, it seems half empty even when it's full.

In the South's case, the action's downstairs. A conglomerate of bars designed to stuff in as many of the summer people as possible. The South stands on a corner of the street and the biggest of the bars runs the whole length of the building on the street side. It's so long there are three separate entrances on the street frontage. No steps up, of course, or anything flashy like that. Just straight in off the street.

I push one of the double doors and walk in.

Inside, out of season, it's got all the charm of a crematorium; as though that's what the architect designed it for, except that on his plans he got the scale wrong. The enormity of the bar is exaggerated by its present clientele, which at the moment numbers four. None of them is a day under sixty. The really depressing thing is that I now know them all, to nod to, in the same way I'll know the others who'll be coming in later, to reach the lunchtime peak of about a dozen customers.

The actual bar counter is almost as long as the room itself, disappearing into the distance to where the four dartboards are placed at equal intervals. From where I enter, the dartboards look as big as bull's eyes from seven foot six.

I cross the industrial carpeting to the bar and Jackie the barman closes and folds his copy of the *Sun;* my drink is waiting for me by the time I reach the counter.

"Morning, Mr. Carson," he says, putting the drink on the soak mat for me. "All right?"

I take some money from my wallet and put a pound on the counter.

"I'm well, Jackie," I say, "thank you. What will you have?"

"I'll just have ten penn'orth, thanks very much."

He gives me my change and sticks his half of bitter under the brandy optic. The act of him doing that and of me putting my money away gives us a natural break so that neither of us will have to carry on talking to each other. I take a sip of my drink and walk over to one of the endless leatherette seats by the window that looks out on to the street. I put my drink down on the table in front of me and begin to glance through the *Mirror*, but as usual there is nothing. There's been nothing for two months now; the news editors, although they've got far more on their files than they can ever print, ran out of new developments ages ago and tried to keep it alive with speculation disguised as reporting, but they finally gave up. The last thing was, I was dead along with some of the others or I'd gone to Australia, or somewhere, and the Law had been extremely glad to be reported as saying that the gangland killings had seemed to serve their purpose, in that those that had been put down had been put down and that was an end of it. Of course, there were still areas under investigation. As for the Law, they were quite happy for the press to clutch at straws, so long as the straw didn't come from the foundations of their own house.

I finish the *Mirror* and I'm just starting on the *Telegraph* when the door is pushed inwards and in comes Eddie Jacklin. A copy of *The Stage* is rolled up in one hand, and with it he beats the palm of the other, as if he's keeping time with the number that's in his head and dancing in his walk. Eddie's around thirty but was born out of time; his soul-era is the fifties, music from which period he re-creates in his various acts. Out of season he runs a Country and Western group round the local pubs, and sometimes at the Dunes when it occasionally gives itself an evening airing; but when the season comes he's resident at the Dunes full time, doing the full bit—playing with his group, doing his Roy Orbison impressions, organising talent shows for adults and for kids, lunchtime shows, compering the wrestling, the full bit. Although he wears the wide lapels and the rest, he's never been able to bring himself to comb his hair other than in a style of the period he really belongs to. And even though what Eddie does is never going to threaten Freddie Starr's corner or get him within a million miles of *New Faces*, he's in his own eyes a local star. In the eyes of the locals, he's a shithouse; the senior citizens patronise him, play up to his ideas about himself, the joke being to treat him as the star he thinks he is. Eddie's totally unaware of all of this; he reacts to the greetings he gets during his progress through the town with the insincere humility all the big stars have. The only person he's different with is me. Oh, he gives me the razzmatazz but he's slightly unsure of his delivery. I both worry him and intrigue him. There's the smell of a different world about me, and he's bright enough to recognise at least one source of the aroma. What am I? he wonders. Some eccentric Val Parnell, taking a break from the pressure of others' international stardom? Whatever he wonders, one thing he's certain of: I'm the kind of person who knows some people.

So as usual, when Eddie enters, he pretends at first not to clock my presence as he swings on his way across to the bar and by the time he gets there he's thrown out a couple of distracted "Hi's" to the customers.

"Morning, Eddie. How's it going?" asks Jackie, because Eddie wants him to.

"Oh, you know," Eddie says. "You know what it's like on amateur night. They let you have their music beforehand, but you never get time to go through it with them. So on the night, when they lose, they blame the backing for not doing it right."

Slight non-glance in my direction to see if I'm clocking his routine. Jackie puts a pint in front of Eddie.

"That's why I'm setting up this morning, just in case the lads can get in early tomorrow so it might give one or two of the punters a chance to go through their paces."

Eddie drinks, then acts his recognition of me over the top of his pint. He lowers his glass and walks over to where I'm sitting, sits down.

"Busy?" I ask him.

"Busy? I'm trying to get the acoustic balance right all by myself," he says. "That's the trouble. The other lads are only semi-pro; during the day I have to do their work for them. And some of them are married, and they can't go home at night and have their tea and come straight out again. So that leaves me driving the equipment to the gigs during the day so's we're not wasting half the evening setting up. Sometimes Cyril can get an hour or two away to give us a hand. He works for the Electricity Board."

"An impresario's work is never done," I say to him.

"Yeah," he says, laughing only to show me that he's the kind of fellow who can take a joke.

He takes another sip of his drink.

"Take tomorrow night," he says. "I'm organising the whole fucking issue. A lot of work. Twenty different acts. We've even got somebody reciting poetry; 'If' or something. But it's all a waste of time."

"Why's that, Eddie?"

He leans towards me slightly.

"Well," he says, "I know you wouldn't let on, but the winner's already fixed up."

"Really?"

"Oh, yeah. Not that she doesn't deserve it. She's great. I've asked her if she'll join the group for the summer season."

"That good, eh?"

"Fan-bloody-tastic. The group's rehearsing tonight. I'm hoping she'll be able to drop in and go through her numbers with the lads."

"She a local girl?"

"I dunno. I think she did Butlins at Skegness last season. I think she is."

A fellow in Electricity Board overalls comes in, looks around. Eddie clocks him.

"That's Cyril," Eddie says, downing his pint. "Better not hang about; he hasn't got long."

As Eddie moves off, he says, "If you're around tonight, why not drop in and catch the rehearsal? Unless you're already doing something else."

"Thanks. I might do that."

"Great."

Eddie and Cyril go out. I smile to myself. As if I'm not doing anything else.

No, I'm not doing anything else.

Only time.

THE SMOKE

I DECIDED TO TALK to Mickey about it. He had nothing to do with the collectors other than on the odd occasion I'd had reason to send him to go and talk to one or two of them.

"After what the accountant said," I told him, "it doesn't look like the kind of pilfering we allow for anyway. So we've got to make a decision on the odds. Because of the amount involved, I'd suggest starting at the top, with the ones who are the last to collect the money before it's delivered here. At any rate the accountant thinks that way."

Mickey thought about it.

"Do you really think they'd try it on? I mean, Hales, Wilson, Chapman, Warren. They make a lot of bread. Would they risk what they already get? And risk what they'd get if they were sussed out?"

"Money has a funny effect on people, Mickey," I said to him. "Corrupting. Sometimes it makes them act very peculiar."

Mickey thought some more.

"And the accountant's sure that's what the books say?" he said.

"As sure as he could be. Naturally he didn't have everything entirely at his disposal."

"And supposing all four of them are at it?"

"Then we'll find out all four of them are at it, won't we?"

Mickey lit a cigarette. "So what do you want me to do?"

"I want you to talk to them. But if I invite them here and they're the ones who're at it, they might not come, if you get my meaning, and once we've talked to one, and supposing it's not him, and the others get wind, then there'll be nobody to talk to at all."

"So you'd like me to bring them along to Sammy's?"

"That's right."

"Who would you like to see first?"

"I don't know. Try Ray Warren."

Mickey blew smoke from his cigarette upwards towards the ceiling.

"I think," Mickey said, "I *think* Ray's gone to Bolton for a few days. His mother's in a terminal situation."

I shrugged.

"I'll leave it to you, then."

Mickey nodded. There was a short silence.

"I don't know," Mickey said. "People. They never cease to amaze me."

THE SEA

IT'S ONLY A QUARTER of an hour's drive from Mablethorpe to the bungalow, but after I've finished reading the papers in the South and get back into my car and drive along the street and out of the town, I don't turn off the main road and head for the bungalow; instead I keep going and without doing above fifty I'm in Grimsby inside three-quarters of an hour.

Grimsby is a place that looks exactly the way it sounds; life imitating art, so to speak. A huge chunk of its centre's been cleared out in recent years and replaced with an enormous self-contained shopping precinct, with piazzas, the lot. Piazzas in Grimsby. Still, they have cod and chips in Benidorm. It's a small revenge perhaps.

I park the car in the multi-storey and when I've found my way out of this tower I make my way on to the confines of the basilica and wander through the pedestrian thoroughfares until I come to a built-in pub called the Monastic Habit. It's got a restaurant that is not quite half bad; young execs and a big demand for prawn cocktails from their escortees.

I take my place at a table for two against the gauze-draped picture window that offers me an uninterrupted view of Sketchleys and John Menzies and the Vallances on the other side of the pedestrian thoroughfare.

A waitress comes to take my order and I order the fish. When in Rome.

I also get her to send over the wine waiter and I choose the wine and ask for it to be brought straightaway; when he returns with it he pours it for me to taste but I waive the ritual and he adds some more to my glass and retires hurt.

While I'm waiting for my meal to arrive I turn my attention from the commercial aspect outside to the cluster of the better halves of young marrieds at the small cocktail bar across the room. They're all wearing credit-account machine tailoreds and drinking halves of keg. There's a couple of groups of them, and in each group there's the token secretary brought along to remind the collected marrieds that each one is still singularly a bit of a lad.

A man of the same ilk except five years on and perhaps with an office all to himself is sitting alone on one of the high stools, nursing a tomato juice, doing a crossword in the newspaper that's folded and balanced on his legs.

I take a sip of my drink and while I'm doing that a girl in her early twenties comes into the restaurant and goes over to the cocktail bar. She looks good in one of those double-breasted PVC macs, trench-coat length, leather boots that stop just below the knee. Beneath her maroon coat I can see the rolled top of a white cashmere sweater softly emphasising the clear line of her jaw. Her fair hair would be about shoulder length if it hadn't been dressed so that it turned under, hiding the back of her neck in a soft inward-turning wave. As she crosses the room her walk is confident, unhesitant, expressing a certain self-containment, all combining to give her an air of authority that she obviously feels she doesn't have to work at.

When she reaches the bar, she sits down on one of the bar stools so that there is just a single stool between her and the man with the crossword. The barman steps forward and waits. She takes her purse out and puts a five-pound note on the table and gives the barman her order; he goes off to work the vodka optic. While she's waiting she takes out a packet of Dunhill's and lights up. Meanwhile, her arrival has not gone unnoticed by the man with the crossword. He gives her an up and down but returns to his crossword when he sees that she's impassively clocked his appraisal.

And you can't really blame him. She's a very good looking girl, very even features, excellently made up, the kind of look of the girls who hand over the prizes on the quiz programmes on TV, or decorate the latest models at the Motor Show.

I cast a professional eye over her and along with considering the former association of ideas the possibility of her being on the game roams through the corridors of my mind. In the Smoke, it would have been a certainty; but here, the air of respectability very carefully prepared to cloak the nature of her business until she herself revealed what she wanted the prospective punter to know, here, in a town like this, all that would be a waste of time. A brass here would be highly polished in a different way, to express her occupation, not to conceal it.

So although I conclude that that particular possibility is virtually not on, there is an aura about her that doesn't make me close my mental book on her entirely, and although not normally a gambling man, I keep the book on her open as a way of passing the time. I also run a little side bet on the man with the crossword. Will he or won't he, and if so, how?

He gets his chance when she checks her wristwatch against the clock above the bar. An enquiry as to whether she's waiting for someone or not. Her reaction to that is neither a frost nor a come on. Although I can't hear what either of them is saying, from that point on the conversation appears to flow fairly smoothly, with just the faint expression from the girl to the man that it is not a conversation that in any way will lead to a discussion concerning territorial gains. In fact the closest he appears to get to her is when he buys her a drink. To do this he stands up and when the drinks have been replaced he hands her hers and sits down on the stool that previously stood between them.

By that time my fish has arrived and for a while, because it's so good, I devote my attentions to that. I don't look across at the bar again until I've finished eating. Sipping my wine, I now see that the girl is no longer there. So perhaps I was wrong. Or perhaps he couldn't afford the asking. In any case, so what? I have to pass my time somehow but . . .

Vaguely irritated, I refill my glass, and the waitress appears to take my order for dessert. I order ice cream and when the waitress goes away, the girl has returned to the bar and is again sitting on her stool. She's only been to the powder room. And so now I begin to re-speculate, even more irritated with myself. Whoever she's waiting for, if she's waiting for anyone, is by now very late. She's showing no irritation at the lack of arrival, and appears to be enjoying the conversation, though not perhaps as much as he would like her to.

I shake my head. Even though my instincts still nudge me towards a different conclusion, sense tells me that if she was a brass they would have left together at least a quarter of an hour ago.

The ice cream arrives and I eat it in a couple of minutes flat; my obsessiveness is really beginning to get on my nerves. I call for my bill and get up and leave the restaurant and go out into the precinct, in search of a movie to occupy my mind for the rest of the afternoon.

THE SMOKE

HENRY CHAPMAN WAS THE first. When Mickey brought him in he looked a very worried man, but then anybody being picked up by Mickey and being brought into Sammy's house would look worried, innocent or not.

The room was set up as before, and, as before, Jean was there.

Henry was asked to sit down in the chair. He declined my offer of a drink.

"All right," he said. "Just what the fuck is going down?"

I lit a cigarette. "How'd you like living out at Marlowe now, Henry?" I asked him. "The missus got used to the neighbours yet? Kids settled in at the new school all right?"

"Look, George, fuck the fun and games. I'm here for a reason. First off, I want to know what it is."

"Maybe you already do?"

"I know all sorts of things, George, as you are very well aware."

I nodded.

"Those apart," I said. "The new house, I mean as I mortgaged it for you, I know what it's costing you a month. And the school fees, those are a couple of good schools. And then there's the Algarve, and Las Palmas, and—"

"I can afford all that. As you pointed out, you know all about my financial situation."

"Do I?"

A short silence.

"This is about money, isn't it?" Henry said.

"You're getting warm."

Henry considered what he was going to say. Then he said, "George, I've been a member of this firm a long time. A very long time. And I'm not stupid; I know how well paid I am. I don't go out on fourhanders any more, not even for you; I don't have to. Failing a financial situation of the kind that happened in Germany before the war, not only am I set up for the rest of my life, but so are my kids. So, would I, in my right mind, put all that down the pan for sake of creaming a few extras?"

"So you know that's the area we're going to be talking about?"

Henry shakes his head.

"George, give me the kind of credit you give me for being able to do my job."

"All right. Supposing it wasn't you. What about the other three?"

"I don't know, do I? I should imagine they're as happy in their lot as I am in mine."

"And those you collect from?"

Henry shrugged.

"They know me. They know what'd happen if I caught them at anything. That's one of the reasons you gave me the job."

I poured myself another drink. There was a long silence.

"Does the missus know about the cottage outside of Saffron Walden?" I asked him.

Henry went the colour of cream cheese.

"And does she know how much it costs to keep Millie Rowson there fifty-two weeks a year? Not to mention what it costs when she comes up to town shopping or goes on her holidays."

Henry didn't bother asking how I knew about Saffron Walden. Instead he said, "The cottage is an investment. When I decide to sell it I'll be quids in."

"So why didn't you come to me for the finance?"

"I didn't need to."

"You didn't need to about the house."

"You offered. You look after your best people like that."

"And if you'd told me about the cottage, I would have offered again, wouldn't I?"

Henry didn't say anything.

"So why didn't you tell me about it?"

Henry breathed in.

"Look," he said. "All right. I'll tell you."

"Do that, Henry," I said to him.

"Look," he said. "It's like this. I don't know quite how to put it. Supposing something goes down. Supposing there's an earthquake. Old Bill suddenly has to start eating people. I mean I heard about the Shepherdsons' latest stroke."

I waited for him to go on.

"So I got this place," he said. "It's a place to go. Millie's neither here nor there. Well, I mean, you've got to have somewhere to go, don't you? I mean, even you must have made contingency arrangements for whatever goes down, if it ever does."

"Must I, Henry?" I said.

Henry seemed a bit embarrassed.

"Well, what I mean is, I didn't think anyone knew about mine. In your case . . . well, you know what I mean."

I didn't tell him that I knew what he meant. Instead, I said, "That place cost you seventeen thousand five hundred pounds."

"That's right."

"You put it all down at one go."

"I could afford it."

"Still a lot of money. All at one go."

"I'm telling you. I could afford it."

I stubbed out my cigarette.

"So that's as far as you're prepared to go?" I said.

"That's as far as I can go," he said. "Except to say that whatever's going down, you're talking to the wrong man."

I topped my glass up. Henry was a very convincing fellow. And up to now he'd been like Caesar's wife. That was why he was in the job I'd given him. I took a drink. I liked Henry. I looked at Jean. She was standing still, by the blanket-muffled curtains. She liked Henry too. I remembered once asking her if she fancied him. She'd said, yes, she'd fancy Henry if I wasn't around. It was the kind of thing we used to ask each other about other people. Of course it was academic, just part of a general gee-ing up process in our mind games. Not that she hadn't had sex with other men since we'd been married. But those times were with different kinds of people, of both sexes, and on occasions different to having sex singly with someone because she wanted that particular someone. Those were the occasions committed to video-tape and to film, the cast of supporting players as anonymous as was possible; Henry was a fantasy to Jean, a shared mind experience with myself.

Now, Henry was here.

Jean's face was deliberately void of all expression. Which meant I knew exactly what she was thinking.

I gave Mickey the nod.

THE SEA

AFTER THE MOVIE, I cruise slowly out of the town and back along the main road, in the direction of the bungalow and of Mablethorpe. Cars continually rush by me, the drivers now office-free, rushing headlong home to get back to wives they probably are not particularly eager to see. Stupid haste to risk getting yourself smashed up.

Dawdling along, I remember Jean's questions when we'd got back to the Penthouse, after Mickey'd worked on Henry.

After we'd made love.

No, I'd told her. Henry was safe. In both ways. There was a point beyond which Henry could not have remained silent had he been the one. Henry had told us the truth. And what now, she'd said, now that he'd had that done to him? Could he still be trusted; could I risk keeping him on after what had been done to him? Look, I'd told her, Henry was a pro. He knew what the score was. He'd been the victim of an occupational hazard. He wouldn't bear a grudge, consider revenge. After the doctor had spent a week with him, Henry would continue as before. He would be free to go about his business on my behalf, to return to the bosom of his family or to the bosom of Millie, whichever he preferred. But now, knowing that he'd once been under suspicion, he'd be twice as scrupulous in his modus operandi, so that his activities would cast not even the tiniest of shadows in my direction. Because next time, he would know, condolences to the immediate family would be in order. No, I'd told her; an excellent soldier would become a perfect one.

I'm about half a mile away from the turn-off to the bungalow, and I begin to wonder whether or not to go back. There's no immediate reason for going straight back, but then there's no reason at all for carrying on into Mablethorpe. My mind is made up for me by headlights flashing in the tea-time dusk of my driving mirror. I pull over slightly to let the following car pass me and by the time I've repositioned my motor more centrally I've gone past my turn-off, so I just carry on towards Mablethorpe.

As I drive down it, the street has a slightly warmer feel to it. Although the evening is not yet dark, the lights are on in the few shops that are open, particularly bright in the big supermarket, and at intervals one or two sodium street lights, bronze against the deepening plushness of the blue sky neutralise the garish coldness of the marine paintwork.

I park the motor where I parked it before, at the foot of the ramp that leads the concrete horizon with its row of bollards.

I sit in the car and take a couple of pulls from my flask and consider the few early stars that twinkle in the darkening uniform curtain that soars beyond the rim of the ramp. The twinkling of the stars soon becomes boring so I slip my flask in the pocket of the anorak that's lying on the seat beside me. Then I get out of the car and take the anorak off the seat. I close the door and lock it and when I'm slipping the anorak on I look down the street. The lights from the South's tall windows stretch across the street's width, and nearer, just opposite me, the arcade on the corner of the street and the promenade provides both street and promenade with the generosity of its Friday-night light that blazes out into the evening to become quickly diffused by the very slight, almost imperceptible sea mist that is drifting in through the gap at the top of the ramp;

in fact it is only the diffusion of the arcade's light that makes me aware of the mist at all.

From where I'm standing, I can see into the arcade through its broad plate-glass windows that look out onto both the street and the promenade. For Mablethorpe, its interior dimensions are fairly big, a flattened-down and squared-off area similar in volume to that of the South. There's hardly anyone about, just handfuls of kids running from machine to machine, a few wandering adults, separate, looking at the machines as if they're exhibits in the wrong museum.

I cross the promenade and walk through the open doors and into the arcade.

The old boy in his white coat is just about upright in the change kiosk. I walk over to him and get a pounds-worth of ten-pence pieces and go over to the aerial Dogfight machine, and spend a quarter of an hour trying to top my previous personal best, which tonight I don't happen to be able to do. After I've failed to do that I decide to go over to a pin-table I particularly like to play. While I'm getting some more change from the kiosk, I clock that this particular machine is already in use, being operated by a dark-haired girl in dark glasses. She's wearing one of those Afghan coats and a pair of deliberately patchy jeans and white plimsolls. A newspaper is sticking out of one of the pockets of her Afghan. I pick up my change and walk over and lean against the machine next to hers and watch her manipulating the flippers. She's wearing a T-shirt which reads: I'D RATHER BE HANG-GLIDING. She's clocking up quite a good score and she's still got a couple of ball-bearings to come. She takes no notice of my interest. What I notice is that the paper sticking out of her pocket is a copy of *The Stage*, and also she's beautiful in a way that goes with the clothes she's wearing.

She shoots her final ball. I watch as she juggles the machine as close to Tilt as she can without actually tilting it. In the end, she finishes up with a very good score.

"You almost got a free game," I say to her.

Beginning to move off, not looking at me, she says, "You didn't."

I smile to myself. It was one way of getting onto the machine.

I insert a coin and press the button that sets up the five ball-bearings and then for no reason at all I think there was something about the girl that was vaguely familiar. I look up from the machine in the direction that the girl had gone. And that's it. She's gone. Nowhere to be seen. Out into the night and all that. Anyway, why shouldn't there have been something familiar about her? The town is full of girls. Why should I even care she seems familiar? I shrug my shoulders, like a dog shaking off rain. I'm obsessive about everything these days. I need a new obsession like I need a win on Littlewoods.

I pull back the spring mechanism and start the game.

THE SMOKE

THE DAY ON WHICH I was going to have a talk to Mal Wilson, I had lunch with my lawyer, James Morville. As usual, it was pleasant and relaxed. As long as you allowed him a half an hour to discourse on his two hobbies, opera and the movies, James was happy to spend the rest of the allotted time meandering through any subject you cared to slide at him, giving gentle exercise to a mind that was as sharp as his exterior was smooth. He was forty-two years old, and extremely wealthy. He enjoyed taking out girls but not on a regular basis. Perhaps his legal mind was a disadvantage to the naturally advantaged young ladies in which he specialised; like a chess player, he was always the requisite number of moves ahead of whatever the young ladies had in their minds. But he was much loved by them; on the other hand he was much hated by the Law. It was ironic really; there was no better criminal lawyer in the country. It wasn't only his courtroom performances that made him unique; it was his backroom tactics that had all that could afford him knocking on their doors for him to let them out. And this was the area at which the Law's hatred was directed, and not only the straight law. It was as if the immaculate public presentations of his backstage deals, deals which not only saved the faces of his clients but the faces of the Law themselves, it was as if this very perfection got up their noses most of all; it was similar to the money syndrome. The debtor never forgives the person who is the source of his credit.

And there was nothing James didn't know; perhaps this was why they hated him most of all. There was nothing he didn't know about the villains, either, and that knowledge made him safe; he had no family to threaten. Only his own life was on the line. And if any derailment were ever effected James had made it common knowledge that his will provided that the Attorney General received the key to the safe deposit box that contained his memoirs. There would be more about me in that little box than I could ever remember myself. I often used to say to him, if he ever retired, he should take up biography. There was a big market in biographies.

Nothing he didn't know, nothing he couldn't find, nobody he couldn't locate. He had his ways, just as I had mine.

He was a member of the best clubs, and his appearance would have graced the Opposition front benches in the House. And he really loved his work, and the knowledge that he possessed. There was very little I hid from him; and as my lawyer, the more he knew, the better it was for me, should the unforeseen happen. He wouldn't thank me if it was only while he was standing up in court he discovered I'd sold him a dummy.

So he already knew of the fates of Philips and Carpenter and Butcher. I'd told him all about it over lunch.

"Yes," he said, considering the wine in his glass, "you were quite right. Nothing else you could have done. Not that I can see."

He drank some of his wine, savoured it.

"Farlow's such an idiot," he said. "Can't understand the fellow, screwing it up the way he did. One can only put it down to megalomania. Sheer megalomania."

"Well, it's tough at the top," I said.

James smiled and said, "I saw him in Muriel's the other day; of course he was well aware that I'd know all about it. We had a few words."

"What did he have to say?"

James smiled again.

"He bought me a drink. You know what he's like; in buying me a drink, he wasn't conceding defeat. He was demonstrating that in the larger battle, he'd be the final winner. I sometimes wonder why he doesn't wear a pair of six-shooters."

"And he said?"

"Oh, nothing specific; the usual heavy irony, not disguising his real meaning. He mentioned he knew of a flat just gone vacant in Brighton. Ideal for the weekends. Sounds super, I said. I asked him for the number of the estate agents. He said how would he know?"

I shook my head.

"Poor chap," James said. "He's never been the same since he discovered the meaning of the term *Macho*."

Then I told James about the business over the accounts. He asked me what I thought the outcome would be.

"Well," I said. "I don't doubt I'll suss it out, wherever it's happening."

"Oh, of course. What I meant was," he said, "would you say that the final outcome will prove fatal?"

"It couldn't be otherwise, could it? You know every possible consequence if I just put him in the hospital. Not everybody's a Henry Chapman."

"Oh, naturally."

There was a silence.

"But?" I said.

James shook his head.

"Look," he said. "I know in one respect it would be perfectly safe. With you, one doesn't assume anything else. The only thing that occurs to me, in the present climate, so soon after the last unpleasantness, is that perhaps you could afford not to pursue this particular business with your usual thoroughness. Of course, Farlow's stupid. But at the moment, and particularly at the moment, he's simply not going to stop thinking and looking and even shithouse rats can see in the dark."

James's using that kind of language always disturbed me in a vague kind of way.

"Do you know the kind of money that's involved?"

"Well, I can imagine, of course."

"In any case, it's not the money. It's the principle I can't afford."

"Quite."

"I'm not going to sit up there on the top floor while there's someone down here on the street smiling at my expense."

"I can quite see that."

"And as you say, I don't own a building contractor's for nothing. Those concrete mixers cost me a lot of money."

"Nothing," he said. "I'm worried about nothing. Everything you say is absolutely true."

"Then what?"

James drank some more of his wine.

"Well," he said, "this time, he's already looking. The last time he cocked it up himself, and before he'd even realised it, you'd moved and then everything was as before, in other words, purely academic."

"Go on?"

"This time, supposing one of your men disappears off the streets, he'll know it's not the Shepherdsons, not least because of his involvement. Therefore—however long it takes him is neither here nor there—he will conclude that your man is no longer on the street because of you."

"I can't see that it's any different from the previous situation."

"It's just that he's already looking; that's all I'm trying to say."

"James, last time he and the Shepherdsons went to the trouble of setting up Arthur and the other two, Christ, if he couldn't nail me then . . ."

James waved a hand in the air.

"I know. It was only a thought. I knew you wouldn't mind my mentioning it."

"Of course not. I appreciate the concern. But, honestly. Don't worry. I'm a very careful driver."

James smiled and took out his cigar case. He opened it and offered me one, as he always did, and I declined, as I always did.

"By the way," he said, "I meant to ask you. Have you seen the new Russell movie? Honestly, it's unbelievable. Beautiful. Quite his worst so far. It's so gloriously bad. I've seen it twice already."

While he went on to describe the movie in detail, I considered what James had been proposing to me. Not of course the actual words, the stuff about Farlow; the only way Farlow and the Shepherdsons were going to break me down was to put their own heads on the Attorney General's block first. No, James, being the extremely clever fellow he was, wasn't conveying me the literal meaning of his words; the words were just words. And whatever the purpose behind them, it wasn't necessarily a warning; if I ever went down he'd move on to representing the Shepherdsons without bothering to change his carnation, before he'd even collected his final payment from myself. On the other hand, if he ever let me go down, it would never be because he'd withhold from me any knowledge he had which I ought to be in possession of.

But whatever James was saying, he certainly wasn't saying it.

Curious.

For the moment, I dismissed any alternatives that might have entered my thoughts. I tuned back in to the description of the Russell movie; James had just got to the point where he was describing the homosexual rape.

THE SEA

IN THE SOUTH, UNDER the harsh evening lights, the regulars look older than ever. They're dotted about the leatherette, at angles reminiscent of ventriloquist's dummies without the support of the ventriloquist's hand. I cross over to the bar and as usual Jackie is ready with my drink.

"What sort of a day you have?" he asked, taking my money.

"Fine," I say. "And one for yourself."

"Thanks, Mr. Carson," Jackie says. "I'll have the usual."

After Jackie's worked his optic and given me my change, instead of retiring to the leatherette, I ask Jackie for the darts. He doesn't give me the usual Sailors' Aid ones; instead he lends me his own personal tungstens. He even takes them out of the wallet and inserts the flights for me himself.

"I'd give you a game myself," Jackie says, "only the governor doesn't like it at nights. It's all right at dinner times."

He hands me the darts and by the time I've crossed the yards of carpeting and reached the seven-foot-six marker, Jackie's operated the switch behind the bar and the board is already lit up. I set my drink down on a nearby table and begin to go round the board in doubles.

Sanity, I think as I pluck the first handful out of the board and go back to the marker. That's the name of the game. Sanity. The trick is, in an asylum, to try and remain sane. I float three more darts at the board. Sanity. Therapy. Control.

By the time I've got round to the nines, Eddie hustles into the pub as I'm pulling the darts out of the board. He waves and I acknowledge his wave. While I'm throwing another handful I overhear Jackie suggest to Eddie that he give me a game.

After the next handful, Eddie joins me, sipping at his pint.

"Winning?" he says.

"I'm up against tough opposition," I tell him, going on from twelves, getting the thirteen, narrowly missing the fourteen. "Fancy a hiding?"

Eddie takes his darts out of his breast pocket and while he's fitting them together he says, "You dropping by tonight?" I must look blank because he says, "The Dunes. The rehearsal."

"Oh, yeah. Well, I may not be able to."

"We're starting early. We won't be going on late."

"I'm not sure yet," I tell him.

"Waiting for somebody?"

"You ever seen me waiting for anybody, Eddie?"

"Er, well, no, I can't exactly say I have."

"No, I don't suppose you can," I say. "You want a practice, or shall I throw one for middle?"

"No," he says. "No, you go ahead, Mr. Carson."

I throw one and get a twenty-five. Eddie's lands just outside the circle. He takes the two darts out and hands me mine.

While we're halfway through the first game, the girl from the arcade comes in, the girl in the Afghan coat. She clocks Eddie and Eddie clocks her. Eddie slips into his promoter's habit.

"Er—can you excuse us a minute?" he says. "I just want to get Lesley a drink. I'll be right over."

"Sure," I tell him. "I'll wait."

I throw a ton and leave the darts in the board so that when Eddie comes back he won't just have to take me on trust. I pick up my drink and look at the girl as she joins Eddie at the bar.

She's still wearing the heavy dark glasses. And she's still

looking to me as though I've seen her before. And the irritating thing is that it's irritating me.

Jackie draws her a half of lager and I watch Eddie explain to her that he's just having a game of arrows. Perhaps he thinks she wouldn't have managed to guess that all by herself.

Then Eddie walks back to me, the girl a few yards behind him. She sits down on one of the wall seats.

"The star of the show," Eddie says, cocking his head in her direction. "The one I was telling you about."

"Oh, yes. That one."

"I'm afraid I'll only be able to play you best of three," Eddie says. "She doesn't want to leave too late."

"That's all right, Eddie," I say, taking my ton out of the board.

The girl sits there, reading the copy of *The Stage* I'd clocked in her pocket earlier.

I finish the first game on double sixteen.

"Like another drink, Eddie?"

"Yes." He downs the remains of his pint. "Thanks."

"And the star turn?"

"I'll ask her."

Eddie walks over to her.

"Lesley, like another half?"

She looks up from the paper.

"No. I'll have a vodka and tonic."

"I see," Eddie says.

By that time I'm already on my way over to the bar. Eddie catches me up.

"She says she'll have a vodka and tonic. That all right?"

"Of course it's all right, Eddie."

While we're waiting at the bar, Eddie says, "You should hear her. You really should. You can forget Elkie Brooks."

"Ah, but will the punters buy her, Eddie?"

"Well, of course, for the season, she'll give them Anita Harris. If she decides to hang around."

Jackie gives me the drinks and we carry them back to where the girl is sitting.

"This one's with Mr. Carson," Eddie says. "Mr. Carson, this is Lesley."

"You found someone to play with you then," she says to me.

"Men or women," I say to her. "They're all the same to me."

Eddie looks puzzled.

"A brief encounter," I say to him. "In the arcade."

Eddie clocks.

"Oh, yeah," he says. "She loves the machines, Lesley does. She loves all the games."

THE SMOKE

"Heart attack," Mickey said.

Finally certain that Mal Wilson was dead, Mickey straightened up and stood back from the still body.

"That's what must have done it," he said. "Heart attack. The old ticker gave out."

I looked at Mal's features, already begun to blur into the unfamiliarity born of death.

"Who'd have thought it?" Mickey said. "A big lad like Mal. You never can tell."

Mickey reached up and unscrewed the wires from the central light-socket, then began to wind them up.

"That's a bastard," I said.

"How's that, gov'nor?" Mickey said.

I shook my head.

"I don't think it was him."

"No, I thought that."

I lit a cigarette.

"Of course, you can't be entirely certain."

"Oh, no," Mickey said. "You can't be entirely certain."

He emptied the ashtray into a small paper bag and put the bag in his pocket.

"A bastard," I said again.

Mickey drained scotch from the remaining glass and began polishing it with his handkerchief.

“He was a good man,” I said. “He’ll be difficult to replace.”

“Yeah,” Mickey said. “A good lad, Mal was.”

I drew on my cigarette.

“Still,” Mickey said. “No family to worry about. No steady or nothing like that.”

“No,” I said.

Mickey bent down, began to untie the ropes from around the chair legs and Mal’s ankles.

“Look,” Mickey said, “if you and Mrs. Fowler want to be getting off . . .”

“Yes,” I said.

“I’ll have tidied up and I’ll be away by the time Sammy gets back.”

“Right,” I said.

Behind me, Jean finished packing up the video recording machine.

THE SEA

I CAN HEAR THE tinny booming of Eddie's group even as I walk up the ramp. At the top, I pause for a moment, stationary like the bollards. The blue of the sea and the blue of the sky are now almost identical in shade; here, the only chance the sea gets of being close to blue is when it reflects the deep almost purple of the evening sky. In contrast, the orange light from the Dunes' picture window does a fair impression of an eastern sunset.

I walk along the mini-promenade towards the Dunes. A couple of leathers are sitting on one of the seaward-facing seats, doing nothing, their visored helmets parked beside them on the slats of the seat like spare heads. As I pass by them, the music stops issuing from the Dunes.

I climb the zig-zagged concrete steps that lead to the theatre's entrance and then I pass through the small lobby with its payphone and its opposing toilets and through the double doors and into the auditorium. It's cold.

They may air it out of season but apparently the rising damp can find its own level.

Directly in front of me on the far side of the auditorium is the stage. To my left is the bar. Only the lights from the bar and those concentrated on the stage illuminate the auditorium. From the bar an area of around fifteen feet stretches towards the main well of the auditorium. Then there is a drop the same height as the stage opposite. Between these two levels the folding seats have been folded for tomorrow night's entertainment. The girl is sitting on one of these seats. Still in her Afghan, still in the dark glasses.

The group is on the stage; I don't have to describe the group.

Howard, the ex-thespian, is standing behind the bar, studying whatever is or isn't on the shelving unit. In the broad mirror to which the shelving's fixed, his reflection tut-tuts back at him in sympathy for his problem.

My reflection joins his and Howard turns to attend to my needs. In the reflection I can see Eddie, his instructions to the group crackling round the cold auditorium like footsteps in a sharp frost.

"And what can I do for you?" Howard says. It's more of a challenge than a question.

"You can turn the heating up for a start," I say to him.

"Are you cold?" he says, massaging one of his neatly rolled up shirtsleeves.

"No. I'm only bloody freezing."

Howard massages the other shirtsleeve and shakes his head.

"Well, it's always damp out of season."

He stops massaging.

"Still," he says, "I'm used to the sodding place. For me sins."

I light a cigarette.

"Anyhow. What can I get you?"

"A scotch. Large."

"And very warming it'll be," he says, going for a glass.

"And yourself?"

"Thanks very much. I'll have a drop of Rin Tin Tin."

He works the gin optic on his own behalf.

"Thanks very much," he says.

I look at my reflection in the mirror. Without the moustache and the sideburns I look a totally different person. It's a constant surprise.

On the stage, Eddie slides on to the obligatory high stool, guitar hung round his neck.

"Okay, fellers," he says. "Let's run through 'Green Green Grass of Home.'"

"Green is right," Howard says. "Look at him. Roy Rogers without spurs."

"They do their best," I say.

The irony is lost even on Howard.

"That's the trouble," he says. "Of course, when I was doing the shows—"

Howard's imminent reverie is cut off in its prime by the group's opening chords. Eddie does the number as you'd expect, Tom Jones monologue and all, giving it the extra because he's got a captive audience of one.

When the number's finished, so's my scotch. I treat Howard and myself to another optic-ful. Eddie, Presley-style, makes a few comments to the group, then jumps down off the stage, has a brief word to the girl, then makes for the bar.

"Three pints of lager, a half of lager and two bitters," he says to Howard. Then to me, one man of the world to another: "Of course, we got to get another bass guitar. Dave's all right but nothing comes through. Not enough power."

"Well, of course the acoustics in here," I say. "And then, you're playing cold."

"Yeah. Tomorrow night'll be different. Nothing like an audience to gee you up. 'Course, tomorrow, we'll only be doing a limited session. Numbers here and there among the amateurs."

"Well, it'll be a relief," I tell him. "The occasional oasis."

"Oh," Eddie says. "Yeah. You going to make it tomorrow night?"

"I'm not sure yet," I say to him.

"You'd really be able to hear the group then."

"I'll see what I'm doing."

Howard places the drinks on a tin tray and Eddie picks it up, and just as Eddie's going Howard says, "Eddie, about tomorrow night."

"What's that?"

"When you introduce 'My Way,' don't dedicate it to me again, Eddie. Not again."

"Always gets a laugh, Howard. Always gets a laugh."

Eddie walks off with the tray.

"He'll do it once too often," Howard says bleakly.

Eddie gets to the stage and puts the tray down just beyond the unlit footlights. The group dissembles and advances on the beer, bending low, like an exaggerated curtain call. Eddie takes the half of lager off the tray and hands it to the girl, has a couple of words. She takes a sip of her lager and gets up and walks to the side of the stage and climbs the steps, glass in hand. Eddie vaults up over the footlights and they meet at the vocalist's mike.

"Are you going to use the stool?" Eddie asks her.

The girl looks at the stool, then draws it a little closer to the mike, hands Eddie her lager, supports herself rather than sits on the stool, still in her Afghan, still in her dark glasses. The brightness of the spotlight neutralises her face even more, the dark glasses remaining her one and only distinguishing feature. And still my nagging irritation.

"She'll never get the mums and dads to vote for her if she comes on looking like that tomorrow night," Howard says. "In that coat she should be on a lead. That's the trouble today; no style. Where are the Garlands, the Dietrichs, I ask myself."

"Have you heard her?"

"No. But I can imagine."

"All right, fellers," says Eddie. "'She's Leaving Home.' A one, a two. And."

The group begins the backing. The girl takes the mike from its stand. Then she begins the number.

When she's finished, the following silence isn't just because she's stopped singing. Howard says, "I don't believe that."

I don't say anything.

"That," Howard says. "That, what I've just heard."

I take a sip of my drink.

"She's very good," I say.

"Good?" Howard says. "The last time I heard anything like that, well, I can't remember the last time. Like one or two other aspects of my leisure activities."

"She can certainly sing," I say.

"That's not singing, mate," says Howard. "You don't just call that singing."

Meanwhile the girl has asked Eddie if that was all right. Eddie says, offhand, "Yeah, fine. Want to do the other, the encores?"

"If you like."

She does "If You Could See Me Now," at a quarter its usual pace. Very effective. Then she does "The More I See You," with the standard Chris Montez backing.

"Amazing," Howard says, dreamlike.

The girl says, "That's that, then."

"Yeah," Eddie says. "Great."

"I'll see you tomorrow, then."

"You not sticking around for a drink after?"

"No, I've got to be going."

She picks her glass up off one of the amplifiers, takes a sip.

"It's Friday night. We'll be going to the South for a bevy."

"Wonderful."

She finishes her drink, gives her glass to Eddie.

"I'll see you tomorrow. Seven?"

"Yeah, kicking off seven-thirty. Can't keep the geriatrics out too late in the cold night air. Can't afford to lose any of our public."

"See you then, then."

She walks to the side of the stage, goes down the steps and out of the side exit.

Eddie puts her empty glass back on the amplifier.

"Right," he says to the group. "Let's give 'Viva España' a run-through."

THE SMOKE

"Bad news about Ray Warren," Mickey said. "Or for him. Or for us, temporarily."

"What's that, Mickey?" I asked him.

"His old lady. He phoned last night. She snuffed it. He's staying up there for a few days, until after they've put her in the ground."

"Sorry to hear it," I said.

"Yeah, I knew you would be," Mickey said. "You want me to organise a wreath?"

"Yes, I should do that."

"Shall I get two made up while I'm at it?" he said.

"Let's leave that open till he gets back," I said to him. "We can check on him after we've talked to Hales."

"When do you want to do that?"

"As soon as possible."

"He's picking up in Birmingham at the moment. He'll be back in the morning."

"Tomorrow night, then."

"Yeah," Mickey said. "About that."

"What about it?"

"Sammy. He's in a constant state of macaroni at the moment."

"So what's new about that?"

"Nothing. But, you know. Maybe we ought to use another place."

The patina of what James had said the other day drifted into my mind.

"He doesn't know what's gone down," I said. "Not what's really gone down."

"Oh, no. He knows nothing. But—"

"Perhaps you're right Sammy's the instinctive type. Yes. All right. Any ideas?"

"Well," Mickey said. "There's always my drum."

Mickey had two places that I knew of. One was a flat in Covent Garden. The other was a house in Notting Hill.

"Which one?"

"The flat."

"Why?"

"Safe as houses, if you'll pardon me. I mean, top floor; nothing below me but offices. Everybody's gone home by six o'clock. Anything untoward happens, like with Mal, just down the stairs and out the back with him."

"I thought you'd just re-carpeted throughout."

"Can always put polythene down, can't we?"

Again James's words hung in my mind. I shook my head.

"Farlow," I said. "He's creaming himself at the thought of evening up after the last lot."

"Farlow?" Mickey said. "What does he know?"

"He knows where your flat is."

"So?"

"At the moment he'll have got eyes out all over the place."

"Again, so?"

"If anything goes wrong, he could pick it up."

"Look," Mickey said, "he's not going to be watching the place himself, is he?"

"No."

"So it'll be a minion, right?"

"Right."

"So the minion would be in full possession of the facts, wouldn't he? What he'd seen."

"Yes."

"Well, supposing Farlow wanted to use the facts to squeeze us on behalf of the Shepherdsons. He couldn't just tell his minion to tear a page out of his notebook, could he? Not if it was like with Mal. The minion might rush straight upstairs. Farlow wouldn't chance it."

"Perhaps."

"I mean, it's not like with Sammy. The trouble with him not knowing the full score, we don't know whose office he might stumble into. In this case it's safe because Farlow wouldn't risk the same kind of facts being carried into the same kind of office, because if he was squeezing for the Sheps and we went down he knows Morville'd make sure Farlow and the Sheps played the ukelele when the ship went down."

"Perhaps. But I understand the brothers are unhappy with the way he fucked up the last stroke."

"Same difference. Without them giving him full support, he's not exactly going to be motivated to try and get the Commissioner's job, is he? If that was the case, he could have tried to hang one on us a dozen times over, before he decided on going for the kind of promotion the Sheps dish out."

I lit a cigarette.

"Yes," I said. "I take all those points, Mickey."

"So," he said. "My place then."

I blew smoke across the top of my desk.

"Find another place, Mickey."

There was a silence, very short.

"Yeah, well, all right," Mickey said, standing up. "I'll find another place, then."

"Thanks, Mickey," I told him. "And for tomorrow night, eh?"

After he'd gone, his eagerness to use his flat remained behind, mingling in my mind with the words James had spoken a day or so before.

THE SEA

BETWEEN THE TREES, THE path that leads to the bungalow is just wide enough to accommodate the width of the Marina; untrimmed branches scratch at the bodywork like the fingers of harpies against a passing tumbril.

Then the branches are gone and the headlights illuminate the almost blank brickwork that forms the side of the bungalow facing the access from the copse. In this wall, there is one small window, high up, and the garage door, only the top of it at present visible above the rim of the short slope that has been cut to drop below the normal level of the ground. The only other feature is the flashing glass of the front door as the headlights sweep across it.

The Marina dips down the short slope and passes through the photo-electric eye and the garage door rolls up, then down again, behind me.

I don't switch off the headlights until I've switched on the garage's main light. When I've done both these things, I take the flask from my pocket and have a long drink. It's not just the coldness of the concrete that makes me drink now, before going through the door that gives access into the house; it's because this moment, this switching off of the car, this cold immobility, this homecoming, this is the worst moment of all. The deadness, the quietness, the still starkness of the light, the termination of the movements of the day. And beneath my feet, below the trapdoor on which I stand, the other deadness, the other quietness, that can be revived by the threading of a sprocket and the revolving of a spool and the unfolding of a strip of celluloid.

Jean's down there, rolled up in a film can, waiting to be revived.

I take another drink and then I walk over to the door that leads into the house. The switch for the photo-electric eye is on the wall by the door, beneath the switch for the garage and the switch that turns on a light on the other side of the door. I unlock the door and operate all three switches and step through the door and lock it behind me.

In the main room, I operate the switch that curtains the picture window. Then I climb the steps to the upper level and switch on the TV for *News at Ten*. Then I go over to the drinks and pour myself a large one but I don't immediately sit down. Somehow, the finality of sitting down always seems to act as a breach in my defences against the night thoughts that are waiting to flood into the front of my mind.

I go over to the window and part the curtains slightly. Apart from the narrow strip of light thrown out by the gap I've made, everything is a void. Only where the stars stop at the horizon is the blackness complete. I close the curtains and go and refill my glass and drain it and fill it again.

So easy. It would be so easy.

So easy to go downstairs, to get a couple of films, the private ones, run them, face the reminders of Jean, try and exorcise her memory. But after the last one, the last one . . . there would be no exorcism after that. At least that one wasn't there, to tempt me with.

Another drink. Another drink and watch the news. Leave the ghosts. Leave them in the basement. Leave them in their winding sheets, in their circular coffins.

Another drink. Stop them advancing, up through the trapdoor, across the garage floor.

THE SMOKE

"MICKEY," I SAID. "ABOUT tonight."

"Yes, Mr. Fowler."

"After you've brought Hales along, you don't have to stay."

"Mr. Fowler?"

"I don't think we'll need you. At the place."

"How do you mean?"

"I'd like you to wait for us outside. In the car. After he's been settled down. Just in case."

"In case of another Mal?"

"Yes."

"I see."

"I don't think so."

Mickey didn't say anything.

"There's no need to sulk. We just won't be needing you. You know Hales, if he has anything to say, he won't be long in saying it."

"I know that," Mickey said.

I smiled, and poured him some champagne.

"I know it's one of the perks of the job, as far as you're concerned," I said. "But there'll be other times."

"Of course."

"Come on, Mickey."

He doesn't say anything.

"It's not because of Mal, if that's what you're thinking."

"I'm not."

I drank some of my champagne.

"Will Mrs. Fowler be there?"

"Yes."

Mickey didn't say anything.

"Look, I know you don't like women, Mickey, but—"

"Don't include Mrs. Fowler in that. It's different with her."

"—I know you don't like women, but these days, women's lib and all that . . ."

More silence from Mickey.

"And Mrs. Fowler's shy about some things. You understand."

"I understand."

He drank some of his champagne.

"By the way," I said. "The place. It's very good."

"It wasn't difficult to fix up."

"No, it wouldn't be," I said. "Not for you."

After Mickey had left, Jean came into the lounge.

"How did he take it?" she asked me.

"How I expected him to take it," I said.

She poured herself a drink.

After a while I said, "You're certain about tonight?"

"Yes, I'm certain," she said.

"I mean. Watching it's one thing."

"I know that."

"You want to go ahead, then?"

"You know what I want."

"Yes," I said. "I know what you want."

THE SEA

Another drink.

Turn down the TV, turn up the stereo. Loud. *New World Symphony*. Chords deep and warm. Warmth, to fill the bungalow. That's what it needs, to counteract the chill of memory. Turn it up louder. I walk over to the stereo. Louder. Another drink. The booze and the noise. Keep the Eumenides where they belong, rolled up, cold in their cans. Canned Eumenides. I smile to myself. Just open the cans and reheat.

I sit on the top of the steps, drinking, cloaking myself in the sound, rocking backward and forward like somebody who's been punched in the gut.

Then the music stops. The room is full of silence. Just the clicking and the whirring of the stereo machine as it dies.

And then I'm aware of another sound, a light tapping. A light tapping, but not in the room; it's outside.

Outside, at the window.

I stand up and go over to the piano. I put down my drink on the closed lid and pick up the gun.

If they were ever to come, they wouldn't do it this way; if they were ever to come. I'd be dead before I passed through the photo-electric cell.

The tapping stops for a moment. Then it starts again.

I walk down the steps into the lower level of the room,

below the level of the window. I wait next to the door, by the switches.

Again the tapping stops, and again it starts again.

From where I'm standing below them, I press the switch that operates the curtains. I'll be able to see them, but they won't be able to see. Not soon enough, anyway. And then there was the plate glass. By the time they've blasted through that, I can take anybody out who happens to be out there. I shake my head. Whoever they were, they weren't professionals. And not even the local fourth division would tap tap tap as an overture to taking me out. So I press the switch that operates the curtains and the switch that operates the outside light.

The curtains slide apart and the lights illuminate the figure of Lesley, in her Afghan coat and her dark glasses, the light again, like the spotlight in the Dunes, blanking the relief of her features. And the soft inside light combines with the harshness of that outside to diffuse and at the same time double her image in the double glazing of the glass between the two sources of illumination. And my present alcoholic vision doesn't help in clarifying her appearance.

Thoughts of why she's here, what she's doing, seem frozen by the surprise at being presented with her vision.

She stands there motionless, looking into the apparent emptiness of the room for any signs of life.

I press another switch, and, just for the moment, I don't move. Just in case.

A section of the window slides open, letting in the cold night air. For a moment, she just stands there; then she steps forward, into the room.

I press the switches again. The window closes, and so do the curtains.

She stands still, a foot in front of the curtains.

"Do I have to say, coming, ready or not?" she says.

I slip the gun into my jacket pocket, then step away from the wall. She looks down into the well at me.

"So," she says. "You saw the Bond movie, too."

I still don't say anything.

"I'm not standing on a hidden trapdoor or anything like that, am I?" she says. "Or is it the crocodile's night off?"

I move forward to the foot of the steps. She still doesn't move.

"What are you doing?" I say to her.

"Waiting," she says.

"Waiting?"

"To be offered a drink."

"Here," I say to her. "What are you doing here?"

She shrugs.

"I don't know really. I was walking on the beach."

I look at her, not saying anything.

"I often walk on the beach when I can't rest. Mablethorpe's only a mile from here if you walk along the beach."

"But what are you doing here?"

"I saw your light. I was going to turn round and walk back, but I saw your light."

"How did you know it was mine?"

"Yours is the only house here."

"You knew where I lived?"

"Of course," she says. "Eddie told me."

"Why should he tell you that?"

She looks at me. I begin to mount the stairs.

"You're pretty drunk, aren't you?" she says.

I reach the top of the steps and pick up my drink off the top of the piano.

"Why did Eddie tell you where I lived?"

"No reason. Except to impress me, I suppose; I can't think why."

I take a sip of my drink and look at her.

"He's impressed by you," she says. "So I suppose he thought I would be."

"But you're not."

She shrugs.

"Then why come?"

"I told you; I saw your light. I thought I might be offered a drink. I mean, as you tried to pick me up. As it happens . . ."

She walks over to the window, then stops, turns to face me.

"Or do I get to go out through the front door this time?"

"The drinks are over there," I tell her.

She looks at the shelving, then crosses the floor between me and the silent flickering of the TV set and begins to make herself a drink.

"Don't you have any lemon?" she says.

I don't say anything.

"Vodka's not the same without a slice of lemon."

"Why didn't you ring the bell?" I ask her.

"I did," she said, dropping some ice into the glass. "You had the music on loud. You do remember the music?"

She walks over to the fireplace and stands in front of the unlit logs that have been set in the grate.

"I don't believe you," I tell her.

"What, particularly?"

"People don't walk on the beach at night."

"Only first thing in the morning?"

I look at her.

"I've seen you. A couple of times. Once you sat on an old tank. Another time I saw you climb up on to one of those pillboxes and sit on top of that."

"I've never seen you."

She shrugs.

"It's a big beach."

I go over to the drinks and pour myself another.

"One thing I *have* noticed about you," she says.

"What's that?"

"You drink every drink as though you need it."

"You notice a lot."

I go over to the TV, switch it off, then walk just beyond it to the panel of switches on the brick wall. As I pass the TV, I sway into it, almost knocking it off its stand. I get to the panel and as I'm trying to turn up the heating a few degrees to compensate for the entry of the night air I accidentally activate the movie screen. It begins to descend from the ceiling. I reverse its procedure and it slides back up again.

"Every possible home comfort," she says.

I don't answer her. Instead I put a cigarette in my mouth, light it, walk a little closer to her. She steps back slightly. I shake out the match, throw it into the grate.

"Eddie says everybody round here thinks you're in property or something."

"I am."

"Eddie doesn't think so."

"Eddie knows nothing."

She takes a sip of her drink. I try my hardest to focus on her. In spite of myself I say, "I know you. I know you from somewhere."

"God," she says, walking over to the piano. "Why use that line when you're in your own house?"

"Listen," I say. "I don't give a fuck about you."

"That's good," she says. "Because I didn't come here to get laid."

There is a crackling behind me. I couldn't have shaken the match out properly; flames are rolling up from the newspapers, licking round the logs. Lesley clocks the picture of Jean on the piano.

"Your wife?" she says.

"I'm not married."

She places her fingers on the keyboard, plays a single chord.

"What do you do?" she says.

My focusing is getting worse; there seems to be a triple image of her as she stands at the piano.

"Property."

"Yours or other people's?"

The images of her turn to face me.

"Do you mind if I have another drink?"

THE SMOKE

HALES WASN'T THE ONE either.

But Jean had enjoyed herself. The video proved at least that.

Watching it, afterwards, Jean had gone crazy. She made love as though she'd been touched for the first time. And after that we'd watched the tape again. And after that, again, love.

The following day I talked to Mickey about Ray Warren.

"He should have been back by now," Mickey said. "The funeral was last Thursday. He didn't have anything to hang around for."

"Have you phoned his lady?"

"No," Mickey said.

"Why not give her a ring now?"

"What, now?"

"Why not? She might be worried too."

I pushed the phone towards Mickey. He took his little black book out and dialled Glenda Warren's number. I flicked the amplifier so I could hear both sides of the conversation. Glenda came on the line.

"Hello?"

"Hello, Glenda. This is Mickey Brice. I'm phoning on Mr. Fowler's behalf. Ray's not there, is he?"

"Ray? No, why?"

"I mean, he's not back from Bolton yet?"

"No, he's not. Why?"

"Just business. Mr. Fowler's got some ideas he wants to talk to Ray about."

"Well, he's not back yet."

"When did he say he'd be back?"

"He said either yesterday or today, depending."

"Oh, that's all right, then. When he gets back, ask him to give us a bell, will you?"

"Sure, I'll tell him."

"Thanks. Goodbye, Glenda."

"That's all right."

Mickey put the phone down. We looked at each other. After a while I said, "Supposing Ray *has* retired to the sun?"

Mickey shrugged.

"If it's him, he'll have enough money stacked."

"He doesn't know we're looking at him."

"He could have decided it was time, independent of us."

"Well . . ."

"There's two alternatives. Glenda'll either know or she won't know."

"Ray wouldn't trust a bird. Not with this."

"He might. Ray's usually a seven-bird-a-week man. He's been with Glenda eighteen months. Her name's even on the lease."

"In that case she'd have flown with him."

"Not necessarily. As I say, there's two alternatives; if he's cleared off without her, she'd be mad enough to talk to us; if she knows what he's been up to, how much money he's been salting, she'll be even madder. All we've got to do is to tell her he's cleared off, then await further developments."

"And if he's not cleared off?"

"Same difference. We still tell her he's cleared off."

Mickey had a few thoughts.

"Of course, she could be about to join him, wherever he is. If he's put her in this one."

"So we'd better go and talk to her straight away, hadn't we?"

"We?" Mickey said. "What's the need for us both to go?"

"No need, Mickey."

Mickey stood up.

"All right," he said. "I'll go and get the motor out."

"Good lad."

He stood there for a moment. Then he said, "Funny. I never knew Ray was shacked up."

"Nobody did," I said. "Except me."

"I wonder why?"

"Didn't want to spoil his image, did he?"

Mickey shook his head.

"Men," he said. "I'll never understand them, not if I live to be a hundred."

THE SEA

In the dream, the shotgun that's being pointed at my face is growing larger, so that the ends of the barrels grow so large that whoever is levelling them at me is totally obscured by the size of the black tunnels. And when the triggers are pulled, there is not an immediate boom; the shells seem to originate from miles away, down in the depths of the shotgun, beginning with a high-pitched scream, rushing forward up the barrel, expanding into a shattering explosion as pellets the size of bowling balls spread outwards from the barrels' rims. And not just twice. The double process is repeated again and again. Again, and then I wake up.

But the screaming and exploding of the shells doesn't stop.

I'm not in bed. I'm laid out on the settee that's set at right angles to the brickwork and its fireplace.

The first thing I notice is that the TV's still on, the snowstorm on the screen giving out like an audible rash.

I get up and make it to the set and switch it off. I just manage to do that.

That accomplished, I drag myself across the face of the shelving to where the drinks are. I manage to get some scotch into a glass. And then I manage to get some of it into myself.

The screaming and the exploding still go on.

I make it over to the window and part the curtains slightly.

A couple of jets screech low, almost on a line with the sea's horizon, loose their rockets at a piece of the charred hardware on the beach.

I look at my watch. It's quarter past seven. Christ.

I take another drink and go over to the wall panel and activate the central heating. Normally it's programmed to come on at eight, but I'm cold, frozen from passing out and spending the night where I've spent it.

Then I go over to the fireplace and sink down in front of it and light the rolled paper that peeps out from between the logs. I stay where I am for ten minutes, until the fire's properly going, absorbing its warmth, my mind concentrating vice-like in an attempt to keep out the noise of the manoeuvres outside.

Then, when I feel slightly more fit, I raise myself and make it back over to the drinks.

While the second one's going down, the image of the girl comes into my mind.

But I'm still not fit to think in any kind of shape or sequence.

The girl. She came in. She had a drink. She came in, she had a drink. Through the window. She had a drink. And the next thing those bastards outside are bombing my dreams. Or had she been in my dreams, while I'd been bombed out?

The gun.

I look at the piano. It's where I always keep it, next to the picture of Jean.

She'd seen the gun; Jean's picture, a different one, had been in the papers, months ago. The girl had seen Jean's picture, here. If she was here.

I walk over to the piano and slam Jean's picture face down.

"Fuck it," I say out loud. "Fuck it."

I sit down on the piano stool.

Just think, I say to myself. Think things through.

If she'd come.

If she's where she could be from, I'd be dead. I wouldn't have risen off that settee. I wouldn't be sitting here thinking about it.

That aspect was out. And Jean's photograph. Nothing like the one that'd been in the press. No real resemblance at all.

No, I wouldn't be sitting here, drinking, staring at the flames—

The fire. Hadn't I thrown a match in it, last night? Had I? Or hadn't I?

I began to wonder whether she came at all. I couldn't remember her going, I was that pissed. Why should I remember her coming? Except maybe in a dream. The kind of dreams I've been having these days. And the nagging of her familiarity. That could have caused a dream. Christ knew. After what I've seen, I'm capable of seeing anything. After Jean. Working my imagination in reverse. But later I'd know. There was the Dunes tonight. It was tonight, wasn't it?

Stop thinking. Stop thinking until I'm together. Later, when I'm human again, when I'm back to appearing as I appear to the world outside.

And in the world outside, the jets keep zapping the charred hardware out on the beach, and making direct hits on the inside of my head.

Tonight, I'll find out what happened. Until then, Christ alone knows, and I doubt very much whether he cares, one way or the other.

THE SMOKE

IT TOOK US AN hour to go through Ray's flat, but there was nothing. Oh, there were plenty of clothes in the cupboards and in the drawers she hadn't bothered to close. She hadn't had time to pack much. She hadn't taken any of her cosmetics; even the toothbrush was still in the bathroom. But. There were none of Ray's clothes, and there were no suitcases. Not even a small cheque stub.

I sat down on the double bed.

"His mother in Bolton," I said. "No wonder he said it was terminal."

Mickey opened an empty box file, closed it. It made a noise like a door being shut.

"Cunt," Mickey said. "That's the word to describe him."

Ray had certainly gone prepared. There'd been nothing for Glenda to do except close the door behind her.

"Stupid," I said. "Why the Christ did I phone?"

"Like you said," said Mickey. "He'd no reason to suspect we were on to him. Must have been coincidence. Like you said. They were all set to go."

"Like I said."

"I notice she left the safe open. Two fingers and all that."

"We could have beat her to the door if we hadn't phoned."

"One of those things," Mickey said. "Couldn't be helped."

"Stick the philosophy," I told him. "I helped it. I got you to call her."

Mickey went out of the room and came back with a couple of glassfuls of scotch. I stared at him.

"We may as well," Mickey said. "Seeing as how, and all that."

I took one of the drinks from him. We drank.

"Absent friends," Mickey said.

"They won't be absent for long."

"It's a big world," Mickey said.

"Not the one we live in," I said. "He's not going to Angola or Cambodia or Iceland, is he? A friend of ours'll see him, somewhere, some time."

"Well," Mickey said, "let's drink to that."

THE SEA

ON SATURDAYS, PEOPLE DRIVE into Mablethorpe to do their weekend shopping. It makes it look as though people actually live there.

I have a couple in the South but there's no sign of her, and for the brief time in there, Eddie doesn't make his usual Command Performance, so I drink up and make my way to the Dunes via the arcade on the corner. This is full of kids spending their hard-earned pocket money, but she isn't there either. However, I wait a while, passing the time with a pound's worth on my favourite machine.

The ritual of the machine and the fresh morning air and the sauna I'd managed back at the bungalow have all combined to straighten out my mind. I must have been pissed last night. Christ, I'd almost been out of my mind when I'd got back to the bungalow. If I'd had much more I'd have imagined Farlow coming down the chimney dressed like Father Christmas. They say things like that happen to you alone at sea, or in the desert, and this was certainly the desert, with the sea thrown in as well. In any case, real, imagined, or dreamt, I want to know which. If she'd been real, it still gave me things to think about; if she hadn't been, if I'm going crazy, I want to go crazy in full possession of my faculties. That or change the brand of booze I drink.

Besides, there's still the nagging, the near recognition. That, if nothing else, I am going to lay to rest.

So, she doesn't appear in the arcade. So I walk out and up the ramp and walk along the mini-promenade towards the Dunes. Kids scamper up and down the mean grass of the mound, creating even bigger bald spots with their heels. On the broad flatness of the beach, people singly or in pairs stride up and down under the clear sky like figures from a Lowry painting.

Inside, the Dunes looks less gloomy than usual, the plate glass glowing in the morning light. Howard must have cleaned the windows. He's even got his toupee on straight. I buy us both one and we get on to the subject of the evening's impending entertainment, and thus, Lesley.

"My God, though," he said. "She was good though, my God she was good."

"Praise indeed, Howard," I say to him.

"Oh, I've had me moments," he says. "*And* I've seen the best. But last night. I couldn't believe her."

"Any idea where she lives?"

"Hello," Howard says.

"No, I don't mean that," I lied. "Is she a local girl?"

"No idea. Eddie's talked about her, but I never seen her before last night."

I take a sip of my drink.

"I can give you the addresses of a couple of fellows if you're interested," Howard says.

"Howard, would I try and cut in on you?" I said. "I mean, out here. I'd hate to queer your pitch."

"Funny. You should be on tonight."

"You never know. I might win."

"You could easily," he says. "Dead and alive lot, I can tell you that now."

THE SMOKE

"ALL RIGHT," JEAN SAID, "assuming Ray's collectors, or some of them, were involved—"

"No assumption. A couple at least had to be. Ray would have told us. If I hadn't have fucked things up."

"Assuming that, the natural course of events is to talk to them. Is that it?"

"Of course that's it."

"The whole business all over again."

I looked at her.

"Don't tell me you're getting tired of it."

"Look. At the moment, I'm talking business."

"All right; talk business."

"Right. There's five collectors, right. All in the Birmingham area. Right?"

"Right."

"And we've got arrangements among the Birmingham Law. But it's not like it is down here, is it? Anything goes wrong up there, our Law can only sweep up so much. Beyond that, the Regional will be down on them like a ton of bricks. They like things like that."

"Nothing will go wrong."

"Nothing'll go wrong? Look, we go through the lot of them, trying to find out what we're trying to find out. They're not all like the fellows down here, stoical and all that, they could start rabbiting before they've got their plasters on."

"They know what would happen if they did. They've got relatives."

Jean sat down.

"In any case . . ." she said.

"In any case, what?"

"At the moment we only have to hire one replacement. The way this thing is going we'll have to start advertising in *Exchange and Mart.*"

"So you'd rather let it rest and have some second division Foxy Fred sitting in his office knowing he's screwing us and getting away with it?"

"Do you think whoever it is is going to carry on with Ray gone? He was their protection; they'll be scared shitless now."

"It's not only that. We may get some information on Ray."

"You think he's going to scatter travel brochures all over the place?"

I didn't say anything.

"Why don't we let it rest? Wait until we get home thoughts from abroad."

"If we do," I said.

"Well, if we don't, what else can we do?" Jean said. "Look. It's over. It's stopped. Let's let it lay."

I lit a cigarette.

"It's over," she said. "Finished."

THE SEA

THE DUNES IS FULLER than I've ever seen it. Which isn't surprising, as I've only ever seen it empty.

The show hasn't started yet but most of the seats are informally filled, people having turned some of them round, facing away from the stage, so that they can support their beer on them.

Everything's set up on the stage, ready to go; Howard's engaged some half-wit to get in his way behind the bar.

Eventually Eddie makes his entrance, looking even less like a great entertainer in his stage gear. He joins me at the bar so that he can mingle with his public, allow them a brush with the famous.

"What does he look like?" Howard says to me, while Eddie's momentarily distracted by an OAP. "Montague Burton's answer to Des O'Connor."

Eddie disengages himself from the OAP and returns to my side.

"Well," he says, "quarter of an hour to curtain up."

"If we had a curtain," Howard says.

"How do I look then?" Eddie says. "What do you think of the gear?"

"You look a treat, Eddie," Howard says.

"I got it for the Season, really," he says, "only I thought I'd give it an airing."

"Your top of the bill," I says to him. "You fixed her up for the season yet?"

"I wish I had. She hasn't made her mind up. If she doesn't soon, she won't get booked anywhere else."

"You're joking," Howard says. "With that voice?"

"Well, maybe," Eddie says. "I just hope I can persuade her to stay, that's all."

"And talking of staying," Howard says. "Mr. Carson was asking me where she lived."

Eddie looks at me.

"Just out of interest."

"Just out of interest," Howard says.

"Er—well," Eddie says. "I'm not sure. I think she's got a van on the park. She's done a couple of gigs with us and that's where she's asked us to drop her off. But I'll ask her definite if you like, when she turns up."

"No, don't bother, Eddie. I was just making conversation."

"It's no bother, honest."

He looks at his watch.

"Eddie—" I say, but he cuts me off.

"Better go backstage and check they're not all arse about front."

Eddie ostentatiously makes his way through the audience towards the stage.

"A Star is Born," Howard says, watching him go. "Every minute."

Howard picks up my glass.

"Let's have another," he says. "We'll be needing it."

The show is unbelievable, which is of course entirely to be expected. The acts range from the deathly to the embarrassing. Once, Howard puts his hands to his face and asks me when it is safe to look again.

It isn't until towards the end that she comes on.

Before she does, Eddie gives her an introduction which leaves the audience in no doubt of what he thinks about her.

"That's sunk her for a start," Howard says.

". . . and so without any more ado from me, Miss . . . Lesley . . . Murray."

And then, after the introduction, she appears, and she looks completely different to any of the previous times I've seen her; she isn't wearing the Afghan or the dark glasses or the T-shirt or the jeans.

And she isn't wearing her hair the same way either; it isn't even the same hair. It's tucked up beneath a blonde wig that curls gently inwards at the nape of her neck.

It is this, more than anything else, that makes me realise who I'm looking at.

The clothes help to define her, of course; the style of the dress, the leather boots; they help to draw together the strands of her persona. The clothes make her movements different. And the makeup, altering her mouth, and around her previously unseen eyes.

But it's the wig, the way it falls at her neck, the way its forward waves redefine the shape of her face. I'm farther away from her than when I'd seen her the first time, but I'm certain.

I am looking at the girl from the Monastic Habit, the girl who'd been talking to the man with the crossword puzzle.

THE SMOKE

COLLINS SAID, "THE LOCAL lads are very interested in Ray Warren's disappearance."

"Are they?" I said.

"And his missus. Well, you know what I mean."

"And?"

"Going at it like a bull at a gate, they are."

"Bulls," I said.

"You what?"

"They," I said, "it's bulls, at gates. Forget it."

Collins attempted to forget it.

"They're leaving no stone unturned, so to speak," he said.

"Which means they know he worked for me and all the rest of it, yes, all right, get on with it, Dennis, for fuck's sake."

"Well," Collins said. "I haven't got a great deal of influence at that branch."

I was beginning to get sick and tired of Dennis, the money I was paying him.

"What do you mean, Dennis?" I asked him.

"Like I say," he said. "Parsons is the top man down there. You know what he's like."

"That's right," I said. "I know what he's like. Is that what I pay you for? To tell me I know what Parsons is like?"

Collins didn't say anything.

"What I pay you for, Dennis," I said, "What I pay you for is *not* to come here and tell me how little influence you have in the world today. I pay you to come and tell me what you've sorted, after you've sorted it."

There was a short silence. Then Collins said, "It might help if I knew what was going off."

"They've fucked off," I said. "That's what. They've fucked off."

Collins looked at me.

"I'm telling you," I said. "They've fucked off. That's all there is to it."

Collins began picking at his thumbnail, concentrating on it as though it was the most important thing in the world.

"If I may say so . . ." he said, but I cut him off.

"I know, Dennis. People have gone missing before. This is not like that; on those different occasions you've always been put in the picture."

"Not entirely always," Collins said.

I didn't say anything for a moment or two. Then I said, "Look, Dennis, just get your fire extinguisher out and get over there and turn it on them. Christ, they're nobodies. Traffic artists."

"I'll see what I can do," Collins said.

"Too bloody right. And don't come back until you've done it."

"I ought to say Farlow's been fanning the flames with Parsons."

"Of course he has. That's what he'd do, wouldn't he? I don't pay you to tell me that either."

Collins stood up.

"I'll be in touch," he said.

"Yes," I said, "but if you decide to use the post, put a first-class stamp on it, will you?"

THE SEA

I SIT IN THE car, on the other side of the promenade, opposite the caravan park. There is no sign of life whatsoever.

After the show finished and she'd won, she'd gone backstage, got out of her gear and disappeared. Eddie'd told me that. He'd also told me he'd asked her where she lived, on my account.

So I'd made my excuses and left, as the Law says about the obscene exhibitions they're forced to attend all in the line of duty.

I'd got in my Marina and driven straight down the promenade to the caravan park and I've been waiting here ever since, but either I didn't beat her to it or she's gone elsewhere.

I light a cigarette and consider my stupidity, why I hadn't thought of it before; not the fact that she was almost certainly the same girl as the one in the bar in Grimsby. That I couldn't have realised, not until I'd seen her up on the stage. No, it's not that, it's the possibility that has come to me since; the possibility that she could be Press.

It came to me while I was watching her doing her act in the Dunes, while I was wondering what possible reason there could be for her Mablethorpe disappearance, in both senses of the word, and her appearance in Grimsby.

If I hadn't been entirely out of my mind the previous evening, and what I can remember is indeed a fact, then it all fits. And if it was so, she'd been clever. She hadn't immediately tried to pick me up. She'd done the opposite; even to rejecting what she'd imagined was my advance in the arcade, then just being around, creating a bit of interest.

And when she'd appeared at the bungalow, even then she'd started off by playing it cool; but when she'd seen the state I'd been in, my final collapse had made it even easier for her; she hadn't even had to pretend to be seduced. She hadn't even had to steal the photograph of Jean. All she'd had to do was to have taken out her little pocket camera and take a little snap of it, along with one or two of me, dead to the world, and the bungalow's interior, to make up a set together with the daytime ones she'll have taken of the exterior of the bungalow and me going in and out of it and walking up and down the beach.

I can just see the headline: MY NIGHT OF LOVE WITH MISSING PORN KING. And the outline: "How could I ever have imagined that a casual evening's sex would lead to . . ." Etcetera.

I wonder which of the Sundays it would be. The idea sounds more like one of Craig's front pages than the others.

Anyway, even if I'm wrong, she's not from the Law; if I'm right, the last thing Farlow and the others want is it splashed all over the front pages that I'm not dead or living in Australia. The last thing they wanted was that. That would mean they'd have to reopen things they won't want reopening.

As for the others, well, like I say, I wouldn't be sitting here in my motor considering things.

Of course, I realise, after Eddie's discreet enquiries she's probably halfway down the motorway by now. But for that, she'd probably intended sticking around a day or so more, so that we could have been photographed together.

But if I'm right about her, she's got enough. And if she's gone there's nothing whatsoever I can do about it. It's only half-past nine now: I could be all over the breakfast table by tomorrow morning.

Unless she's not clocked. Unless. All I can do is to sit here and hope she hasn't. And isn't.

THE SMOKE

I ASKED PARSONS IF he'd like some champagne. To my surprise he accepted.

"Well," I said, sitting down. "I won't ask you what I can do for you."

"No," Parsons said.

He drank some of his champagne.

"Very nice," he said.

"We like it," I said.

"We?" he said. "Oh, you mean you and the wife."

"That's right," I said.

"To you and the wife, then," Parsons said.

This time we both drank.

"Anyway," I said, "I'm in no hurry, but we may as well get down to it."

"Yes," Parsons said. "Why don't we?"

I allowed him his pause for effect.

"I realise I'm not on my patch—"

"We both realise that," I said.

"Yes. But Ray Warren and Glenda Hill were."

"Were?"

"Let's just say they're not there at the moment."

"You can say what you like. Because whatever you're going to say will be a waste of breath."

"Very probably."

"So why come all the way over here to waste it when you could be wasting it in familiar surroundings?"

Parsons smiled. It was the kind of smile an RSM gives to a new arrival of squaddies.

"I realise that Ray and Glenda are probably cemented up in some City redevelopment by now," he said, "but that won't stop me trying to trace the cement back to you."

"Feel free," I said. "I'm not stopping you."

"No," he said.

"I mean," I said, "I don't have to remind you of all the thousand bits of luck you're going to need to build even half a case that even then would depend entirely on association."

"Yes, I know," he said. "I know all about that. Actually, although Ray and Glenda are central to my being here, it's one of the side effects I'm really here about."

"Really? And what would that be?"

"'What' is correct. When one's talking about Collins."

"Collins?"

"I don't like Collins talking to me."

"You'll be surprised to know that makes two of us."

"I don't like him coming over to my branch and suggesting holidays in the sun, etcetera."

"You should take them; then you'd have more chance of finding Ray and Glenda."

"That's what you'd like me to believe."

"Whether you believe it or not makes no difference whatsoever."

"Quite," Parsons said. "However; Collins. Don't send him over again."

"I won't; not now you've told me how stupid he's been."

"Yes, he has, hasn't he? That's always surprised me about you and him."

"He's not always been stupid."

"Not always; but ultimately."

"You have to be very stupid to have his kind of bank balance. If you wanted to be that stupid you could have one yourself."

"I know. I should never have taken the Mensa tests."

"Resign. Take the money instead."

"I can't," Parsons said. "That's my great trouble in life."

He finished his champagne.

"Like some more?" I said.

He stood up and put the glass down on the table-top.

"No, thanks. I've got to be going. I just dropped in to tell you about Collins. What I felt about him."

"You could have phoned."

"I would have," he said. "But I wanted to see you. Extra motivation and all that kind of thing."

"Well," I said, "any time you feel like being motivated . . ."

"Thanks. I'll do that as soon as possible."

After he'd gone I picked up the phone.

THE SEA

THE MAN WHO TAKES care of the caravan site lives in a low box by the site's entrance. There are a lot of caravans but only one or two of them are illuminated.

I knock on the door of the caravan-site man's house. He's a long time answering. Yellow light from the hall behind him mingles with the sound of the TV and drifts into the night air.

He doesn't ask me what I want. In fact, he doesn't say anything at all. So I tell him.

"Could you tell me which is Lesley Murray's caravan?"

"Lesley who?"

"Lesley Murray."

He thinks about it.

"What's he look like?"

"It's a she. Lesley. Young bird."

He shakes his head.

"No."

"You certain about that?"

"Yes."

"You don't have to check your book?"

He shakes his head again.

"There's only three vans occupied at the present. Weekenders."

"She couldn't be staying with any of them?"

"No, I know them all. They're all regulars. Retired people. Their own vans. I'd know if she was with any of them."

"Well, she did say that this was where she was staying."

He looks at me.

"She's shot you a line, then, hasn't she?" he says.

"You're absolutely certain she couldn't be on here without you knowing?"

"No, I'm checking all the time. Hippies are always trying to get into them, the bastards."

"Well," I say, "that's that, then."

"Yes," he says. "Better luck next time."

"Thanks."

He closes the door.

I go back to the car and get in and drive back to the Dunes. Although the show's over, the audience and most of the performers are still there living it up, being entertained by numbers from Eddie and his group.

I fight my way through to the bar and when Howard gets me my drink I get him to give me a couple of quidsworth of two-bob bits then I go into the lobby in the vain hope of getting James on a Saturday night. At this moment he's probably in his box, halfway through his hamper, halfway through the full production of *The Ring*.

But I dial his number anyway and of course he's not in.

And it's not a clever idea to phone O'Connell myself.

So I put the change in my pocket and go out of the Dunes and back along the mini-promenade and get in my Marina and reverse and point it in the direction of Grimsby.

There's one or two possibilities I may as well pursue until such time as I can raise James and ultimately O'Connell. For instance, if she's been sent up here the way I think she has, there's the possibility she may have been staying at one of the town's two decent hotels or its new motel. And following that, there's the possibility that she might be still hanging around; they might have shipped the stuff down earlier today, the original intention maybe being to wait until she'd progressed in her relationship with me until they printed. But if there was a possibility I tumbled, they might have told her to clear out of it and satisfy themselves with what they'd got. And another possibility being that she hasn't necessarily tumbled to me having clocked her for what she is; after her charade at the Dunes, just to keep up appearances, she could easily clear off to her hotel and relax the remainder of the weekend, not knowing, of course, I've already clocked her in Grimsby.

But everything is academic. If the material is with the paper, then all the thoughts in the world won't make any difference; the bungalow is blown. I'll have to stay in Grimsby tonight before entering into any of my other contingency arrangements.

For the moment I'll just fill in the time between now and James.

THE SMOKE

"I DON'T THINK," JAMES said, "that at this stage we should do other than consider the possibility."

"Why not?" I said. "Why not do it, and get it over with?"

"Because there's no *need*, George. That's why not."

"There'd be nothing to it."

"Oh, I know that."

"Well then. One more Christian Soldier marching on a little too far."

"Look, George," James said. "There is no reason so to do. Ray and Glenda are not permanently missing, so, to begin with, he's not going to discover their mortal remains, is he? He has to begin with those, doesn't he, otherwise where can he go?"

I didn't say anything.

"I mean," James said, "he can be fitted up any time; the machinery is just waiting to be switched on. Why use it when we don't need it? Remember the energy motto. Save It."

I lit a cigarette.

"It's Collins you should really be concerned about," said James. "Parsons wouldn't have came to see you if it weren't for him."

"I know," I said.

"But that doesn't mean to say," James said, "that you should go tearing into him, either."

I didn't say anything.

"With the earlier business, and Farlow and the Sheps getting their balls burnt, things are very delicately balanced at the moment. We don't want to add Parsons and/or subtract Dennis and get the scales tipping in the wrong direction, now do we?"

"No, we don't, James," I said. "But I don't see what harm there'd be in fitting up Parsons. Christ, it'll come to it eventually."

"You're absolutely right," James said. "But just wait for something to give it cause. Let it happen in the natural order of things."

THE SEA

SHE'S NOT BEEN AT either of the hotels, so I go to the motel.

At the desk, I pursue my usual enquiries, and although the money makes the desk clerk eager to help, she hasn't been there, either.

So after I've been established in my room and ordered a tray carrying a bottle and a glass, I don't use the phone by the bedside. Instead I go down into reception and try to get James on one of the pay phones. There's still no reply.

I didn't think there would be, not unless the midnight movie's something he wants to see. I ring him at four more regular intervals; the fourth time I get through.

"It's me," I tell him.

"Yes," he says.

"I may have had a visitor."

"What kind?"

"Journalistic."

"That's a pity."

"It looks like Sunday stuff. It could even appear tomorrow."

"Oh dear."

"If I'm right, I can't go back to where I am. So I want you to phone O'Connell now. He'll still be at the paper and he'll know what all the other front pages are going to be by now."

"Yes, I'll do that."

"Get him on the phone but don't talk to him there; get him round to your flat."

"I think I'll be able to do the job properly."

"And if there's nothing in tomorrow's, give him anything he wants to find out whatever he can. It might even be one of the daily rags. If there's anything, he'll know about it."

"Of course. When will you be calling again?"

"In an hour."

I put the phone down and go back to my room, where the bottle is.

THE SMOKE

"THE TROUBLE IS," MICKEY said, "we can't really promote anybody to replace Ray. Not from that particular area, can we?"

"No," I said. "It'd mean taking someone from somewhere else. Any ideas?"

"Not offhand. Some of them in similar lines in different branches of the business aren't the world's most discreet people. Luckily they only ever come as far up in the water as me so they don't know a lot; but I wouldn't fancy running an entrance examination on that crowd."

"No," I said. "The only real candidates for the job are in the straight business."

"And that's why they're there; because they're straight."

"They'd bend very easily at the sight of a tenth of the money Ray was making."

"And that's the trouble," said Mickey. "Like giving Indians fire water; we'd never know where we were with them."

"Not like we did with Ray, of course."

Mickey shrugged.

"We can't win them all," he said.

There was a silence.

"The only thing, for the moment," I said, "is for you to look after it. For the time being."

"Whatever you say," Mickey said.

"I know it won't cut into any of the other things you're doing."

"Oh, no. I'll do it standing on my head."

"The thing is," I said, "at the same time you might be able to pick up something connected with Ray."

"I thought Mrs. Fowler and you had agreed to let that lay for a while."

"We have."

Mickey smiled.

"All right," he said. "I'll see what I can do."

"But only sniff," I said. "No pressure. I mean that."

"I'll just sniff," he said. "On that you can rely."

"I'm very glad to hear it," I said.

THE SEA

WHEN I PHONE JAMES again, he says, "O'Connell's here. Would you like to talk to him direct?"

I tell him that I would and O'Connell comes on the line.

"There is absolutely nothing," he says.

"How can you be so sure?"

"I'm absolutely certain. Not this week anyway. I've seen every single one. Not a thing. And as for the dailies, none of the papers in our group is doing it. And they'd have got their own team up there if the opposition was doing anything like this, trying to pick up the scraps."

"You're certain?"

"Positive. You know what this business is like."

"It must be next weekend, then."

"Not necessarily. We're all treading very lightly on the Law at the moment, since the last lot. I mean, we don't want the great British public to think the police are all bloated capitalists, do we? And they'd be reminded of that if you go on the front pages again."

"It wouldn't stop this story."

"Maybe. But I've never had a story break over my head, ever. I'll let James know the second I hear anything."

"Thanks."

James comes back on the line.

"Make it absolutely clear that what you're going to offer him is worth far more than Investigative Journalist of the Year."

"Naturally. When will you phone again?"

"Tomorrow morning. After I've read the papers."

"You seem pretty certain about this," James says. "You're sure you're not—"

"No, I'm not fucking stir-crazy, James. Not yet."

"All I was going to say was, perhaps you're overreacting."

"Do you know any of the facts?"

"No, but it might help if I did. And for the moment, where you are."

"Not even you, James. You're in charge, the businesses are still running nicely, thanks to you. But not even you, James."

"Very well. I'll hear from you in the morning, then."

"You will. Thank you, James."

Back in my room, I sit on the bed and refill my glass. I can just imagine them sitting there in James's flat, drinking James's best and my health, comfily mulling over my present state of mind.

I take another drink. It's not their arses that are on the line. Fuck them, the pair of them.

THE SMOKE

"I DON'T KNOW WHAT you're so worried about," Collins said. "Ray and Glenda have merely gone missing. There were no charges pending, no reason why they shouldn't have gone away. So that avenue's shut. And as they've not been topped, that avenue's never even going to open."

I looked at him without saying anything.

"I mean, that's why I was so open with Parsons. There was no reason not to be. I just told him he was wasting his time. That it was right what I said, Ray and Glenda have genuinely gone on their holidays. I mean, knowing the way he is, would I risk going to him direct and giving him a load of horse shit?"

"Dennis," I said, after a while, "did you know Jack Warner's retired from *Dixon of Dock Green*?"

"Yes," he said. "Why?"

I shook my head.

"Never mind," I said. "Just do me one favour, will you?"

"What's that?"

"Nothing," I said. "Precisely that. I want you to do nothing. I want you to say nothing. For a while I don't want you to do anything. Just sit behind your desk and only open your filing cabinet when you want to get your scotch out of it."

"Look—"

"No, Dennis. Don't do that either. Don't even look. Just do nothing. Nothing."

Collins was quiet for a while. Then he said, "Whatever you say."

"Thanks, Dennis," I said. "It's a relief to hear you say that."

THE SEA

IN THE distance, churchbells are ringing.

The motel room is even less charming in the Sunday morning light. But after I've had a few belts of scotch and I've gone through every single Sunday paper it doesn't look quite so bad.

O'Connell was right. There is absolutely nothing. Not even on the sports pages.

Which doesn't mean a thing. There's always next weekend and the dailies.

I light a cigarette and reposition the pillows and sit there and consider things.

Of course, I could be entirely wrong. But I can only act as if I'm right, the way I've already acted.

The prospect of shipping everything cross-country to Wales doesn't fill me with a great deal of pleasure. I'm not exactly in love with where I am at present, but the next move I make I want to make straight back into town. When James has soldered up a defence for me so solid they'd never even chance writing anything down on a charge sheet. Not that they would anyway without putting half the force up there in the dock with me. But justice has to be seen to be done; unseen, the formalities and the procedure have to be observed, but not by the public, nor even by its nominated prosecutor. Before my return as figurehead, James still has a great deal of work to do. But both of us are confident of the outcome. Until then I prefer to stay where I am.

Of course, Ibiza is out. The photographers will be at the villa in shifts even now.

Which, on a permanent basis, leaves Wales, and I don't like the thought of it.

But at the moment, I'm in a variation of my day-to-day existence; suspending my animation until events beyond my control take their course. It's a situation I'm not used to and it almost drives me mad.

But what else can I do? Just keep going through the time from minute to minute, instead of from hour to hour.

I sweep the papers off the bed and have a shower. I dress and leave the motel and after I've exhausted all the different possibilities of driving round Grimsby on a Sunday morning I park the car and make for the Monastic Habit, and not only because they do a passable Sunday lunch.

As I was hoping, the same fellow is on duty at the cocktail bar as was on duty when I'd seen the girl for the first time.

It's just gone twelve and the restaurant is almost empty, and there's no one at the cocktail bar but me. Which gives me plenty of time to buy him a few drinks and get him in a good mood. If they'd used a talented local artiste instead of one from the city, Derek, as he's called, would know her.

But she wasn't, and he doesn't. I remind Derek about the conversation with the crossword-puzzle man.

"Now him I know," says Derek. "A semi-regular. By that I mean, once a week. Hardly ever more than once a week. Funny you should have mentioned him doing his crossword. Now you mention it, he always does his crossword. Something I'd never thought of before."

"Who is he?" I ask.

"Oh, I've no idea. Except, as I say, he comes in Fridays, once a week."

"You don't know what he does?"

"No idea."

"He couldn't be press; local, like?"

"Oh no, they don't use here for their headquarters; they do their drinking in the King's Head. No, he's definitely not one of that lot. I'd say he worked in one of the shops in the precinct or he was a sales rep or something like that."

"Yes, probably."

"Any particular reason? Why you're interested, I mean."

"No, not really. It was just the girl. She was—well, you don't get many pretty girls round here, do you?"

"You can say that again. I've worked all over, and this place is definitely bottom of the list. Still, I've got the Canaries lined up for summer. That's something to look forward to; twice nightly there."

"Knowing how you feel," I say. "I'm surprised you didn't notice her. I mean, the way I did."

"Yeah. I know. Can't figure that. I'm probably so used to clocking rubbish, I've got my blinds down on automatic."

"Yes, probably," I say to him, and get him to fix us a couple more drinks.

THE SMOKE

SVEN UNZIPPED HIS BRILLIANTLY coloured PVC windcheater and reached into the lining and put the envelope on the glass top of my table.

"Mr. Pedersen couldn't be sure it's the right one, but as it certainly isn't to do with us or with any of the others, he thought you ought to have the chance to make sure yourself."

"Thanks, Sven," I said. "Thanks very much."

"You've moved very quickly," Jean said. "We'll be telling him ourselves in due course, but you must thank Mr. Pedersen the minute you fly back."

"I will." Sven looked at his watch. "Couldn't have made it if Mr. Pedersen hadn't sent me in his own plane. Even now the early evening editions will be on to it. It'll certainly be on TV tonight."

"How did you manage to get there first?" Jean asked, while I took the photographs out of the envelope.

"Well, of course eventually we could have got the police photographs, but in this case we were very lucky. Mr. Pedersen had passed it down for people to be on the look out, right down to the gutter. I have to say, I didn't personally think anything would turn up so soon. I didn't expect carelessness; not straight away. But as you can see, it wasn't carelessness at all. Well, not in that way."

"No," I said, looking at the photographs.

"So, we were lucky. We got this call from the hotel, saying it was a possibility, so I got right over. All I was intending to do was photograph her if she came out. But when I got there and checked at the desk I was told she'd had two visitors who'd been and gone. So I went up and found this and took these pictures. The police were there half an hour later."

Jean walked round to my side of the table and picked up one of the photographs, one of the head close-ups. The one I was looking at was wider, taking in the whole room.

In this picture, Glenda was tied down, spreadeagled on the bed, covered in blood, most of her clothes torn off her, her throat cut. Her unpacked suitcases were on the shelf at the foot of the bed. In this picture the gag that had been forced down her throat was still in place; for easier identification, Sven had removed it before he'd taken the close-ups. But even with the gag, it was very definitely Glenda Hill.

"No doubt about it," Jean said, flicking the photograph on to the glass surface and going to pour herself another drink.

"So we are right?" Sven said.

"Yes," I said. "We are right."

THE SEA

MONDAY AND TUESDAY COME and go. So does Wednesday. But the motel room doesn't change; that remains the same, and more so with the dragging of minutes.

I got out, but I have to come back again; the room is a hundred times worse than the bungalow to come back to.

But there is nothing in the papers. Nothing at all.

And I'm in constant touch with O'Connell via James, who assures me there is nothing, not a jot, nor will there be. James keeps telling me how absolutely one hundred percent certain O'Connell is, and to stop worrying. He tells me I'll make myself ill.

If I told him the full story, one girl posing as two, perhaps he wouldn't think I was so barmy. Perhaps he'd think I was more so.

Friday comes.

Again the papers are of no interest to me whatsoever.

So I prepare myself for the day outside and when I've done that I drive around for an hour or so, out in the country, inland across the tops of the gently swelling wolds. The day is clear and any stray clouds are soon shoved across the face of the sky by the hurrying wind.

But by late morning, before the lunchtime crowd has filled it out, I'm back at the Monastic Habit, but not at the restaurant cocktail bar, in one of the other bars through which everyone has to pass if they want to go in the restaurant.

I've positioned myself on the inside of the doorway, on one of the wall seats, myself and the entrance reflected in the wall mirrors opposite. Anyone coming through on their way to the bar won't see me but I will see them. Derek is already in possession of half his readies and I hope he can remember his lines or he'll be returning his advance unspent.

At about a quarter to one the crossword man comes in, slapping his newspaper at his thigh as he walks through into the cocktail bar.

I wait for another three-quarters of an hour. When he comes back, I can see him use the phone booth in the foyer reflected in the mirror opposite. When he's finished his call, he goes out of the pub and out into the precinct.

I follow.

We've not been walking long when I realise he's making for the multi-storey car park.

When he's confirmed that, I don't go in after him; there's only one way out. I wait opposite, out of sight, and when his rust-coloured Cortina comes down the helter-skelter I make a note of his number.

Back at the Monastic Habit, Derek says, "I reckon you're on to something."

"Really," I say, slipping onto the stool.

"Shall I get you a drink first?"

"Yes, do that, and of course, yourself."

Derek does that, serves another customer, slips back.

"Well," he says. "I done it like you suggested; laid right back."

"Go on," I say to him.

"First off I just pass the time of day with him; haven't seen you since last time sort of thing. I always have a word with him, even if he is a-couple-of-tomato-juices-and-that's-it man. We cover a couple of things, the weather, the midweek match, and after that I say to him, on your own today, are you? He says, how do you mean? I give him the wink. Your friend, I say; the young lady. A lovely lady. Oh, he says, her. You what? I say to him. You dropped lucky there. I wish I'd been sitting at that side of the bar when she drifted in, I can tell you. Oh, it wasn't like that, he says. It never is, I say. No, seriously, he says. Sure, we got talking, he says, and, well, I'd have to be blind not to realise how tasty she was, but I'm a married man, he says. Aren't we all, I say. Honest, he says, I'd never risk it with my old lady; she's telepathic. Give over, I said, that's what the afternoons are for, these days. If you got a job that gets you about a bit. It was nothing, he said, they just had a couple of drinks, and when she was leaving I asked her if I could drop her anywhere. Which according to him, he could, and he did."

"Did he say anything about her; who she was, what she did?"

"He was close about her. As close as he could be without appearing to be. He said she was some kind of demonstrator. I said I bet she was. No, he said, she was in cosmetics, ran a group that demonstrated house to house. For one of the big nationals."

"And that's all he said about her?"

"That's all he said about anything. He waited a bit longer, so's not to seem to rush off. An' then he rushed off."

"Well," I say to him, "thanks a lot. You did well."

"So what do you think?" he says.

"Like you say, I think you got on to something. That's probably why he used the phone, to rearrange the meeting place."

"He used the phone?"

"Yes. On the way out."

"Well," Derek says. "There you are then."

I nod, at the same time reaching into my inside pocket.

"Thanks a lot," Derek says, slipping the envelope discreetly into the back pocket of his trousers. "If there's anything else I can do . . ."

"Sure," I tell him. "I'll let you know."

He shakes his head.

"I dunno," he says. "This divorce business."

"You're right," I say to him. "Be warned."

THE SMOKE

IT WAS ON THE ten o'clock news. Shots of the exterior of the hotel and the room, after Glenda's body'd been taken out. Plenty of close-ups of the bloodstained sheets and the splashes on the headboard. Glenda was described as having been a dancer. She'd booked into the hotel at two o'clock that afternoon. Since then she'd remained in her room. According to the desk clerk, to his knowledge she had no visitors. But, said the man with the microphone ominously, as he stood in front of the hotel, Glenda Hill *had* had a visitor. Or visitors. Who they were remained to be seen. It was believed that Dutch police were examining certain items they had removed from the hotel bedroom. What these items were the Dutch had so far declined to disclose; but it was a possibility that due to the very savagery of the attack, the killer may have left some vital clue as to his identity which he'd overlooked in his haste to escape from the scene of the crime. And because of Glenda's nationality, the possibility that her killer was British could not be excluded. Andrew Webber, *News at Ten,* Amsterdam.

The first phone call was from James.

"Have I ever held anything back from you, James?" I said to him. "What do you think I am, stupid?"

"I just wondered if perhaps something had gone beyond your control. Out of hand, so to speak."

"I'll repeat what I said; the last time I had anything to do with her was on the phone this morning. And when we got there, she was gone."

James was silent for a moment.

"It's very off colour, isn't it?" he said.

"That's one way of putting it."

"Have you talked to our friend?"

"I should imagine he's poised with his pennies over the slot at this very moment. Not that he'll have anything to tell me. He'll be phoning to see if it's safe for him to turn up to work in the morning."

"I'll get off the line, then. I'll be round in about an hour."

I put down the phone. I was right. It began ringing again immediately.

"Hello, Dennis," I said.

"What's going on?" said Collins. "I've just seen —"

"I know what you've just seen. And I don't know either."

"But you told me—"

"What I told you was right."

"Look, if I'm to help you—"

"You're the second person that's said that tonight," I said.

"What?"

"Forget it. Listen. This isn't down to me, right?"

"Then who—"

"All in good time, Dennis. Christ, as yet, it's nothing."

"At the moment, but—"

"At the moment, Dennis," I said, "just put your slippers back on and stop worrying. I'm not involved."

"That's not the point," Collins said. "People could—"

"I know what people could do, Dennis," I said. "There are some things I do know. So stay there until I phone you."

I put the receiver down.

Yes, I thought; I certainly knew what people could do.

THE SEA

All right. So maybe I've been wrong. Maybe she wasn't press. But what else could I have done? Just stand around hoping I wasn't right?

Of course, I'm still not ninety-nine percent certain. You can never be ninety-nine percent. That's why I phoned James earlier in the afternoon with the number of the crossword man's Cortina; after he's checked the number with the contact in Records I'll be able either to associate him with the girl as a fellow member of the press or accept what he'd told Derek at its face value.

As to the girl, I've nothing to associate her with whatsoever. James, when I'd phoned, once again told me that as far as O'Connell was concerned, Fleet Street is still becalmed; not a ripple, not a murmur to disturb the stale air. As far as James and O'Connell are concerned, the girl doesn't exist, except in my stir-crazy imagination.

Let them try it, I think to myself. Let them try living the way I've been living these last months, after what I've seen.

I blink, as if to guard against a glare that can only be shielded by something in my brain, and then I concentrate on the road as a temporary screen.

After I'd talked to James, I'd had a few more drinks. Then I'd gone to see another movie. After that, I'd picked up my motor from the multi-storey and I drove out of Grimsby, on to the coast road that leads towards Mablethorpe. I want to see if there's any sign of life around the bungalow. I don't expect there will be, not now. And if there isn't, then I've decided I'll spend the night there and phone James to check again about the papers in the morning.

So I drive slowly along the coast road, its slightly elevated position between the dykes making the coastal plain seem like a tideless imitation of the placid sea beyond the dunes, a mile away to my left.

Ten minutes out of Grimsby and the late afternoon traffic begins to thin out; it's not quite late enough for the early starters to be off their marks from their shops and offices. Still, one or two of them scud past me as though the weekend starts here. The trouble with this road, although the surface is new, is that it follows the old route, which dog-legs its way down the coast, twisting and turning, hardly a straight stretch longer than two hundred yards. Of course, the minute there's more than a couple of yards in a straight line, the cowboys in their Escorts and their Allegros start playing at Brands Hatch between the beads, which you're pushing on this stretch of road if you go into them at more than twenty-five. And even though there isn't a great deal of traffic about, it doesn't take much more than two or three at a stretch to create a racetrack. So as usual on this road I stay at my steady speed, letting those who wish to chance meeting their maker sooner than I do pass me by with plenty of room to spare.

I'm just the other side of Marshchapel when the tail back starts. At first I can't see to what extent because of the trees that surround the unused church that stands silent on the bend. At present there are only eight cars as far as I can see. Then we all shunt forward and the first car in my line of vision slowly disappears around the bend. This process continues for about five minutes, until it's my turn to round the corner.

Then I can see what the blockage is all about.

There are two cars involved and a transit van. But they're not all together. The transit van is half on its back, in the dyke. The only way they're going to get the two cars to the breaker's yard is the way they are now, fused together. One of them must have tried overtaking the transit at just the right moment. From the way the Law and the fire-brigade and the ambulance men are working there must still be people in the motors although I doubt very much if they'll be in the singular any more. The petrol tank of one of the motors must have gone up, but from where I am, all I can see is smoke drifting back across the flat fields towards the dunes. A couple of bodies are lying on the grass verge, under blankets; the authorities are too concerned with whoever is left alive or dead in the motors to shift the bodies any further. An officer of the Law is holding us at bay, while some of his partners and members of the fire brigade work away at the twisted metal like ants on a dead spider.

The traffic controller waves two cars at the front of the procession forward and they move past the accident at a funereal pace. I move forward too and that leaves me in second place behind the leader. The bodies under the blankets are a few yards ahead of me on the grass verge, just the feet and the lower legs showing, two men. One of the men has lost his shoes; just the remains of his socks, burnt and fused to him like nylon blisters, point upwards to the clear, cold sky. Protruding from the other blanket, the nearest one, are the bloodied legs of a pair of overalls. I can see part of an ankle between the top of a boot and the bottom of one of the overall legs, burnt the deepest of possible reds.

I turn my attention to the soldered motors. It is hard to say which was coming from what direction. They must have spun half a dozen times, locked together. One is a Vauxhall Viva, but that is not the one they're presently working on, the one presumably with somebody still inside. That one's the other car, a Cortina, but it's impossible to see inside it because of the concentrated activities of the authorities. There are a few flames licking out from between one of the no-longer-flush rear doors of the Cortina, the boot of which is pointing in my direction. One of the firemen is squirting in foam through one of the shattered windows. The whole frame of the Cortina has been twisted, like an empty cigarette packet that's been squeezed in the middle. Its number plate is parallel to my windscreen but at an angle to the horizon.

It takes a minute or two for me to realise where I've seen the letters and the numbers before.

Just to be certain, I take the piece of paper from my breast pocket and unfold it. The letters and the numbers are the same.

I look up from the piece of paper and through my windscreen at the Cortina.

Two things happen at the same time: the fireman with the extinguisher shouts something and hurls himself away from the car for a second, leaving a gap through which I can see into the car. There's someone moving in there in the passenger seat, a girl in a maroon PVC raincoat. Before the total realisation registers completely, the second thing happens; the interior of the Cortina fills with a sheet of flame, lightning-like, then billows out of the shattered windows like a soundless explosion. Now everybody around the car hurls themselves backwards, and then comes the real explosion, as the flames hit the petrol.

Involuntarily, although the blast is relatively small, I twist my body away from the flash, screwing my eyes tight shut. When I open them again, I'm looking at the grass verge. The blast has lifted a corner of one of the blankets, revealing the face of the shoeless man, the man with the crossword puzzle, eyeless as well as shoeless, because of the glass and metal he'd absorbed on impact, the sockets just blood-black, blood streaked down his cheeks, as regular and as sharply defined as the motley of a clown.

I look back at the Cortina. Everybody is standing back, helpless and motionless in the face of the flames. The figure in the passenger seat is still mobile, though not because of any brief retention of life, but because of the effects the flames are now having on the girl's totally fire-enveloped shape, like a coarse charcoal drawing as it totters slightly to one side, already becoming one with the carpet and the upholstery and the melting plastic.

THE SMOKE

"I've just heard," Mickey said, sitting down. "So that's where she went."

"That's where she went," I said.

"A bit close to home, wasn't it?"

"In more ways than one," I said.

"I mean, they couldn't be much nearer home if they tried."

"You're right about that," I said.

"Parsons'll be happy."

"That's what I thought."

Mickey drummed on the table with his fingers.

"I'm surprised at Ray," he said. "Involving himself with a slag and then knocking her off like this. I mean he could have told her to stay put and let us do the job when we went round to see her. I mean, if he'd already gone, what could she tell us: that he'd already gone?"

"Perhaps she could have told us all sorts of things he didn't want us to know."

"Stupid," Mickey said.

"You haven't seen the photographs?"

"No."

I pushed the envelope across the desk towards him. He took the photographs out and leafed through them, shaking his head.

"Stupid," he said. "Crude. Not the Ray we all knew and loved. Not his style at all."

"No," I said.

Mickey slung the photographs on the desk.

"Stupid," he said again.

"How do you reckon it?" I asked him.

"Well, it's obvious, isn't it? She calls Ray to say we're coming over. He tells her to get out of it and join him in Amsterdam. When she gets there, he knocks her off, or has her knocked off, because of things she may know that we don't, and also seeing as how he's decided that with the kind of money he's got stacked up he can in future do better than the Glendas of this world."

"They'd been together eighteen months. Like we said, it could have been love."

Mickey shrugged. "Maybe she did it a new way that he'd never come across before. In any case, all good things come to an end, in time."

"There's certainly a lot of truth in that, Mickey," I said.

"So what you want me to do?" he asked.

I shook my head. "At the moment, nothing. James is coming round shortly. I'll send for you after he's gone, if I need you."

He stood up, and looked at the top photograph. "Now if I'd been doing a job like that . . ."

I nodded. "I know. They wouldn't even have had to change the sheets."

THE SEA

ONCE I'M IN THE bungalow, with the doors locked behind me and a drink in my hand, I sit opposite the picture window and stare out at the broad sky as it changes from late afternoon to early evening and think about the events outside Marshchapel.

Could it have been just what it appeared to be? That she'd got talking to the crossword man and they'd got something started and he was so shit-scared of his missus that the minute even a barman makes a few remarks he calls her up and changes the meeting place and they drive out into the country for a session of al fresco, resulting in a permanent end to the affair?

Just that, that simple?

But what about the Mablethorpe Lesley? What is she playing at, slumming around local Amateur Nights looking like an out-of-season hippy, then appearing in Grimsby all wigged up and well turned-out, like a different person altogether? Maybe she was a different person altogether. Maybe—

I take another deep drink of my scotch, then another.

If only I'd had one more look at her, just to be one hundred percent certain, the way she'd looked the first time I'd seen her, not the way she'd been this afternoon, her body shuddering because of the blanket of flame that wrapped itself around her.

I have to stop thinking like this, or I'll begin to be like I was the time when I was shown what had happened to Jean.

THE SMOKE

"ALL RIGHT," JEAN SAID, "let's pursue all the propositions to their logical conclusions."

"You sound more like James every day," I said.

"Good," she said. "That means I'm likelier to arrive at a reasonable solution."

"All right," I said, "go on. State your case. Or cases."

"Right," she said. "From the beginning; it wasn't coincidental that Ray went when he did, and he didn't go because he was frightened we were on to him; there was no way he could know; Henry Chapman wouldn't, Tommy Hales isn't in a fit state to talk to anyone yet, and Mal Wilson isn't in a fit state for ever. And why should they? If they knew anything they'd tell us, not Ray. He was responsible for their having to undergo the treatment. And his mother, he'd been setting that story up for a long time. He knew nobody would check it because he didn't know anybody suspected he was up to anything."

"He couldn't be totally sure."

"Quite. So when Glenda gets the unscheduled phone call enquiry into his whereabouts, she phones him, as he would have instructed her to."

"Which means she knew what he was up to."

"Not necessarily. Two alternatives here. If she was in it, she phones him, he tells her to join him quicker than arranged. They hadn't wanted to go together, to attract that kind of attention."

"Or?"

"Or she wasn't in the picture at all."

"So why does she fly off to Amsterdam?"

"Leaving to one side the fact that a lot of people would fly off to Amsterdam or elsewhere after an enquiry by Mickey on your behalf," Jean said, "leaving that to one side, I have no sodding idea."

"There's what Mickey said," I said.

"Oh yes. Supposing Ray wants to top her: because he's fed up with her and she might tell tales or whatever. So, not wanting to agitate the locals, he waits until he's on foreign turf. So he can get rid of her nice and quiet, without drawing undue attention to himself."

I get up and go over to the drinks.

"You do see what I mean?" Jean said.

"Yes," I said. "I do see what you mean."

"So somebody else had Glenda topped."

I dropped some ice in my drink.

"If so, the immediate question not being who or why," I said. "Because there only seems one possibility in that respect. The question is how did they know what was going down?"

THE SEA

I DRIVE INTO MABLETHORPE.

The evening paper comes in about a quarter to six.

So I park my car at the foot of the ramp and cross the promenade and walk down the street towards the paper shop. The lights from the arcade flop limply onto the pavement. On impulse, for no reason whatsoever, I drift over to the arcade and into it and get some change and go over to my pin-table and try to beat my previous best. But I get nowhere near. I seem to have lost my touch. All I keep getting is Tilt.

So in the end I give up and go out into the street again.

Across the street, a bit farther down, the double frontage of the newsagent's is illuminated as if for all the world they're still using gas mantles inside.

I cross the street and open the door and walk over to the counter and take a copy of the evening paper from off the pile.

"I don't know about you," the old girl says as she takes my money, "but I think it's gone ever so cold this afternoon."

"I hadn't noticed," I say to her. "But now you come to mention it, I suppose it has a bit."

"Wicked," she says. "I thought we'd had the last of the winter. We don't want another season like we had last year."

"Cold, was it?"

"Cold and miserable. It's all right for the arcades and the

bingo and the pubs, but we've still got stuff out the back from last season."

"Well," I say, "let's hope for a bit of sunshine, eh?"

"Yes," she says. "Let's hope."

I tuck my newspaper under my arm and go out of the shop.

In the South I get the hero's return from Jackie.

"Well," he says, "hello stranger. Beginning to think you'd gone into hibernation. Mind you, couldn't blame you, what with the weather."

I tell him to take for himself, which he does with a fair amount of swiftness; he must have been dry for the whole week. While he's getting his and mine, I notice he's got a copy of the evening paper spread out on the counter, front page upwards. I look at the upside-down picture of the smash-up.

Jackie places the drinks on the counter and clocks me clocking the photograph.

"Nasty, isn't it?" he says. "Still, there's a bright side to everything; somebody'll be getting a visit from the insurance people."

"Yes," I say to him. "Everything's got two sides to it."

THE SMOKE

"APART FROM ANYTHING ELSE," I said, "there is too much of Mickey committed to film and tape for him even to begin having nightmares about that kind of a deal; my thirty years would be his thirty years."

James studied his brandy.

"All we can do is examine the facts."

"There aren't any."

"Well," said James, "to begin with—"

"To begin with, all else apart, he might be able to do a deal with Farlow and the Sheps. But this is Parsons's case. And nobody, not even Jack Jones, can do a deal with Parsons."

"George—" James began, but I cut him off.

"I know what you're going to say; Jean apart, Mickey was the only one who knew we were having the investigation, the only one who knew we were on to Ray. He phoned her up, we went straight over. But he went to get the car out; he'd got time to make another, quicker, phone call."

"That is one of the facts, yes."

"So that the Sheps can take her over to Amsterdam and point her, us thinking Ray did her in, so that Parsons can blaze a trail to our front door. Behind which door is not only Jean and myself, but also Mickey. He gives us all to Parsons, including himself, just for the pleasure of having the next thirty years watching Farlow and the Sheps carve up our operation, of which, I might add, he's not exactly a minor shareholder."

James drank some of his brandy, savoured it.

"That is all so," he said. "But you are in the middle of an attempt to incriminate you. The biggest piece of evidence at the moment being Glenda, and only you and Mickey knew you were going to visit her."

"Excepting," I said, "excepting Ray."

THE SEA

THE NAME OF THE driver of the transit van is Malcolm Tunbridge, twenty-eight, of Marine View, Mablethorpe. Superficial injuries, released from hospital.

The name of the driver of the Escort was Ernest Emerson, garage proprietor, of High Street, Tealby. A widower.

The crossword-puzzle man's name was Colin Hewitt, a sales representative, of Western Avenue, Grimsby. A wife survived him.

According to the driver of the transit van, who had been proceeding on his way from Mablethorpe to Grimsby, the accident had been down to the driver of the Cortina. He'd begun to overtake with plenty of time to make it past the transit van before the bend, but the Cortina had seemed to lose power as it drew level with the transit van and then the Escort appeared coming round the bend from the opposite direction, and then there'd been nothing anybody could do. Just before the collision the Cortina had bumped the van and the van had gone on to the verge and finally into the ditch.

The girl, the passenger in the Cortina, had yet to be identified.

Lucky for Malcolm Tunbridge, twenty-eight, of Marine View, Mablethorpe.

I look at the photograph again. In monochrome, the smash seemed to have a greater reality than when I'd actually seen it, the way that black-and-white movies used to appear more realistic than those made in Technicolor. The blackness of the burnt-out metal looks much starker than it had in fact, made even more like crumbled charcoal by the rough grain of the photographic block. The number plate is diffused by the crudeness of the reproduction, but not enough to blur entirely the numbers and the letters; they're still the same ones.

I fold the newspaper, photograph inwards, and drain my drink and get up and go over to the bar. Jackie refills us both and I'm just about to go back to my seat when Eddie comes in and makes it to the bar in about five seconds flat, the worries of his show-business world appearing to distract him even more than usual, but he's not distracted enough to prevent him giving me the kind of welcome return I got from Jackie. I pay for his pint and, the formalities over, Jackie says to Eddie, "You're in a mucksweat, aren't you?"

"Too bloody right," Eddie says. "We've got a gig at North Somercoates tonight and no bloody transport up to now."

He nods at the newspaper that's still lying on the bar.

"Thanks to that," he says. "Jerry only lends it out for the afternoon, the silly bastard, and now look what happens."

"It's not written off, is it?" Jackie says.

"Oh, no, it's not written off," Eddie says. "It'll only need a couple of hundred quid to put it right, that's all. Which of course we haven't got right at the moment."

"So what are you going to do?" Jackie says.

"I've been running round trying to organise one," Eddie says. "I've even tried persuading Cyril to let us have one of the Electricity Board ones."

"Have you tried Grafton at Central Garage?"

"Yeah, I've tried him, the mean old sod. He wants fifty quid deposit apart from the hire."

"Miserable old bugger."

"Yeah," he says. "As if what happened to the other van was something to do with me."

THE SMOKE

JEAN SAID, "WE'VE ALREADY been through that one."

"I know we have," I said. "And I've been thinking. Supposing when she calls Ray, what better way can he think of to stop us proceeding too immediately in his direction than to do what we're assuming the Sheps have done: leave Glenda in a showroom window, to slow us down a bit while the Law attempts to take its course."

"It's a thought," said James. "But not one I would consider worth pursuing."

"All right," I said. "Let's hear your contribution."

"Well," he said, adding some more brandy to his glass, "I would imagine that the Shepherdsons and Farlow are content to await developments following their initial contribution and leave Parsons to pick up anything else they've left around to be collected for your file."

"Which could be just about anything."

"Yes," James said, "but I wouldn't worry unduly. Even if it comes to you going into court, there'd be no case for you to answer. It would only be circumstantial, whatever was planted. In fact I'd quite enjoy a session with Parsons in the box."

"Would you?" I said.

James smiled.

"I expect he's already over there," I said.

"It would help to know what the items were the Dutch police removed from Glenda's room."

"I talked to Pedersen," I said. "He's already doing what he can. He got on to his people in the department before Sven had even developed his snaps."

"Well, that's something," James said.

There was a silence.

"What does worry me," Jean said, "is Ray. If Glenda was meeting him in Amsterdam, why didn't they do for him as well?"

"Ray would have stood back for a while," James said. "To make sure Glenda hadn't led anyone to him."

"Or it supports my argument," I said. "That Ray did for her himself."

There was another silence. This time nobody broke it. We all sat there thinking our thoughts.

Then the phone rang.

THE SEA

WHILE JACKIE'S AWAY SERVING someone else I say to Eddie, "You got time for a quick word?"

"What?" Eddie says.

"A moment," I say. "For a quick word."

"Yeah," Eddie says, "sure."

"Let's go and sit down."

"Sure," Eddie says. "Yeah."

We go and sit down on the leatherette seating.

"That was bad luck about the transit van," I say to him.

"Yeah," he says, "but what can you do?"

"The driver," I say. "Is he a mate of yours?"

"He's no mate of mine," Eddie says. "I'd never have lent the silly bugger it in a million years. I could murder him."

"Unreliable, is he?"

"Between me and you," Eddie says, "I would say it's lucky for him the others didn't come out of it alive."

"Why do you say that?"

"I wouldn't be surprised if it was down to him. He drives like a madman. I think I'll send him a headstone for Christmas. Should come in more useful than a pair of socks."

I take a sip of my drink.

"Incidentally," I ask him, "had any joy with Lesley? I mean, about getting her on a permanent basis?"

"No," he says, "I'm being facked about in that respect as

well. She can't make her fucking mind up what she wants. Which is just about anything with her talent. I suppose I'm lucky she's even thinking about doing a spell with us."

"When did you last talk to her about it?"

"I dunno. I haven't seen her all week. In fact, now you come to mention it, I haven't seen her since the amateur night."

"She's not been around?"

Eddie looks even gloomier.

"No," he says. "I expect she's like the rest of the Seasonals; as reliable as a two-bob watch. She's probably fucked off to Skeggie or Yarmouth or somewhere to see what's going on. If she's done that I got no chance, have I?"

"I suppose not," I say to him.

"No," he says. He takes a sip of his pint. "No chance."

We sit there in silence for a minute or two. Then I say, "So what are you going to do about tonight?"

"Christ knows," he says. "And it's not just tonight; if we can't get the other van on the road, we're going to lose a lot of bookings; there's plenty of second-rate groups waiting to jump in."

"How much do you need?"

"I beg your pardon?"

"Well," I say to him, "the fellow at the garage wants fifty quid, and you say the work on the van'll be about two hundred."

"About that, yeah."

"How much is it to hire the other van? Without the deposit."

"Ten quid a night."

I take ten tens from my wallet and fold them neatly and tuck them under the beer mat beneath Eddie's pint glass. Eddie looks at the money and what I've done with it as if he's never seen fingers folding money in his life before.

"What's that?" he says.

"That should cover the van hire till next weekend. By then you'll probably have got your own fixed up."

Eddie looks at the money.

"I don't know what to say," he says.

"That's all right," I say to him. "When you get a price on the van, let me know what it comes to."

"But I can't—"

"Don't worry," I say to him. "I don't want it back all at once. Let me have it whenever you can."

Eddie looks at the money again.

"I'll pay you back out of each booking," he says.

"I've told you," I tell him, "when you can."

"I don't know what to say," he says again.

"Forget it. You'd better pick it up and get round to Grafton's before he hires the van out to somebody else."

Eddie takes the money and puts it in his inside pocket and drinks his drink and stands up.

"Each booking," he says. "I'll pay you back out of each booking."

He clears off, not quite bowing from the waist down. I get up and go back to the bar and get myself another drink. Jackie has, of course, seen the passage of the money but he can't think of any way of finding out what it's all about without asking me point blank, and that he doesn't do. And if he had asked, I don't know what my answer would be. Of course, I could tell him what. But I doubt why. Perhaps I felt somehow responsible; the accident wouldn't have happened if the crossword man hadn't changed the venue, due to my indirect enquiries. Eddie was not only out of a van, but out of a star attraction. Perhaps it's just because I don't want anything else on my conscience at this present time.

"Anything on at the Dunes tonight?" I asked Jackie.

"Yeah, there's some wrestling on. Starts at eight."

"How could I ever miss that?" I say.

"Yeah," says Jackie. "All good clean fun."

THE SMOKE

I PUT THE PHONE down.

"That was Pedersen," I said.

"So we gathered," Jean said.

"What did he have to say?"

"The items removed from the hotel room," I said. "They've also been removed from the local nick."

"That's good news," James said. "What were they?"

"Mainly identification belonging to Ray. Bankers' cards, deposit numbers, etcetera. But the main thing being a notebook including my name and various connected addresses."

"Christ," Jean said.

"There's no need to worry. They were only at the nick half an hour before they were transferred out. Everybody knows what's in the book, naturally, but nobody was able to make a copy before it got mislaid, along with Ray and Glenda's other personal effects."

"Well," James said. "We can drink to that, at least."

I watched Jean as she thought things out in the light of the phone call.

"Ray's things, and the notebook," she said.

"Right," I said. "My theory isn't all that stupid, is it?"

"Yes," she said, "because if you were right, and he'd done Glenda that way to calm us down, he wouldn't have chanced implicating himself. That part would have been very clean."

"The items being planted as additional material to link it with us," James said.

"But to do that, to get those items from Ray, the Sheps would have to know what was going on, and in good time," I said.

"Quite," said James. "Which makes my own theory not quite so stupid, does it?"

I poured myself another drink.

"It's no good putting your head in the sand," Jean said. "It's got to be considered."

THE SEA

I STAND IN THE lobby at the Dunes, listening to the ringing-out signal until at the other end the receiver is lifted and James says, "James Morville speaking."

I tell him that it's me.

"Christ, George," he says, "you don't expect me to have the number this soon, do you? I mean, it is Friday night."

"I know what time it is, whatever you think, James," I tell him.

"Well, George, and I say this in all friendship and sympathy, you haven't exactly sounded yourself the last few times you called."

"Well, forget my state of health for the moment, James," I say. "I'm only phoning to tell you not to bother with that registration number."

"Oh?" says James. "How come?"

"Never mind," I tell him. "It's no longer necessary."

"I see."

"I don't think so, but it doesn't matter."

There is a slight pause.

"You haven't done anything that might be termed a little bit extreme?"

"No, I haven't. It's just that it is no longer of any importance."

"I've heard you use phrases like that before."

"In this case you can take it at its face value."

"I hope so. Because things are going well down here and the last thing either of us wants is for you to draw any untoward attention to yourself."

"Quite, James."

"I'm sorry to sound like a dutch uncle, but after everything that's happened, the way everything's been smoothed out, it would seem ridiculous to say the least, at this point—"

"James," I say to him, "there's nothing to worry about. I'm telling you."

There is another slight pause.

"Look," James says, in his most diplomatic manner, "it hasn't been me that's been worried. It has been yourself who's been telephoning, out of concern."

"All right, James," I say. "Point taken."

"I realise after all that's happened you're probably—"

"Whatever I'm probably, let's not go into what's happened, eh?"

"No. As you wish. You're quite right. I'm just concerned. That you're—that you're quite yourself."

"Don't worry, James. No need to worry about that. I am. I'm quite myself."

THE SMOKE

"WHAT WAS MICKEY'S REACTION," James said, "when you told him about Amsterdam?"

I told James what Mickey's reaction had been.

"Rather simplistic, don't you think?" James said. "I mean, knowing Mickey."

"I repeat," I said. "Mickey would have to be totally insane to imagine that bringing me down would do him any good whatsoever."

"At the moment," James said, "motivation is rather beside the point; the point is that if I were a gambling man, which I am not, on the basis of the facts, the odds are on Mickey."

"But not the form," I said.

James was silent.

"And it's not a matter of facts," I said. "It's circumstantial, James, if I might put it that way."

"George," Jean said. "Forget the semantics. Listen to James. He's not saying what he's saying just for fun."

"And you think," I said to her, "that after all this time, after all Mickey's been to this firm, all it's worth to him, he's going to throw in with a circus like the Shepherdsons?"

Jean didn't say anything.

"There is no deal he could do with them that could prevent him going down with us. You above anybody know that."

James took out his cigar case.

"So what do you intend to do?" he said. "Nothing? You hardly lay back and thought of England in the case of the collectors."

"That was different."

Jean didn't look at me and said, "Well, what *do* you intend to do, George?"

"I don't know," I said. "Naturally, I shall take everything into consideration, and I do mean everything. And I shall look into everything. But with the greatest of care. I don't want to be falling down any manholes."

"That, at least, is very wise," James said. "Although at present, thanks to our member from the Common Market, Parsons is without evidence, I'd advise a low-profile situation."

"James," I said. "You didn't start representing me yesterday. I had arrived at that conclusion myself."

"Because God knows what else the Sheps might have in their possession to put in Parsons's pocket."

"I realise that."

"And in the meantime," Jean said, "if it's Mickey feeding the Sheps, that's very handy, isn't it?"

"Well, there's one thing for sure; in establishing the rights or wrongs of Mickey's case, we don't proceed in the manner in which we proceed against the collectors. Horses for courses."

"Well, let's hope this course isn't Aintree," said James.

"Look, the pair of you," I said. "If it's Mickey, I'll find out. You both know that, for sure."

I poured myself another drink.

"I mean," I said, "I do take it you consider me reliable in at least that department."

THE SEA

AFTER I'VE MADE THE phone call to James, I go back to my drink, and to Howard.

The wrestling ring has been set up in the centre of the auditorium, the packaway seats boxing it in, some of them set in rows on what is normally the stage. As yet the place is totally empty.

Howard, naturally enough, is in a buoyant mood. As he's said earlier, he looks forward to his bit of wrestling; the nearest thing he gets to his kind of fun around here. Mind you, he told me, the women are the worst; a couple of pairs of well-hung bollocks thrashing about underneath the spotlight, and well, the castration complex is nowhere in it; it's as if they want to take them home and hang them on the wall along with the flying ducks, he'd said.

You don't say, I'd said to him earlier.

But now the topic of conversation is a different one.

"Eddie told me what you done," he says. "Come in here earlier on like he'd got a sixpenny-bit up his backside."

"That dates you," I tell him.

"What doesn't?" he says. "Except fellers."

I help him along in his routine by smiling a little.

"You, er, you're not masquerading under false colours, are you?" he says.

"How do you mean, Howard?"

"Well, you know."

"No, Howard, I'm not."

"No, I thought not. I was going to say, if you were, I could have seen my way clear to helping you get rid of the odd fiver."

"Sorry, Howard. And all that."

"Ah well, I can dream, can't I?"

"Dream away."

Howard refreshes himself with his drink.

"The only thing is," he says.

"What, Howard?"

"Well, I mean. Eddie. Why? I mean, he's not going to be able to settle up with you first thing Monday morning, is he?"

"I suppose not."

"And you don't strike me as being your actual philanthropic type. Not, I hasten to add," he hastens to add, "that you're not always generous to me, you are; you know what I mean. There, I've done it again. Come out all wrong."

"I know what you mean, Howard."

Howard goes into a theatrical production of wiping his brow and flicking the invisible sweat from his fingertips.

"You know what I mean," he says. "Honestly, if Sam Spiegel walked in here and offered me the lead in *Lawrence of Arabia* I'd probably tell him I was Jewish."

"Howard," I say to him, "I understand you."

"If only you truly meant that," he says, doing a fair enough Janet Gaynor.

"Optics, Howard," I say to him. "To the optics."

"But what I can't understand," he says, zipping the glasses up and down, "is you knowing what you're doing and yet lending money to Eddie, which is like injecting capital into British Leyland."

He sets the drinks down between us.

"Don't ask me," I say to Howard. "Perhaps it was a momentary aberration."

"We all have those," Howard says. "Only some less momentary than others."

Howard picks up his glass.

"Anyway," he says, "to our aberrations. Whatever they may be."

We drink.

"Men," says Howard. "I'll never understand them."

Which Mickey said, once.

I drain my glass.

"Another?" Howard says.

"No," I tell him. "I've got to be going."

"Not staying for the wrestling?"

"No, not tonight."

"It's not something I've said?"

"No, it's not anything you've said," I tell him.

THE SMOKE

In bed, while we were making love, Jean began to talk to me, the way she often did, about other people, about what she'd like to do to them, in fantasy, what she'd like them to do to me, what she'd like them to do to her, would I like it, would I like that, would I like to do something like that, would I, would I, and I would say yes, yes, to elevate her excitement, to help to lift her mind and her body, to help in opening the floodgates, and this time, it was Mickey. Would I like to do that to him, she'd like to see him do that to me, what would I feel like if I did that to him, would I, would I, really? Christ, would I, God, my God, would you, Christ. Christ.

Afterwards, I brought us drinks to the bed. She was very quiet, and so was I.

Eventually, I said, "It's not because of that, is it?"

She didn't reply, and therefore I knew what her answer would be.

"Because it's not that kind of situation," I said.

"I know," she said. "You didn't think I was serious, did you?"

I took a sip of my drink.

"It didn't seem difficult to convince you that it's down to Mickey. When it was being discussed."

"James neither, if you remember."

"That's true enough," I said. "But I know you even better

than I know James. So, with you, I have a broader range of motives to select from."

"Come off it, George. You may know what I'm like, in that respect, but you also know what I'm like as far as the business is concerned, and through that, our mutual self-preservation. And that particular preservation is not coloured by any artificial flavouring."

"No," I said. "I suppose not."

"Although," she said.

"Dispense with the although," I said. "Save the although if and until it's necessary."

She didn't say anything.

"And after all is said and done," I said, "I don't believe, in your water, or even in your blood, that you believe, that this, in any way, is down to Mickey."

THE SEA

I AWAKE.

I'm lying on top of the bed, still wearing my suit. The far-off sound of the sea murmurs in my ears like sounds from seashells. On the bedside table, the scotch bottle is almost finished, the morning sun shining through its transparent emptiness.

I sit upright, reach for the glass and complete the work I started on the bottle the night before.

When I've done that, I swing my legs off the bed and stand up. It is not too much of a shock to my system, but I stand there for a moment or two without moving, until my body's completely sure that that is what it's meant to be doing.

After that's been ascertained, I take off my clothes and pick up my robe and walk into the bathroom and while I'm standing under the shower I look at my multi-faceted reflection as the water teems off me. Considering everything I'm still in good shape. The old scars still show, but those are very old, and over the years have almost assumed the same tone as the rest of my skin. Almost, but not entirely. It's never entirely.

I towel myself down and put my robe back on and plug in my razor and put the toilet seat down and sit on it and watch myself in the mirrors as I shave. As the razor moves over my skin it seems to solidify the slight signs of flabbiness that have appeared over the last few months, and when I switch off the razor and examine my face a little bit closer, I'm not displeased with the way I'm looking; I'm looking better than I've looked for ages.

It must be all the sea air I'm getting.

I have breakfast and when I've done that I go back into the bedroom and put on some fresh casual clothes and then I go back into the kitchen and take the jug of iced orange juice from the fridge and take it into the lounge.

I climb the steps and go over to where the champagne is and as I'm crossing the upper level I notice that the screen is half in and half out of the ceiling and that one of the small lamps that is operated from the same panel is still switched on from the night before. I shake my head and put the jug down on top of the piano and go over to the panel and switch off the lamp and operate the screen back up into the ceiling. I swear quietly to myself as I walk back to the piano. These days it's not unusual to forget switching off lights and to fall onto the bed rather than get into it, but you would have thought, despite the bottle of scotch, that I'd have noticed half-setting off the movie screen.

But really, I think, as I'm mixing the champagne with the orange juice, that's what it's all about, the bottle of scotch. A lot is down to that, these days.

I raise my glass in celebration of that profound thought, and drink.

THE SMOKE

"So you mean we're going to do nothing," Mickey said.

"That's it," I said.

"What, fuck all?"

"That's right."

"Well," Mickey said. "I don't know. What can I say?"

"Not a great deal."

"But, that bit about the address book. I mean, what does it look like?"

"What do you think it looks like, Mickey?"

"Oh, come on."

"Exactly. That's why we're not doing anything. Let them let the shit fly for the moment; we'll content ourselves with fielding it."

"But why? We could dryclean the lot of them in twenty-four hours. Half that time."

"I know. Which Parsons would highly enjoy."

"So we fit him up at the same time."

I shook my head.

"No," I said. "That way we may clear the decks but we still haven't flushed out what's doing down in our own operation. Plus Parsons would need a lot of fitting up. No, the time is not appropriate. But it will be."

"Well," Mickey said, "at least I can still talk to Ray's collectors."

"I'd like you to leave that as well, for the moment. For the time being, just collect from them. Give whoever it is a false sense of security."

"I know what I'd like to give them."

"Yes, but that's a pleasure to be savoured at a future date."

After Mickey had gone, Jean came in.

"How much did you tell him?"

"As much as I said I would. Just enough."

"So if it's Mickey the Shepherdsons will know we're not doing anything at the moment."

"Correct."

"Which gets us where?"

"Which gets us the Shepherdsons not expecting us to do anything."

"You promised James."

"What I said was, I'd keep a low profile until it was worth doing otherwise. And at the moment, it isn't, is it?"

THE SEA

I UNLOCK THE DOOR that leads into the garage and open and close it behind me and lock it again. Then I switch on the photo-electric mechanism and walk across to the Marina and as I'm doing this I stub my toe on one of the bolts that fasten down the trapdoor. Involuntarily I look down, and I notice that the lifting handle of the bolt is not flat to the floor, but sticking up at right-angles.

Looking down at it, I think back to the last time I checked the bolts, which was probably last night. Because I haven't been down there since I put away the stuff I brought up with me from London. For various reasons.

But checking the bolts has developed into a habit with me; each time I bring in the Marina, I look at them and sometimes even get down on my hands and knees and perhaps slide one of them in and out, as if by doing that I'm making that which lies beneath the garage floor that bit more secure. And I only usually manipulate one, as if to stop myself from going any farther, from sliding back all the bolts and actually lifting the trapdoor and going down there.

But last night I can't remember doing it. Which isn't surprising as I can't actually remember getting into the bedroom and on to the bed.

So I kick the bolt flat and go over to the Marina and unlock it and get in and switch on the ignition.

THE SMOKE

THIS TIME, PARSONS DIDN'T accept a drink from me. He even thought quite lengthily about whether he was going to sit down or not, but eventually he did.

"You don't mind if I do?" I said, indicating the drinks.

He didn't say one way or the other, so I helped myself and sat down opposite him.

"Well," I said, "I suppose this time there won't be such diffident politeness."

"Possibly not," Parsons said.

"So," I said.

"You've been very efficient," he said.

"In which particular way?"

"Getting the evidence away from my colleagues in Amsterdam."

"Did you think I wouldn't be?"

"I was hoping you wouldn't, no."

"But," I said, "I was. And now, what you're going to say is—because even though you've become involved by association with the worst team in London apart from Queen's Park Rangers, you're going to play the game—what you're going to say is that you're surprised by my initial inefficiency."

Parsons didn't say anything.

"That's what you were going to say," I said to him. "Weren't you, you fucking thick copper?"

Parsons remained silent.

"Listen, you cunt," I said, "try and fit me up all you want. There's a filing cabinet through in the office; go and have a browse through. Feel free. But don't come here playing the Shepherdsons' game. It doesn't suit you. You're like a sardine in a trifle. You couldn't pull off a fit-up if they kitted you out to look like Vince Hill, instead of wearing that clerical grey—you must spend hours on getting it to shine just right. Stick to your rules, Parsons. Stay within the guidelines of your striped suit. Have a get-together with the Inland Revenue, or the VAT boys, go after me that way. But don't come in here in a haze of the Sheps after-shave and try and play that game. You are strictly not headline material."

Parsons unbuttoned the lower button of his Gannex and flicked a speck of dust off his trousers; with Parsons, the speck wouldn't have been imaginary.

"That's what you think, is it?" he said.

I shake my head.

"You'll never do it, Parsons," I told him. "Whatever the Sheps give you, you'll never do it."

"You think not?"

"Associating with Farlow and the Sheps? You know what you should be looking at, don't you? You should be looking at what they might possibly be fitting you up for, not me. That, if I was you, would be the first thought that strayed into my mind after I'd been approached by that particular Band of Hope."

"Thanks for the advice," he said.

I looked at him and said nothing. He made me sick.

"Now," he said, "can I speak?"

"Speak away," I said.

"I'm only saying this," he said, "because I like to get things straight."

As the proverb goes, there is no answer to that.

He continued, "I am in no way involved with the

Shepherdsons. I am in no way involved with Farlow. In fact, if there was no alternative to a choice between Farlow and the Shepherdsons, I would choose the Shepherdsons."

I still didn't say anything.

"No," he said, "I'm not involved, as you imagine. You see, to me, in that way, there would be no satisfaction."

"Except that you're quite prepared to pick up anything they happen to leave lying around in a hotel in Amsterdam."

"I would have picked up anything I could use in evidence against you, yes," he said. "But that doesn't mean I could be a party to it having been put down."

"You ever thought of doing a detergent commercial?" I asked him.

"No," he said, "but what I've thought of is this: and that is, you protest too much. However hard you try to steer me towards a fit-up from the Shepherdsons, it won't be hard enough, because I know that Glenda and Ray, if he turns up, are down to you, and it is for that, and that alone, that I will see you eventually at Her Majesty's Pleasure. The day I need to play games with Farlow and the Shepherdsons will be the day I hand in the evidence of my commendations which, as you know, add up to quite a collection."

"It must have been the helmet," I said. "All those years carrying it around on the night shift, in Paddington. Irreversible brain damage. That's what must have caused it."

"That's right, Fowler," he said. "That's what it must have been; but better to have been accidental rather than incipient, wouldn't you say?"

"I'd say what I said to you before," I said to him. "That you are just a thick copper with nobody and nothing in your pocket. Except for your highly scrupulous expenses chitties, which are no doubt neatly folded and are sometimes not even cashed over the counter."

THE SEA

THIS SATURDAY, MABLETHORPE HAS a little more life to it than usual.

The season is one more weekend closer. Easter isn't far away. They're even getting the funfair ready, just in case anybody comes.

I sit in the Marina at the bottom of the ramp and watch them in their many attempts at raising the ferris wheel. For a while, it's pretty good fun, but eventually it palls, becoming too predictable. Anyway, I think to myself, getting out of the Marina, nobody ever goes on it anyway, the prices they charge.

I walk to the top of the ramp. As yet there are no donkeys on the sands.

I look in the direction of the Dunes. The entrance door is open, even though it is not yet opening time. Which in my case makes no difference, whichever way you look at it. But before I go and pass some time with Howard, I walk back down the ramp and cross the promenade and past the arcade and make for the newsagent's. The arcade is not yet open. The sun makes its dusty glass shine like burnished gold.

In the newsagent's I buy the local weekly paper and go back to the Marina and sit in it and unfold the newspaper.

The picture is the same one that was in the evening paper, and the story is pretty much the same. The body of the Cortina's passenger is as yet unidentified.

I drop the paper on to the passenger seat next to me and light a cigarette. I look out of the window. The crane operator has finally got it right; the wheel has been swung into its position and it's lowered on to its pivot, all nice and ready to start turning its circles again.

I take my flask out of my pocket and unscrew the top.

THE SMOKE

THIS TIME ALL FIVE of the Shepherdsons were in the Steering Wheel, and this time I didn't go on my own. This time Mickey went with me. But Mickey was Mickey, and at no time on his way to the Steering Wheel, or at it, or on his way back from it, was there anything that could give me any idea, not one inch, not one way or the other.

It being early evening, the Shepherdsons had not yet gone on to anywhere else they may have been going on to. All five of them were there, almost filling out the booth: Charlie, Walter, Jimmy, Rich and Johnny. Charlie and Walter were the two oldest. They were around my age. Out of the five of them, they were the only two of any consequence. Which out of that five didn't mean an awful lot.

Johnny was sitting at the end of the booth, his artificial leg sticking out at right angles from the table, as if tempting anybody who might be so inclined to try tripping over it.

Drinks and extra chairs were brought, and Mickey and I sat down.

After I had a sip of my drink, I said to them, "You'll notice I didn't come in the way Ronnie and Reggie's boys went into the Barn."

"Yeah," Charlie said. "We're observant like that."

Johhny laughed at Charlie's razor-sharp wit.

"You seem to be observant in a lot of other areas at the moment."

"We keep our eyes and ears open."

"Like regarding Glenda."

"Yeah," Walter said. "We saw about that in the papers. Was it in the *News* or the *Standard*?"

"Wasn't she Ray Warren's lady?" Rich said.

"I heard something to that effect," Jimmy said.

I took another sip of my drink.

"When I was in here the other day," I said, "talking to Johnny, I got the impression he not only understood English but that he spoke it, too."

"Oh, yeah," Walter said. "Johnny told us you'd been in."

"And did he manage to tell you what I said to him?"

"He said you seemed to have some idea that we put Arthur Philips up to talking to Farlow about that four-hander that went down not so long ago," Charlie said.

"That's right," I said.

"Here, hang about," Walter said. "I think I'm just cottoning."

"Perhaps we should all drink to that," I said.

Walter looked at Charlie, all full of hurt concern.

"You know what he's saying, Charlie?"

"What's that, Walter?"

"He's not only come here suggesting we put Arthur up to what he done," Walter said. "He's come here again trying to say that we have some idea as to the way Ray Warren's Glenda shuffled off these mortal coils."

"No," Charlie said. He looked at me. "I mean, why should we want to top a slag like Glenda in order to irritate you? If we was going to do that, there are many other ways we could think of."

"I know," I said.

"Then what?" Charlie said. "What are you talking about?"

Johnny adds his little laugh to the proceedings once again.

"What I'm talking about," I said, "is this. I've come here to tell you that although you probably know already, the Amsterdam charade has been screwed; there is no longer any mileage in it for you. Not unless you can come up with a photograph of me personally cutting Glenda's throat."

"So why have you come here to tell us things you think we already know?" Rich asked.

"To tell you that I know them too," I said. "That's all. And to demonstrate to you that after two attempts I'm still walking around; if there's a third one, you won't be. Not any of you."

Johnny smiled to himself.

"Well," said Walter, "you don't half make yourself clear, don't you?"

"I always try to do that," I said.

"That's a lot of us to put down," Johnny said, "if that's what you were thinking of doing."

"Only numerically speaking. The sum total doesn't add up to all that much."

"So," Charlie said, after a small silence. "That's what you came to tell us."

"That's what I came to tell you," I said.

I stood up. Mickey moved my chair to one side.

"The next time I come, if it's necessary," I said, "you won't even know that I've been."

Mickey and I walked out of the club. In the car Mickey said, "You really think Amsterdam was down to them?"

"I don't know," I said, "but it doesn't do any harm to let them think I do."

Mickey didn't say anything. He just carried on driving the motor. I considered the thoughts possibly going through Mickey's mind, depending on which side of the fence he was on.

Eventually I said, "What do you think?"

"I don't know, do I? It's all too complicated for a simple fellow of the kind that I am."

That was the kind of remark I'd have expected from Mickey, in either eventuality, being the kind of clever fellow he was.

"What I can't understand is," Mickey said, "them being the thick bastards they are, if it was down to them, how they got on to Ray, and what he was pulling, so they'd be able to top Glenda and get that stuff of Ray's and plant it there. That's what I don't understand."

"Leading us to the question of the moment: Is Ray already with Glenda in Paradise? Or what?"

"Yeah," Mickey said. "Or what?"

THE SEA

In the Dunes, Howard is bottling up, an activity he ceases immediately when I appear at the other side of his bar.

Everywhere is activity this morning; the wrestling ring in the auditorium is being dismantled. There is also some gear on the stage that looks as though it belongs to Eddie.

Howard puts the drinks between us.

"How did your wrestling go last night?" I ask him.

"Highly entertaining," he said. "Made my week. Which says a lot for the kind of week I have these days."

"Never mind," I said. "Maybe things'll pick up when the season starts."

"Yes," says Howard. "The monsoon season."

He drinks and for a minute or two we watch the efforts of the workers as they set about the wrestling ring.

"The way they're going on," Howard says, "they won't have it down for next Wednesday week, let alone tonight's down-home get-together."

"Something on two nights running?"

"Oh yes, we don't muck about around here."

"What's going off?"

"Well, from now on, until the season starts proper, Eddie does Saturday nights here. Regular."

"And when the season starts proper?"

"I get him five nights a week, plus the kids' talent shows every dinner-time."

"You'll be looking forward to that then."

"Oh yes. Can't wait," Howard says. "Mind you, if he could have got that girl to stick for the season, at least she'd shine out like a kind act in an unfriendly world."

"Yes," I say. "Certainly a pity, that is."

"Still," he says, "what could you expect? A girl like that, and a group like Eddie's."

"Quite," I say.

I buy us two more and while we're drinking those we watch the men go about their business with the wrestling ring. After a couple more, the spectacle loses whatever fascination it may have had earlier and I decide to have a wander.

As I'm about to go, something occurs to Howard and he says, "You going to the South?"

"Probably. Why?"

"I should have thought, earlier, when we were talking about him. Eddie was in, setting up. Said if I saw you, tell you he wanted to see you, if you were around."

"About what?"

"Well, I doubt if it's about paying you back what you doled out to him yesterday."

"He didn't say what?"

"No, he didn't. He just looked as chuffed as a pussy that's been on the rhubarb. Mind you, so would I, if I'd been on the end of that kind of generosity."

"You never know, Howard. Maybe some day."

"You never know."

"Anyway, I'll probably be in the South later, if you see him before I do."

"I'll tell him that."

I walk out of the Dunes in the bright Saturday morning sunshine. The sea glitters beneath it, appearing almost inviting. Almost, but not quite.

THE SMOKE

HOWEVER MUCH SPECULATION WAS going down about a final outcome to what was buffetting the organisation slightly, this speculation in no way intruded into our private lives; we continued to act like the rest of the nation's consenting adults. Only in our case, the props were more realistic, and the productions better lit, the supporting players prettier and more professional.

It was during one of these at-homes, when the central character was Jean, playing the role of a WRAF officer whose barrack-room subordinates stripped and humiliated her, and which I was videotaping, that the phone rang.

Normally, on these occasions, the phone didn't ring. Whoever was on duty out on the Penthouse landing took all calls that came through the switchboard in the club downstairs if they were intended for me. Unless they were absolutely urgent, they never got through to me on occasions such as tonight.

So when the red signalling light came on in the small studio beyond the projection room, I was well pleased; we were only halfway through. So instead of stopping the action I handed over the videotaping to a girl who was only at present marginally involved in the action and went out and through the projection room and into the vastness of the lounge to pick up the phone on my desk. Gerry Hatch was on duty outside that particular night and I said to him, "What the fuck is it?"

"I'm sorry to bother you, Mr. Fowler," Gerry said. "But Mr. Collins is on the line and he's saying to me it's very urgent."

Collins, I thought to myself. There was nothing about Collins at the moment that was urgent except his concern for his own skin. But as he'd interrupted me, and he was still on the line, I wanted to tell him what I thought about him calling at this particular time.

"All right, Gerry," I said. "Get him put through."

Collins came on.

"George—" he began.

"Fuck all that, Dennis. Didn't Gerry tell you I was busy?"

"Yes, he did—"

"And you know what that means, don't you? It means I don't want bastards like you calling me up with nothing whatsoever to say to me."

"George, I have," he said. "I have got something to tell you."

"Oh yes?" I said. "Like what? Like the Bank Rate's just going to be cut by a quarter of a percent or that *Jesus Christ Superstar* is still running at the Palace?"

"George, I'm serious. And I'm shit-scared."

"You surprise me."

"Listen. I know something."

"You still surprise me."

"All right," Collins says. "All right. If you don't want to know, you don't want to know. That's your privilege. Only after this phone call, don't try and phone me. Because by the time all that could possibly go down has gone down I won't be able to be reached, not even by the international operator."

For Collins to talk like this, there must be something, so I said, "All right, Dennis. Go ahead. Lay it on me."

"Not even on this telephone, George."

"It'd be difficult for you to come round here at the moment—"

"I know it would. Bloody difficult. Because I don't want to come round there anyway, not at the moment."

"What are you talking about, Dennis?"

"At the moment, nothing. We'll meet where we've sometimes met before, and then I'll tell you. You know what place I'm talking about, don't you?"

"Yes, Dennis."

"I'll see you there in an hour."

Then he put the phone down before I had a chance to reply.

THE SEA

I WALK DOWN THE ramp and past my Marina. Up at the top of the steps, on the funfair, they've begun to give the ferris wheel a few practice whirls, just to test it out in case it might do something unexpected, like fall over, or something like that. Its height makes the rest of the town look even flatter, its black shadow like an enormous film-spool circling across the ramp and over the promenade and down the street as far as the far west end of the arcade.

I cross the promenade, because now the arcade is open for business, and I have plenty of my customary time to kill.

It's fuller than on a usual Saturday morning; a further sign of the approaching season. Kids run from machine to machine, leaving each machine in a permanent state of tilt. Three kids are giving hell to my favourite machine, so after I've got my change I spend a quarter of an hour on the anti-tank game, satisfying myself as each explosion knocks over a tank as it trundles forward over the desert dunes.

After I've exhausted the entertainment value of that, I spend some money on the grappler machine, manoeuvre the mechanical crane, trying to grab a dusty bar of chocolate or a plastic ring, an achievement I have never yet in my life accomplished, but the regularity of its failure gives the machine a certain compulsion and I'm quite happy to while away some more time swinging the crane as unsuccessfully as the man who had been inserting the ferris wheel.

Eventually I run out of change and go back to the kiosk and while the man is counting out my money I glance over to see if my favourite machine is free yet.

It isn't.

But it's no longer occupied by kids.

It's being played by a girl with long dark hair. Wearing an Afghan coat. And dark glasses.

THE SMOKE

I PARKED THE MERCEDES in the car park and waited. A light drizzle drifted across the dark night sky and around the sodium of the street lamp like swarms of midges on a summer evening.

Eventually headlights appeared, slowed down, swung slowly on to the car park. As the car drew level with mine, I shifted in my seat, so that my arm dangled over the back, within easy reach of what lay underneath the car rug on the back seat.

The door of the other car opened and closed and my passenger door opened and Collins got in and sat next to me. Immediately certain that everything was as it seemed, I removed my arm from the back of the seat and took out my cigarettes.

"Nice night for it," I said to Collins.

"Yes," he said.

I lit my cigarette.

"Well?" I said.

Collins breathed in, like a manager who's just seen his centre-half put in his own goal.

"I've not come to tell you what I know," he said.

I blew out cigarette smoke.

"I see," I said, like the blind man.

"I've come to tell you what I want. When I've got that, then I'll tell you."

I considered things all round. Finally I decided I'd get quicker further if I didn't do what I wanted to do.

"Go on," I said.

"The reason for all this is very simple; it's not because I wouldn't trust you if we worked out a deal."

"That's nice to know, Dennis," I said. "After all these years."

"It's because when I tell you what I know, knowing you, all hell will be let loose, one way or another. And I don't want to be any part of it. I want to be out of it, before it happens."

I didn't say anything. He continued.

"I've got some leave due," he said. "On Friday, I'm taking it. Going abroad. And I'm not coming back. I'm going to spend the rest of my life where my money is. I've got too much at stake to risk going down with you."

"Dennis," I said, "what are you talking about?"

"I've told you," he said. "Before I tell you, I want some more money transferred into the account in Lucerne."

"Assuming I was prepared to do that," I said, "what sort of amount had you got in mind?"

"Fifty," Dennis said.

I inhaled.

"You've already got a lot of money out there, Dennis," I said, "What are you going to do with an extra fifty thousand?"

"Consolidate," he said.

"And what makes you think I'm going to give you fifty grand for telling me fuck all?"

"Because when you know what it is you'll be glad to have paid it."

"Sort of what you might call an *impasse*," I said.

"I think you'll pay me," he said. "Because you know that I wouldn't be getting out of what has been up to now an extremely good situation for me."

"What makes you think the things you know are bad enough to send you off to pastures new?"

"In themselves, they're not. It's what you'll do, when I tell you. The way you'll react. Quite in what form that reaction will manifest itself, I don't know. All I know is I don't want to be around to find out first-hand."

I stubbed my cigarette out in the ashtray.

"And who do I deal with when you're gone?" I said.

"There'll be no problem there, will there?" he said. "They'll probably have a sweepstake."

I thought about things.

"All right," I said. "Phone your account and check it on Tuesday morning. I'll meet you here same time Tuesday night."

"I'll do that," Collins said, and opened the car door.

"And Dennis," I said.

"What?" he said, half out of the car.

"I've got a shotgun on the back seat," I said. "Under a blanket. I brought it just in case. Know what I mean?"

"Yes," said Collins. "I know what you mean."

He got out of the car and closed the door.

THE SEA

I SIT IN THE Marina and cradle the flask in my lap and stare at the bollards on top of the ramp and the sky beyond them.

That I've just seen her, there was no doubt. There was no doubt it was Lesley Murray, Mablethorpe's answer to Carly Simon. But Lesley was the girl from Grimsby, the girl I'd seen crumble to ashes in the Cortina.

Wasn't she?

I take another drink.

Now think rationally. You've just had a shock, seen something you hadn't expected to see. You've seen a girl playing a pinball machine who you thought you'd seen burnt to death in a salesman's Cortina.

That's all.

I try and focus on the faces, the way they'd become different in the different circumstances, the different gear, the different hairstyles.

I can't separate the two images. They keep coming together like the images when you focus a telescopic sight; the contours and features keep coming together and fitting one over the other with complete accuracy. They keep matching up. I shake my head, to re-jumble the elements of memory, but they keep reforming in the same twin patterns.

Which is, of course, completely irrational. There is only one rational answer, that answer being that I was wrong. The two girls were in fact two girls. That is the evidence. But to my own eyes that evidence is inadmissible. My retina continues to retain the two images as one.

Think.

When I saw her, ten minutes earlier, I'd been too bottled to move; I'd just stood by the kiosk, watched her as she'd given the pinball machine a final disenchanted shove as the tilt sign had lit up, and then she'd drifted off, out of the arcade, seeming to be going nowhere in particular.

I hadn't moved until the kiosk man had nudged me and put my change in my hand.

Of course, I have to be wrong. There is no connection between the two girls, not in the way I have imagined. They are two separate entities. There is no other explanation.

But try explaining that to my eyes.

I take another pull from my flask and as I'm doing that there is a great thunderclap of noise and the Marina shakes as if it's been struck by several thunderbolts and then there's Eddie's face grinning in the window at me as a postscript to his having battered on the Marina's roof with the flat of his hand.

I recover somewhat and roll the window down.

"Morning, Mr. Carson," he says. "Hope I didn't interrupt your breakfast."

"Actually," I say, "it's an early lunch."

Eddie shows his appreciation of my great wit and when he's done that he says, "Did Howard tell you I was looking for you?"

I nod.

"I wanted to tell you; you must be lucky for me. Lesley turned up and she's decided to give it a go with us for the season. That's great, isn't it?"

"Terrific," I tell him.

"I'm just off to the South; come with us and let me buy you a drink. That's the least I can do."

"Well, as a matter of fact—"

"I'm meeting Lesley there. It's my chance to do you a good turn for the good turn that you done me. I mean, you did want to get to know her, didn't you?"

THE SMOKE

ON TUESDAY EVENING, AT the same time and at the same place, I waited for Collins.

His car arrived and he got out of it and into mine.

"Thanks," he said.

"Did you think I wouldn't have done it?" I said.

"No," Collins said.

"Well," I said, "I hope it's worth it."

"I think you'll think so."

Then Collins told me what I'd paid him fifty thousand pounds to tell me.

When he'd finished, we sat there in silence for three or four minutes. Then I said, "I'll only ask you once. This is straight up, isn't it? I mean, you're not going into retirement because I might at some point discover you've been selling me a load of shit."

"I think you know that I'm not."

I lit a cigarette.

"All right," I said. "Just, as you might say, to reassure me. How did you get to know all this?"

"One of Farlow's grasses."

"And you'd call that a reliable source, would you?"

"In this case, yes. Because he's not Farlow's grass at all. He's mine. He has been for nearly six years. How do you think I've got you some of your information over the years?"

"I imagined you must have had some sort of method, Dennis," I said.

"Thank you," he said.

"But," I said, "how did your grass get to know? I mean, it's not the kind of thing that's going to get shouted about even in whispers."

"Not in the normal course of events, no. But in this case, we have our friend with the wooden leg to thank. If he hadn't swayed into my grass at the Aerodrome Club in the small hours of last Thursday and needed a hand home, we'd never have known a thing."

"Highly fortuitous," I said.

"It happens," Collins said.

There was another silence.

"What are you going to do about it?" Collins said.

"Right at this moment, I'm not quite sure."

"I'm fucking positive," Collins said.

"And that's why you're geting out."

"Too right."

"Well," I said. "I doubt very much if I'll be seeing you again."

"There's no doubt about it," Collins said, and got out of the car.

THE SEA

I FOLLOW EDDIE ACROSS the industrial carpeting of the South to the bar. Eddie is now in his element; yesterday, all was doom and despond. Today, the sunshine is bringing the season, his element, that little bit closer. And now he has transport, and a new lead singer to give that transport added purpose. And he is going to buy me a drink, to demonstrate to whoever may be in the South that he is the kind of fellow who is used to buying a fellow like myself a drink. When we reach the bar there is great heartiness from him to Jackie, which Jackie receives with all the enthusiasm that he would normally reserve for a representative trying to push a new brand of cigarettes. Eddie, naturally, is unaware of this. His own kind of central heating leaves him impervious to that kind of chill.

"Lesley not been in yet?" he says to Jackie, as he gives us our drinks.

"Lesley? Oh, you mean the bird. No, not that I can recall."

"Women," Eddie says to me. "You can always rely on them, can't you?"

"Yes," I tell him. "That seems to be a fact of life."

"Anyhow," he says, "your very good health, and to your generosity."

As he's saying that, one of the doors is pushed inwards, and Lesley appears.

She crosses the floor towards us. Dark glasses glint with the rose colours of the bar behind us.

"Lesley," Eddie says, before she's anywhere near us. "You proved me wrong."

When she gets to us she says, "In what way?"

"I was just saying to Mr. Carson that if there's one thing in this life you can be certain of, that is you can never be certain of women."

"And did Mr. Carson agree with you?" she says.

Both of them are looking at me.

"Your arrival makes any comment I might have made superfluous," I say.

"Well," she says, "now I'm here, I'll have a drink. If that isn't superfluous too."

"Jackie," Eddie says. "Vodka and whatever goes with it."

"Ice," she says. "And lemon. I can't abide it without lemon."

"So I understand," I say.

"I beg your pardon," she says.

"That night you paid me a visit you mentioned that."

Eddie goes over the top at doing a hello hello routine.

"I'm sorry," she says. "But I don't understand."

"See what I mean," Eddie says to me, "about women?"

"You're saying I came to your house?" she says.

"Well, I haven't seen you since, but—"

She smiles.

"Are you trying to impress Eddie?" she says. "And Jackie? Is that what you're trying to do?"

"Now look—"

"Jesus," she says, shaking her head.

"Excuse me," Eddie says. "I got to see a man about a dog."

He leaves us and makes his way towards the toilets.

"All right," I say to her. "Forget it."

She moves a little closer. Jackie is called to the far end of the bar to attend to one of his geriatrics.

"Look," she says, "don't come all that shit in front of Eddie. I'm going to do the stint, for my sins, all right? He already thinks it's a one two three four and into bed. You understand?"

"I'm sorry," I tell her. "It didn't occur to me."

"Well, it occurred to him, and it occurred to me. Now he probably thinks he can have me between numbers."

"And you don't want him to think that."

"What do you think?"

"I don't know," I say. "I don't know what you want."

"Don't you?" she says.

She looks at me.

"I think you do," she says. "I think you think you know what I want."

THE SMOKE

I TOLD JEAN WHAT Collins had told me. She listened and then she got up and went over to the drinks and came back and sat down opposite me. Instead of saying what she'd every right to say, she said, "What are you going to do about it?"

"What do you think I'm going to do about it?"

There was a silence.

"Don't you think you ought to talk to James first?" she said.

"Fuck James."

"He's got to be told."

"What for? What difference would it make? He'll come in and drink his brandy and tell me what you know he'll tell me."

"Well, he'd be right, wouldn't he?"

"This is different. This isn't a square dance. There's only one way to stop this kind of thing. And that is to stop it. Not to pass it over to the Oxford Union and wait for a show of hands."

"James ought to be told."

"He'll be told."

"I mean before."

I drank some of my drink.

"You didn't answer my question," I said. "What do you think I'm going to do about it?"

"I don't have to answer that, do I?"

"No."

"But there's a question, bearing on that."

"What?"

"Who are you going to use? Because in something like this there's no one you could trust, is there? Not for certain."

"No," I said. "Except you."

She looked at me.

"You're joking."

"No, I'm not joking."

"I mean, what exactly would you expect me to do?"

"What you usually do," I said. "What you've done in the past."

THE SEA

In the evening, the Dunes is fuller than it had been for Amateur Night. But I doubt if it's because word has got around that Eddie's got a new singer with him. It's like everything else; it's just that it's that little bit nearer to the season. In fact, Howard is moved to say:

"The turn-out makes one feel positively gay."

I'm not in the mood for feeding lines to Howard so I nod and, like the rest of the punters, I look at everybody else and wait for the evening's entertainment.

Which tonight should be of special interest.

After Lesley said what she'd said in the bar at lunchtime, Eddie had returned from the gents and even if I could have thought of a reply I wouldn't have had the opportunity to say it, because a minute or so after Eddie's return she downed her vodka and left and told us she'd see us at the Dunes this evening.

And now it is this evening.

At lunchtime, after she'd gone, Eddie'd been very pleased with himself, at the way he thought things had turned out between Lesley and me. He'd done everything but nudge me in the ribs, which, like Howard's repartee, I could have done without, at a time when I'd been propositioned by a girl I'd thought I'd seen burnt to death the previous day.

Now it is evening and I still haven't exactly got used to the idea.

After she'd gone, at lunchtime, I'd left the South and driven back to the bungalow and walked down to the beach and sat on the tank and drunk from my refilled flask and thought about all the possibilities. But all I could come up with was the facts as they appeared to be. That I'd been mistaken about Lesley and the girl from Grimsby being the same. Naturally. No other explanation. That I'd been totally wrong in suspecting that both or either were from the Press. Understandable, considering the alternatives and that the girl fancied me. Simple. After all, from just a look around the bungalow, I'd be the best offer she'd get in this area. And so, not to seem to make things easy, she'd decided on a catch-as-catch-can game, to leave me guessing and keep my interest.

Well, she's certainly succeeded in keeping my interest, although not quite in the way she imagined. And, like I say, if her source had been the aftermath of what had happened in London, I wouldn't be standing at Howard's bar speculating about anything at all.

So. Whatever her game is, I've decided to play it. I'll let her think she's let me catch her. I'll go along with whatever she has in mind. That way, I'll find out what it is she has in mind. I'll appear to play the role she wants me to play in order to discover why she wants to play hers. After the show I'll continue to appear to pursue her and take it from there. And when the show begins, after Eddie's done a half-dozen numbers and he introduces her on the stage, done up in her gear, in her wig, I have to shake my head, because it's still uncanny, the resemblance to the girl from Grimsby.

THE SMOKE

THE REALLY STUPID THING about him, above all the other stupid things, was that he was a Millwall supporter. Every other Saturday he used to go to the match and sit in the directors' box boozing it up and boozing it up after the match with the lads, with whom he liked to mingle. And after the festivities at the ground some of them would go back to the Steering Wheel with him and carry on boozing it up there for the rest of the evening.

Johnny always parked his motor in the official car park. This particular night he came out and his mates got into their cars and he got into his and I waited until he got to Villiers Street before I sat up in the seat behind him and put the shooter into the back of his neck.

"It's me, Johnny," I said, as his eyes confirmed it in the driving mirror.

He didn't do anything except continue driving, there being nothing else at the present moment for him to do.

"Turn left into Plender Street," I said, "and then get on to the Cambridge Road. You know the Cambridge Road, don't you, Johnny?"

He nodded, very slightly.

He drove on for about a quarter of an hour before he spoke.

"You're being stupid," he said. "You know that."

"I don't think I'm the one that's being stupid," I said.

"If anything happens to me, that's being stupid," he said.

"If?" I said.

He didn't say anything for the rest of the journey, until we reached the caravan.

THE SEA

BUT AFTER THE SHOW she disappears again.

After the show's over, Eddie and some of his group join Howard and myself at the bar. Lesley and a couple of the others have left the stage and gone round the back for some reason. For a while I let Eddie bubble on about what a great session he's just had, waiting for Lesley to reappear from backstage and join us at the bar. Which she doesn't do. The other two members of the group join us, but not her. It isn't necessary for me to ask because Eddie gets in first and one of his mates tells him she's gone home. Eddie exercises what he imagines to be tact and doesn't make any cracks that associate Lesley and myself.

After we've had a few more drinks Eddie suggests to his boys that they pack up the gear and then drop down to the South for the last half-hour.

"Are you coming down, Mr. Carson?" he asks me.

"Yes," I say to him, looking at my watch. "I'll see you down there."

"Great," he says. "We'll only be about a quarter of an hour."

I walk along the mini-promenade and down the ramp and get into the Marina and turn it round and point it in the direction of the street and as I coast it towards the South I consider how her non-emergence from behind the stage is all part of the pattern, if I'm reading it right, the build-up, then the let-down. She may be in the South, she may not. She may come in later, she may not.

But whatever she decides to do, all I can do is go along with it, exercise patience. After all, I've got plenty of time.

I park outside of one of the double doors and go into the South.

She isn't there.

I go over to the bar and order my drink. There's twenty-five minutes left before time. Ten minutes later Eddie and the remaining members of the group who haven't gone home to their old ladies come in. Eddie's still in his Palladium mood and it isn't long before he's taking Jackie to one side and setting up an after-hours boozing session. Jackie agrees, probably because I'm around and my presence offers the prospect of a few fivers more than he'd actually take if it was only involving Eddie and his mates. But when eleven o'clock comes round and I tell them I'm going home for an early night Jackie's face drops in ratio to what isn't going to be in his till.

I make my goodnights and walk out of the pub and get into the Marina and pull away from the curb and I'm a hundred yards down the street when from the back seat a voice says to me:

"I hope it's not any trouble, Mr. Carson."

I look in the driving mirror. In the darkness, her image is only recognisable by the shape of the stage wig she's still wearing, defined against the sodium lighting beyond the rear window.

THE SMOKE

I WALKED ACROSS THE field behind Johnny, slowly. I had to, with his leg being the way it was. But being the way it was, he was hardly going to try and run off into the night. And since getting out of the motor I'd changed the Browning for a pump action.

The only lights were the lights from the caravan. Mickey and Jean were waiting inside, as arranged, but only Jean knew who I was bringing.

I tapped on the door and said to Johnny, "Think you'll be able to manage the steps?"

Johnny didn't say anything.

The door was opened by Mickey, the way I'd arranged it should be done with Jean. If Johnny's appearance was going to cause an immediate happening, Jean knew what to do about that too.

But when Mickey opened the door and illuminated Johnny and myself, he was his usual impassive self. He just stepped aside and let us both in.

I closed the door behind us.

"Sit down, Johnny," I said, indicating a bench seat.

Johnny sat down.

Jean took another pump action from the cupboard next to her. Then I put mine down. Mickey didn't do or say anything.

On the circular table, which was bolted to the floor by a

single central support, were a couple of coils of rope. Next to the ropes was a can of paraffin and a roll of cotton wool.

"Tie Johnny's left leg to the table," I said to Mickey. "To the support, at the bottom."

Mickey took the rope and did as I'd asked him. When he'd done that I tore a handful of cotton wool off the roll, unscrewed the lid of the can and soaked the cotton wool in paraffin. Then I dropped down on to one knee and rolled up Johnny's trouser leg and dabbed paraffin all over the lower part of his artificial limb, faintly obscene in its pink, perfectly shaped hairlessness. When I'd soaked enough paraffin onto it, I got up and went and sat down on the bench seat opposite him.

Mickey just remained standing where he was, quiet. Jean stood behind him, slightly to his right.

"Well," I said to Johnny, "there's no point in fucking about, is there?"

Johnny shook his head.

"How long had you had the black on Ray?"

"About two years."

"Apparently you all found it very funny."

Johnny didn't say anything.

"I mean, all that money of mine, going into your back pockets. That's what I heard. All highly amusing."

"How'd you hear?"

"Does that really interest you?"

He didn't reply straightaway. Then he said, "It won't do you any good, topping me. They'll have you for it, one way or another."

"Who says I'm going to top you? I just want you to verify one or two things I've happened to hear."

"Well, I verified them," he said. "Now what happens?"

"You haven't verified them all."

"Like what, for instance?"

"Like Glenda, for instance."

"What about her?"

"How you got to know we were going to talk to her."

"We didn't. That wasn't down to us."

"And like how Ray knew we were looking out for what he'd been doing."

"How should I know? He just found out, didn't he?"

"He just found out, and you didn't have anything to do with Glenda?"

"Right," Johnny said.

"Is that what you're saying?"

He didn't answer. I took out a box of matches and put them beside me on the seat.

THE SEA

SHE STANDS BY THE piano as I pour the drinks.

"Where's the photograph gone?" she says.

"It's being re-framed."

"I see," she says, getting my point, turning towards me and looking at me for the first time without being behind her dark glasses.

I offer her her drink.

"You didn't take your clothes off," I say to her.

She looks at me, impassive.

"I mean," I tell her, "you didn't change out of your stage gear. Not even the wig. Although I notice the Afghan doesn't change."

She takes the drink from me.

"Perhaps I imagined you might prefer me in this gear, being the type of man you are."

"And what type of man is that?"

"Your type," she says, drifting over to the shelf unit.

"And why should you take any interest in what I might prefer?"

"I wonder," she says, running a finger along one of the racks of records.

It's as I thought it was going to be. Almost on, almost off.

"Put one on if you want," I tell her.

"I was thinking it was a bit quiet," she says.

I watch her while she chooses a record.

"You went to great pains not to let anyone know you were coming here."

"I wouldn't exactly say great pains."

"Why does it matter?" I say. "I would have thought you were the kind of girl that didn't give a fuck what anybody thought."

"Would you?" she says, sliding a Carly Simon record out of its sleeve. "You've formed an opinion already, have you?"

"Haven't you?"

She puts the record on the turntable.

"How do you know it wasn't just on the spur of the moment? I saw your car outside the South and decided to give you a surprise."

"I don't know what you decided to do."

She flicks the mechanism and the arm descends on the record. Carly Simon's deep cold voice echoes round the room. For a moment or two Lesley listens to the voice, making mental comparisons.

"In any case," she says, "I meant what I said at lunchtime. I don't want Eddie thinking I'm just another of the group's arrangements. It's going to be a crappy enough season as it is."

She sits down by the unlit fire.

"I meant to ask you about that," I say, going over to the drinks. "A girl like you. You could work anywhere you wanted."

THE SMOKE

"I'M TELLING YOU," JOHNNY said. "All right, Arthur Philips and that stroke we tried to pull there was down to us; I mean, all right. And we been fucking you up and down behind your back with Ray. But when you come in the other night and put Glenda down to us, you got it all wrong. Right, it would have been a good idea, use her to point Parsons at you, but we could have done that without bothering to take her overseas to do it."

"No," I said, "because you didn't know we were on to Ray."

"Right," Johnny says, "you see? We didn't know you were on to Ray."

"Or his involvement with you."

"Right."

"Except," I said, "that you did."

"You what?"

"You did know," I said. "You know all about the matter under discussion."

"I don't know what you're talking about."

"You knew what you were talking about when you talked to Wally Barling."

"Wally Barling?"

"Wally Barling. You remember Wally, Johnny? Farlow's grass. You and your brothers excluded, of course."

"Yeah. What about him?"

"You may not have realised it when you were chatting with him the other evening, but he's not Farlow's grass at all. He's been Collins's grass ever since England had a decent football team."

Johnny didn't say anything. I looked at Mickey.

"Did you know that, Mickey?"

"No," Mickey said. "I didn't know that."

THE SEA

"Do you mind if we light the fire?" she says.

"The central heating seems to be working all right."

"I know. But looking at an empty fireplace makes me feel cold."

I kneel down and pick up the box of kitchen matches off the hearth and strike a match and light the fire. The newsprint crackles like the sound of small bones breaking.

"You were saying," I say as I stand up, "what, with your talent, you're doing taking up with a group like Eddie's."

"I wasn't," she says. "You were asking."

The flames settle into the bark of the logs and some of the bark flakes off like dead skin.

"I mean, you got relatives in this area, or what?"

"I haven't relatives in any area. I'm a single girl."

"So why have you ended up here?"

"Why not? You've got to end up somewhere."

I pour us both another drink.

"You're hardly of an age to end up anywhere."

"Like you, you mean?"

"I'm only here temporarily."

"Like me, passing through?"

"You said you've ended up here."

"No, you said that," she says.

I hand her her refilled glass.

"Anyway," she says. "All these questions. I could be asking you the same ones."

"You could."

"I mean, I could be asking you who you are. Why you choose to spend your time in this dead-and-alive hole."

"Perhaps you don't ask," I say to her, "because you think you already know."

She looks at me, blank.

"Know?" she says. "Know what?"

I smile at her.

"Never mind," I say. "I don't think you'd be that stupid. Not a second time."

"A second time what?"

I shake my head.

"Forget it. It's just a thought I had."

"About what?"

"About you. About why I interest you."

"You interest me, do you?"

"Well," I say, "what other reason would you be here for?"

"Perhaps it's just for the sake of something to do."

"You mean, a way of passing the time?"

"That's right. You don't necessarily have to be interested in someone to pass the time with them."

"Not necessarily," I say, "no."

THE SMOKE

"YOU SEE," I SAID to Johnny, "even Mickey didn't know Wally Barling was on our team."

"That fucking bastard," Johnny says, "I'll—"

"You'll what, Johnny?"

Johnny became silent.

"And I bet," I said, "I bet Mickey'll be even more interested when you tell him what you told Wally."

"Listen—"

"That's what we're doing, Johnny. Listening."

I picked up the matchbox and shook it in the palm of my hand.

"I didn't tell him nothing, honest," Johnny said.

"You didn't tell him, like, how you and your brothers knew we were on to Ray. That that information came from Mickey. Because you'd been blacking him for over a year, because you happened to come across some pictures he had taken in his spare time with a fourteen-year-old who hasn't seen the light of day for the last twelve months."

Mickey looked at Johnny. Behind Mickey, Jean held the pump action pointed straight at the middle of Mickey's back.

"Is that what he said, guv'nor?" Mickey said.

"That's what you said, Johnny, wasn't it?"

"I never."

"Didn't you? And you didn't tell him that the only way you

got to Glenda before I did was because Mickey phoned you up before we set off on our way. You didn't tell him that either, did you, Johnny?"

"Look, I'm telling you—"

"Oh, I'm forgetting," I said. "You also said that Mickey topped Ray, because we were getting too close. But that Mickey didn't know about Glenda until I called her up. And when he phoned you up to get there first, you decided to use her to try and drop me in it. That Mickey furnished you with the effects he'd taken off Ray's body."

"Listen—"

Mickey interrupted him, very quiet, standing very still.

"Is that what you told him, Johnny?" he said.

"Mickey, listen—"

I stood up and took out a match and Johnny stopped talking and looked at the match as I held it against the striker. The caravan was full of silence.

"Guv'nor," Mickey said.

"Yes, Mickey?"

"You don't believe all this shit, do you?"

"Well, let me put it this way. I wouldn't like to think you've been slagging me behind my back after all I've done for you over the years. I'd hate to think after all that I couldn't trust you."

"I thought all that was understood between us."

"That's what I thought, yes."

"But now you don't."

"Well, I'm just going to find out, aren't I?" I said, striking the match.

THE SEA

"ALL RIGHT," I SAY, "if you don't want to tell me why you've chosen this place, where were you before?"

"Before?"

"Where were you working?"

"All over."

"In London?"

"I tried London, yes."

"What happened?"

"What didn't? A chapter of accidents."

"Did you get close to making it?"

"I think so."

"What went wrong? It can't have been your ability."

"It wasn't."

"What, then?"

"Like I said. A chapter of accidents. Instead of being in the right place at the right time I was in the wrong place at the wrong time."

"How old are you?"

"Twenty-two."

I light a cigarette.

"Sounds to me as if you gave up very easy," I tell her.

"Does it?"

"I mean, twenty-two. Hardly too late for a comeback, is it?"

"You don't know what happened."

"What could have happened? You missed out first time round. Who doesn't? And you're hardly going to get a second chance round here."

"Aren't I?"

I shrug.

"Want to manage me, do you?" she says.

"All right. You know what you're doing."

"Yes. I know what I'm doing."

The Carly Simon record stops. Silence.

"You mind if I put on another record?" she says, getting up.

"No, I don't mind."

She picks out one of the albums. It's a Barbra Streisand, *Live Concert at the Forum*. It was Jean's favourite.

"Not that one," I say to her.

"You don't like Streisand?"

"There's some others there of hers."

"I haven't heard this one."

"Another time," I say.

She shrugs, replaces the record, searches for another, pulls out one of Stevie Wonder's, turns to face me with the cover.

"This one in order?" she says.

THE SMOKE

THE MATCH SOUNDED LIKE a gun going off in the caravan.

"Mr. Fowler," Johnny said. "George—"

"It's George, is it?"

Johnny started to try and wriggle his wrists out of the ropes behind his back. I knelt down and put the match to the paraffin on Johnn's leg and retired quickly.

Blue flame danced on the sickly pinkness of the smooth plastic.

Johnny screamed and thrashed about as the flame darted up his leg to the knee part, where the folds of his shoved-up trousers began.

"Christ!" Johnny screamed. "My Christ!"

"What, Johnny?" I said. "Now what have you got to say?"

Johnny was lying on his side on the bench, trying to tug himself away from the table leg, like a man in a gin trap, only in this case the spirit was paraffin.

"Well, Johnny, is that what you told Wally?"

The flame leapt at the squeezed-up cuff of his trousers. I picked up the paraffin can and shook a few drops on to the other trouser leg, the one with his good leg inside, and struck another match and dropped it on the material. A patch of paraffin sprung to life.

"Christ," he screamed. "Yes, yes, Mickey done it, Mickey copped for you. He did, he did, he copped for you."

Mickey screamed even louder, in a different way.

"You dirty fucking cheating bastard," he shrieked, drawing his shooter from his shoulder holster. "You fucking wanker!"

Mickey aimed at Johnny's head.

Two things happened simultaneously.

Mickey fired, and Jean fired. The combined noise was like a bomb exploding.

Because of Johnny's thrashing about, Mickey missed.

Jean didn't.

The barrels were only six inches from the small of his back when she fired. Mickey was lifted up off his feet and thrown across the table and landed on top of Johnny, his blood and insides reaching Johnny before Mickey did, making Johnny's face and shirt and jacket scarlet, as though someone had splashed a full paintbrush all over him. His screams became even louder as Mickey slid off him and lay on his back on the floor, his legs across Johnny's burning legs, a great black-red bubbling hole where his stomach had been.

I opened the door and Jean went down the steps still holding the pump action. I picked up my shotgun and emptied the rest of the paraffin over Johnny, and slammed the door on his screams as the flames began to blossom all over him.

We were almost at the Mercedes by the time the flames got to the Calor gas and the whole caravan went up, illuminating the night sky like the centrepiece of a firework display.

THE SEA

THE STEVIE WONDER RECORD finishes. I stand up.

"Another drink?" I ask her.

She looks at her watch.

"I haven't time."

I look at my watch. It's ten past twelve.

"Got a prior engagement, have you?"

She smiles at me, as warm as ice.

"I might have."

It's my turn to smile.

"Is this the moment you make the move?" she says.

"I'm going to make a move, am I?"

She maintains the smile.

"Actually," I say to her, "it's the moment I ask you if you'd like another drink."

She hands me her glass. Unmelted ice slides about the base.

"All right," she says. "I'll have one more. Before I go."

"Fine," I say, and begin to make the drinks. When I've done that I give her hers and go and sit down opposite her again.

"In any case," she says, after taking a sip, "I'm frigid. So it wouldn't really be worth it, would it?"

"I don't suppose it would."

"Or would you consider that a challenge?"

"Some men might. If they believed it."

"And you?"

"I thought you'd got me all weighed up."

She smiles her smile again.

"There's always rape; meant to be more exciting if the woman's frigid, isn't it?"

"So they say," I say.

"Or are you more of a watcher. Yes," she says, "at your age, I'd say you're more of a watcher."

"Would you?"

She raises her glass in the direction of the screen in the ceiling.

"That's what that's for, isn't it?"

"Is it?"

"Hardly had it installed just for home movies, did you? Although there are home movies and home movies, aren't there?"

"So they say," I say again.

"I did some once," she says. "In London."

She takes another sip of her drink. I don't say anything.

"One of my accidents. The money was good, though."

"It would have to be," I said. "Seeing as you're frigid."

"I'm a professional," she says. "At whatever I do. I always give a good performance."

"I'm sure."

"Besides, it was lesbian stuff. Which doesn't mean to say I'm a dike, because I'm frigid."

"Of course not."

"Are you taking the piss?"

I shake my head. She takes another sip of her drink.

"Is that how you spend the long winter evenings, then? Watching blue movies?"

I shake my head. She smiles the smile again.

"Of course not," she says. She drains her glass. "You don't do things like that, do you?"

THE SMOKE

"YOU FUCKING IDIOT," JAMES said. "My Christ Almighty. After *The Music Lovers*, I'd thought I'd seen everything. It's me that must be stupid, to think you have sense."

I gave him his drink, frowning, hearing James swear like that.

"And you, Jean," he said, after he'd downed half his brandy. "At least I thought you'd be able to prevent something like this. At least attempt to."

He swallowed the other half and I took his glass from him.

"And now I find you were actually a party to it."

"It was quite some party," I said, handing him back his glass, refilled.

He took another drink and sat down.

"I don't know," he said. "I just don't know."

"Well, I do," I said. "We did what had to be done."

"Like what?" James said. "With all the means at your disposal?"

"What means? Mickey was my means of disposal. I trusted him. Who else could I get to do it for me, if I couldn't trust him?"

"I don't mean that. I mean the bodies. Why didn't you do it *Sonet Lumière* at the Bloody Tower? It mightn't quite have attracted the same amount of attention, but I suppose it would at least have been appropriate."

"It was appropriate, all right. It spelt it out in fire, like at

Belshazzar's Feast. In big letters, so that even the Shepherdsons can read it."

"Parsons can read as well," James said.

"And what's he going to do, when all the time I was sitting here in the bosom of my family, entertaining various well-known and well-paid friends?"

"And well-trusted, I suppose?"

"Look, nobody's going to risk talking to their own reflection in the mirror after this. And what's Parsons going to do? Wait for some more secondhand furniture from the Shepherdsons?"

"He will do what he can."

"Which is fuck all."

James had cooled down slightly; this time he only sipped at his brandy.

"And as you mention them," he said, "what do you think they intend to do? Lock the doors at the Steering Wheel and hope you didn't pick up Johnny's key?"

"I've done them a favour. Their best-laid plans were fucked up, thanks to their terrible brother. He was a liability, and now he's proved it. I've done them a favour."

"And supposing they don't think you're intending to stop at Johnny?"

"I'll tell them," I said. "When I go round and see them."

"When you what?"

"When I go round. To thank them for putting me on to Mickey. Without their help I'd never have known, would I?"

James took the rest of his brandy at one go. I raised my glass.

"To absent friends," I said. "The cock-sucking bastard."

THE SEA

SHE STANDS UP AND I stand up and pick up my jacket and she watches me and says, "What are you doing?"

"Putting my jacket on."

"Why?"

"Because it's cold out."

"I don't want you to drive me home," she says.

"What?"

"I want to walk home along the beach."

"Why?"

"Because it's a nice night and I like walking along the beach."

I put my jacket back on the chair.

"I could have you back in five minutes," I say.

"I know."

"Whereabouts exactly is it you live?"

"In Mablethorpe," she says, giving me the smile.

"Well, I'll show you out."

"You'd better. You've got more locks than the Bank of England."

"That's because I've got more money than they have."

"It wouldn't surprise me."

"I don't suppose much would," I say, as we walk out into the hall and towards the front door.

"Not any more, no," she says.

I unbolt and unlock the front door and open it for her.

"Are you?" she says.

"Am I what?"

"Surprised. At the way the evening turned out?"

"I'm neither surprised nor not surprised."

"Wasn't quite what you expected, though, was it?"

"I didn't expect anything. If showing out and holding back turns you on, well, everyone to their own."

"That's what I always say," she says. "Now I've gone you'll be able to run a few movies, all by yourself. Look out for me, won't you? You'll recognise me by the wig, if by nothing else. Good night."

THE SMOKE

I PHONED THE STEERING Wheel before I went round.

When I got there, there were only Charlie and Walter waiting for me.

I sat down opposite them, only this time I wasn't given a drink.

"Do you want to know what happened?" I said.

"You think we don't know?" Charlie said.

"I think you ought to know the details," I said.

"You fucking chancer, you—" Charlie began, but Walter halted him.

"Listen to him," Walter said. "I want to hear what he has to say."

"You what?"

"Just shut up," Walter said.

"First of all, it was through Johnny that I found out about what was going down; so you've only got yourselves to blame."

"Like what was going down?" Charlie said.

"Leave it out," Walter said. "Just listen to what he's got to say."

"So," I said, "like I said, it was through Johnny I found out."

"And you topped him, just for that," said Walter. "Just because one of your blokes—"

"I didn't top him."

"You what?"

"Mickey did."

"Same thing, isn't it?"

"You're not understanding me," I said. "I said Mickey topped him."

"Yeah?"

"I mean, off his own bat."

"Why should he want to do a thing like that?" said Charlie.

I shook my head in despair of them.

"Mickey finds out what Johnny'd been saying," I said. "Right? He didn't know I'd found out. So he didn't want me to hear, so he arranged to meet Johnny and he topped him. So I wouldn't."

"You're barmy," said Charlie.

"Listen," said Walter to his brother. Charlie listened.

"But I found out. I followed Mickey. By the time he'd got there he'd seen off Johnny."

"So who saw off Mickey?" said Charlie. "Johnny?"

"Who do you think?"

There was a silence.

"You?"

"You've got it in one."

"You knocked off Mickey?" Charlie said. "For—"

"Shut up," said Walter.

"You're saying you topped Mickey for topping Johnny, for what he did?" Walter said.

"I'm not saying I wouldn't have maybe topped Johnny myself, if I'd seen him first. But I thought I'd let you know, Johnny brought it on himself. Once Mickey got wind, that was it."

A silence.

"So," I said, "I came to tell you how things happened, before you started getting steamed up over something you started and finished yourselves."

Another silence. Then Walter said, "You're saying you topped Mickey. Because of what he found out?"

"Of course."

Walter took his cigarettes out and lit one up and then watched me.

"You couldn't stand it, could you?" he said. "Not even your best man."

"Could you?"

"You couldn't live with it, could you? Him knowing. So you topped him."

"Knowing?" I said.

"What was going down."

"Of course not. Seeing as how—"

"Hang about," said Charlie. "I'm not with this."

"I am," said Walter. "He's barmy. But that's beside the point."

"What is the point, Walter?" I said.

"The point is," said Walter, "as far as Johnny's concerned, that's still down to you, however you choose to write your memoirs."

"Too right," said Charlie. "Too fucking right."

I was quiet for a moment.

"All right," I said. "But you're madmen. To start all over."

"Not quite as fucking barmy as you are, Fowler," Walter said.

"So I'll be hearing from you?" I said.

"What do you think?"

"Let's get it done now, Walter," Charlie said.

"No," said Walter. "I want time to think. Let me count the ways."

"Apart from the fact you haven't the bottle, just the two of you," I said.

"We'll wait," said Walter. "There's plenty of time. There's plenty of things to remember."

THE SEA

I LOCK AND BOLT the door behind her and go back into the lounge and pour myself another drink.

It's possible. Think.

It would certainly explain a lot. Why I thought I'd seen her before, why I'd transferred my memory to the girl from Grimsby who'd looked so much like her, instead of pointing it towards the real source, a half-remembered face from a blue movie.

It's possible. But is it probable? Consider.

It certainly wouldn't be too coincidental; to the average man, who maybe sees about half a dozen during his whole life, sure. But the odds on coincidence, being in the business I'm in, are much shorter. I've seen thousands. So there, coincidence is probable.

But the coincidence of her being here, where I am. That is where coincidence begins to be improbable.

Removing the coincidental aspect here, the probability is that she knows who I am.

She knows that I am George Fowler. And she has been in a blue movie. Probability again: one of mine. I've seen more of my own than I have of the competition's. Thus the vague memory.

So she's been in one of my movies. And she knows I am George Fowler.

Of course, she wouldn't have known at the time. She

wouldn't have got within a hundred people of knowing who I was then, the way I had everything structured.

But now, the probability is that she does. The probability is that she knows I am George Fowler, and who George Fowler is.

How?

Not even James knew I was here. Not even the number. I never even phoned him from here.

How?

And why?

The probabilities of why are easier to evaluate.

She's been sent. Or she's working for herself.

If she'd been sent, whoever by, I would no longer be here, in one way or another. They wouldn't risk this kind of cat and mouse.

So she's working for herself. And to her, the cat-and-mouse game doesn't seem so much of a risk. She's even dropped a hint to point me in the direction of the Blues. That's why she came. And left at that point, to leave me to consider.

Consider what? Her reasons, her connection?

Her reasons.

In her position, a lot of very very good reasons, hundreds and thousands of them, all signed by the chief cashier of the Bank of England. Because she knows who I am, and she knows enough of what happened in the Smoke to appreciate the value of knowing where I am.

Which would put her in a position of risk from me. Which doesn't seem to worry her one little bit.

Because I don't know where she lives.

Because she'll now have the unlisted telephone number of this place.

And the next thing I will get is the phone call and the proposition and I will probably never see her again.

Certainly never see her again.

Only hear from her, if she's greedy.

No wonder she didn't mind signing with Eddie and his Barren Knights.

Eddie?

The How.

Eddie.

Think about that.

Probable. The probability here being that he's not as pig-thick as he appears.

The probability being that they were closer than they appeared to be.

Much closer.

Eddie had mentioned, hadn't he, that he believed she'd been down the coast last season, at Skegness.

Believed.

Met her.

Met her and got together with her. No secrets. She'd tell him about the Blues.

Then what happened in London happened. The press. After a while I reappeared here.

Eddie had known me from before. When I'd been up here, other times.

This time, when I'd reappeared, he'd clocked.

And they'd talked.

And the result, this.

Eddie?

The How?

Probable?

Probable.

Proof positive lay beneath me, on racks, in the basement.

Where I never went.

Where I'd never been, since Jean. Because the temptation was too great.

Because she was down there, waiting for me to give her life.

THE SMOKE

"DID THEY BELIEVE YOUR story?" Jean said. "About Mickey killing Johnny and you killing him?"

"I don't know."

"Will it make any difference? If they believe it?"

"It might. They know it was all their own fault in the first place. It might cool them off for a bit."

"And if it doesn't?"

"They won't do anything yet anyway. Because of Johnny, Parsons'll be looking in their direction as well. In time, they will, sure. But it was for now I wanted to calm them down, while Parsons is sniffing about. And later on, we'll have had a bit more time to review the position. Entrench, as they say."

"With Collins gone? And no Mickey?"

I poured myself a drink.

"We're well rid of them."

"We've got to replace them."

"Of course; that's why I wanted a little time before the Sheps figure out what stroke they're going to pull next. We've got to have a look at the available material."

I sat down and Jean came and sat next to me.

"Whatever we do," she said, "you'll have to be careful. They'll never let up because of Johnny. I know it."

"Yes," I said. "I know it, too."

We were silent for a while.

"Incidentally," I said.

"What?"

I slid my arm round her shoulders.

"How did it feel?"

"How did what feel?"

She slid towards me, very close.

"You know what I mean," I said.

She was quiet. Her hand began to stroke my thigh.

"You know," I said. "When you shot Mickey."

THE SEA

I WAIT TILL DAYLIGHT.

There's no way I'm going down there in the dark. So I think my way through to the Sunday dawn. Eddie. And the girl. With her, he could be the star he felt he ought to be. With her, and with my money. Some of which I'd already donated to him, to keep him on the road. Nice one, Eddie.

But watch the girl, Eddie. Stardom for you may not tie in with her astrological chart. Keep the ejector seat on safety, Eddie. In this particular case, you can't use breach of contract, can you?

If I'm right.

The dawn comes, and with it the cold, and the sky slowly lightens.

I put another log on the fire and get out of my chair and pour myself another drink.

Irony, I think to myself. Everything is irony.

I mean, I was going to spring this place on Jean. Before everything had gone wrong. As a present, as a surprise.

That was why everything was down there on racks. Everything we'd ever made together, every video, every movie, plus prints of almost every Blue I'd ever had in circulation. For our entertainment, for her surprise. Cross-referenced and neatly stacked. It made the equivalent layout at The Yard look a little bit thin.

And of course there was stuff down there that was not strictly for pleasure. The stuff I'd had to grab and run with when I'd left London. Most of the administrative stuff, the records. Just leaving enough essential copies with James to continue with the aspects of the business he was capable of running. As well as the money. A lot of the money was down there, too. Enough to last me until I became of pensionable age, at least.

And that was the last time I'd been down there, to deposit the stuff. After that I'd shot the bolts and locked the padlock and put the key in my pocket and never taken it out again.

I feel in my pocket. The key feels as cold as the sky beyond the plate glass.

THE SMOKE

"FIRST OF ALL YOU'D have to prove he worked for me," I said to Parsons. "If you like you can look at the files. I don't think you'll find a P45, do you?"

Parsons didn't say anything.

"Second," I said, "if you could prove he worked for me, you'd have to come up with a reason for me having him topped."

"I think the Shepherdsons could furnish a motive, don't you? The collaboration, or whatever it was."

"Oh, sure. They're dying to get on to the centre court, aren't they? Perhaps they'll tell you what happened to Ray Warren's Glenda while they're at it."

"And maybe even Ray Warren."

"No," I said. "They'd only be guessing there."

Parsons looked at the inside of his hat.

"Anyway," he said, "I'm not too bothered at the moment. I've got plenty of time. I'll have you, no danger."

"Glad to hear it."

"No," he said. "I'm more interested in what's going on at the office at present. Collins's retirement has created a vacuum."

"How can a vacuum create a vacuum?" I said.

"Well put," he said.

"Are they taking bets yet?" I said.

"On what?"

"On who's going to be promoted. On to my firm."

"Well," he said, "that's very interesting, because at the moment the field seems a little bit thin. In fact, it seems as though there's really only a couple of front runners in it."

"Being?"

"Now, that's not fair, is it?" he said. "Why should I tell you that, give you that kind of advantage? Why shouldn't you find out the hard way?"

"It makes no difference," I said. "I'll find out."

"I know," he said. "So I may as well tell you. It's between me and Farlow."

I looked at him.

"Now what do you think about that?" he said.

"I think it's as different as over the sticks is from the flat," I said.

"Quite," he said, "and from what I gather, it appears that Farlow's not entirely in favour. Oh, the rank's there, but I don't think they want another Collins in there, not at the moment."

"Why should Farlow want it, anyway? He's well set up where he is."

"One would have thought so," Parsons said. "Although perhaps he thinks he won't be so very well set up if the Sheps happen to go down."

"And why should they happen to do that?" I said.

"I can't imagine," he said. "Can you?"

THE SEA

I STAND ON THE trapdoor.

The trick will be not to be drawn to the section where Jean is. Not to be like when I'd been standing on a pier, pulled towards the current beneath.

I unlock the padlock and slide back the bolts and lift the trapdoor.

I go back to the panel by the door and flick a switch and light shines up through the gaping square in the floor.

Then I go back to the trapdoor and walk down the steps and go past the section where Jean is without looking at it.

The section, in the cross-referenced scheme of things, wherein the evidence of the hint Lesley planted lies, contains around a hundred boxed movies, eight-millimetre stuff. The sixteen millimetre has a section to itself. So, in the eight-millimetre section, the lesbian stretch, there are a hundred movies. Twenty minutes each. Two thousand minutes altogether. But that can be halved, because half the boxes are illustrated on the outside by frame blow-ups from the prints inside, accompanied by a title. So if she's on the inside of one of the illustrated boxes, she'll be identified by the still on the outside. It won't take me long to eliminate the illustrated boxes. Which will still leave me around a thousand minutes to run through the eight-millimetre projector. Assuming she's not in any of the quality stuff. Around fifteen hours of celluloid. Two or three days' viewing, depending how much I can take.

But what else can I do, and what else have I got to occupy my time?

So, in the coldness of the basement, I eliminate the illustrated boxes, because she's not in one of them. Those that remain, I put in a big cardboard box, and carry the box to the top of the steps, and put it on the garage floor, and close the trapdoor behind me, without looking back.

It's a relief to slide back the bolts and re-lock the padlock, so much so that I kneel on the dusty floor for a few moments, letting the sweat fall like raindrops on the dryness of the concrete floor.

As I stand up, I look at my watch. It is a quarter to seven.

THE SMOKE

"THAT WOULD BE ALL we need," said Jean, "Parsons sitting behind Colins's desk. Christ, from there, he could practically wave to us from the window."

"I know," I said. "Anyway, he'll never get it."

"Why not?"

"Because he'd turn over too much stuff that wouldn't be good for the office, that's why. You know that."

"And what about Farlow?"

"He won't either. For the opposite reason."

"Makes it difficult for us to set up anybody at the moment, though. Till it's settled."

"Yes," I said. "It does."

"Anyway," Jean said. "All we can do is wait and see."

"Which I don't very much like doing," I said.

"Oh, I don't know," she said. "You waited for me, didn't you?"

"Bollocks."

She put on her sealskin coat.

"Where are you going?" I said.

"Hairdresser's," she said. "It's Tuesday."

"Oh. Yes."

"Gerry's bringing the motor round."

"Good."

"I won't be any later than two," she said.

The phone went. It was Gerry with the motor. Jean put the phone down and said, "See you later, then."

"Fine," I said. "See you later."

THE SEA

AT ELEVEN, I SHUT the projector off. Four hours of celluloid and no appearance.

And no phone call.

I pour myself a drink and walk over to the picture window and look out over the different perspectives of the dunes and the gorse.

Four hours of it. Four hours of it, without Jean. For whom it was meant. Together, the two of us; without her, it almost makes me sick.

And all I have to do is to go down there and choose from a particular group of movies or videos, and bring Jean back to life, in some cases, along with myself.

I wait another half-hour.

No phone call.

Why? I could have been gone a long time by now.

Maybe they don't give me enough credit. Maybe they don't think it'll get through to me this early. Perhaps they're waiting, luxuriating in their smartness.

Quarter to twelve.

All right. I'll play it their way, if they think I'm that thick. I go down into the garage and get into the Marina and drive into Mablethorpe.

By the time I get there it's opening time.

Sunday lunchtime seems to bring them out; the South is

almost a tenth full. But after my third drink, there's still no sign of Eddie.

Jackie says, "You missed a right old session last night."

"Really?"

"Yeah. Didn't get cleared up till half-past two, did I?"

"That must have been handy."

"Well. I took a few bob, didn't I? Didn't do any harm."

"I suppose not."

"The bird came in later on. Round the back."

"Lesley?"

"Lesley. About half an hour after you left."

"You're joking," I tell him.

"How do you mean?"

"Half an hour after I left? You must have been well pissed."

"I was. Anyway, whatever time it was, she came in and was it worth it! What a bird."

"Eddie here, was he? When she came."

"Of course. Oh, I see what you mean. It's not like that. It's more a business arrangement. I mean, can you imagine, her and Eddie?"

I make no comment. Instead, I say, "Where is the superstar this morning?"

"I should think he's sitting trying to outstare a fried egg. Was he bottled last night! Mind you, we all were, like I say."

"Did Eddie and the bird leave together?"

"Hang about. Yes. Yes, they left at the same time. But not together, know what I mean? I mean, Eddie made a big deal about going at the same time as her, but, you know."

"They playing anywhere tonight?"

"No. He was saying tonight was a dead night. It'll be a dead day today as well, as far as he's concerned. Christ, was he bottled."

"So you say," I say, and order two more drinks.

THE SMOKE

AT FIVE O'CLOCK, I phoned the hairdresser's. Yes, Mrs. Fowler had been, naturally. She'd left at one-thirty.

I broke the connection and rang downstairs.

"Did the car come back yet?" I said.

"No, not yet, Mr. Fowler."

I put the receiver down and looked at it. There was nobody else other than James for me to phone.

"She couldn't have gone anywhere else?" he said.

"Sure," I said. "There's a thousand places she could have gone. She could have gone to the pictures, anywhere. The point is, she didn't say she was going anywhere else."

"What about the driver?"

"If he'd been in on it she wouldn't have made the hairdresser's, would she?"

"Probably not."

There was a silence.

"Do you really think it's down to them?" James said.

"In an hour's time I will do," I said.

"And then what?"

"I'll go looking for her, won't I?"

"You think if they've got her you're going to be able to find her?"

"What else can I do?"

"I think I'd better come round," James said.

He was round inside of half an hour. In that time there'd been no news of Jean.

"They won't dare touch her," he said, taking the brandy glass from me.

"Won't they?"

"They'd have to be insane, at the moment."

"Then why take her? If they don't intend doing anything to her?"

"We can't be certain they have, yet," said James.

"No," I said. "Yet."

The phone rang at six o'clock.

"Sweating, Fowler?" the voice said.

I didn't say anything. There was soft laughter at the other end of the phone.

"Want to talk to her?" said the voice. "To make sure she can still talk back."

"Yes."

There was a short silence and then Jean came on the line.

"George," she said, "I'm all right."

"Where are you?"

The other voice came back on the line.

"You move out of your place and she's dead. Even to get the night paper. We'll phone you back at nine. They tell me Scrabble's good for passing the time."

Then the line went dead.

THE SEA

EDDIE DOESN'T APPEAR ALL lunchtime. Nor the girl. But then I hadn't expected her to appear.

When the South closes, I drive out of Mablethorpe and past the bungalow and on to the track that leads to the beach.

The beach is totally empty.

I walk to my tank and sit on the top and take out my flask and review the flatness.

My different lines of footprints stretch away into infinity which, in that case, is the mouth of the track.

Then it occurs to me.

There'd been no footprints for her at the mouth of the track. No footsteps stretching away towards Mablethorpe, in the opposite direction to mine.

If she'd walked home along the beach, there would have been footprints. Mine are still there, from the day before and from the day before that.

She'd walked home by the beach, all right.

I smile to myself. I expect the bastard thinks it's very funny, picking her up in the van which is only on the road through my money.

It would only have taken him ten minutes. Nipped out the back of the South, over here, back with her, so it looks as though he's been chucking up in the bog and she's just walked in.

Nice one, Eddie.

But what is even nicer is that as yet you don't know I've connected you up. When you see me next you'll still think I haven't clocked it, won't you? And that'll be good fun. Whether I get her phone call before or after I see you next, you'll still be playing the game, won't you, Eddie?

Well, so will I.

THE SMOKE

"WELL, IT SEEMS QUITE apparent to me," James said.

"Does it?"

"They're going to extract their pound of flesh financially," he said. "Quite bright of them, really. For them."

"You think that's what they're going to do, do you?"

"What else? I hate to put it this way, but if they were going to do anything to Jean, they'd have done it, and the only phone call you'd have got would have been to tell you where to find the body."

I poured myself another drink.

"Supposing they intend marking her?"

"I don't think so," he said.

"Why don't you think so?"

"Partly for the same reason I don't think they intend killing her; they wouldn't bother to phone."

"To make me sweat, that's why they phoned."

"If that was the real reason, it would have been far more effective not to have phoned at all, wouldn't it?"

I drank my drink.

"I don't know," I said.

I poured myself another drink and sat down.

"Of course," I said, "they could be using her to get to me. To make an exchange."

"It's possible," James said.

"I hope so," I said. "For her sake."

"How much could you raise?" James said. "If my supposition is correct."

"As much as necessary."

"Good," James said. "Good."

The phone rang at nine o'clock.

"If you want her back, unmarked," the voice said, "it'll cost you three hundred thousand."

"Is she all right?"

"What do you think?"

"Put her on."

"Can't at the moment," the voice said. "Not convenient."

"Listen—"

"No. You listen. You want to see her again, alive, unmarked, that's the deal."

I didn't say anything.

"I take it you want her back?"

"Get on with it."

"I'll tell you the arrangements, then. You want me to do that?"

He told me the arrangements. I agreed to them and put the phone down.

"Just as I said," James said. "They're being very sensible."

"They've never been sensible in their lives," I said. "Why should they start now?"

James took a sip of his brandy.

"No," I said, "it's me they want."

"If that's the case," James said, after a short silence, "what happens next?"

"I follow the arrangements. If they're stuck to, Jean'll be safe and out of it before they can get a crack at me. In the event that they're successful, Jean knows what to do, as far as the business side's concerned."

James was quiet.

"I wonder if we ought not to consider this," he said.

"What's to consider?" I said. "If I don't go, Jean's dead."

There was nothing even James could say to that.

THE SEA

I PUT ANOTHER FILM in the projector. Outside the window, dusk begins to collect at the top of the sky.

I watch the flickering images on the screen.

There's been no phone call.

They can't think I'm that stupid.

She dropped the hint though. So sure of my stupidity, so sure of herself, she'd risked that. But this. Giving me time.

I'm not wrong. It all fits. It's all nice and neat. What are they trying to do, throw me somehow? And by doing that, throw their own plans out the window?

I switch off the machine and decide to go and talk to Eddie. I know I've got plenty of time, but I can't stand killing it like this, being pissed on by a couple of amateurs.

I get in the car and drive into Mablethorpe.

When I get there it's not quite opening time, so I park the car at the bottom of the ramp and walk up and onto the mini-marina and sit on one of the benches at the base of the mound and look out across the half blue to the horizon.

About ten minutes later the lights go on in the Dunes. I turn my head and look at the flat rectangle the huge window makes on the sand.

Then I get up and walk along the mini-promenade and into the Dunes.

Howard is behind the bar, bottling up.

"Didn't know you were opening up tonight," I say to him.

"I'm not," Howard says, straightening up. "I couldn't be bothered to come in this morning."

"What did you come in for anyway?"

"There's some wrestling on tomorrow night. May as well get stocked up now. Anyway it's something to do, isn't it? Better than *Stars on Sunday*."

He wipes two glasses and operates the optics.

"Go to the South last night?" I said. "After you'd cleared up here?"

"Yeah, for half an hour."

"I hear Eddie was well pissed."

"Doesn't take much with him. He thinks he's a boozer. Always throwing up."

I sip my drink.

"Seen him today?"

"No thanks. Not yet."

I drain my glass.

"Not stopping?" Howard says.

"Got to see a man about a dog."

As I walk towards the end of the mini-promenade, a figure turns the corner from the ramp and begins to walk towards me, not quite so jaunty, but unmistakably Eddie.

"Eddie," I say, as he gets close to me.

Eddie jumps slightly.

"Oh, hello, Mr. Carson," he says. "I didn't see you."

"Where're you off to?"

"I wanted to see if Howard was around. He keeps some stuff for hangovers."

"Heavy night, I hear."

"Not half."

"Celebrating, were you?"

"I suppose I was, really. Well, because of the van, and Lesley."

"Yes. Eddie, you got a minute? For a little chat?"

"A little chat?"

I indicate one of the bench seats.

"Yeah, sure," he says.

We sit down.

"Look," he says, "if it's about the money, I'll be—"

"No, it's not about the money, Eddie. Not about that money."

"I beg your pardon?"

"I said, not about that money."

"What money, then?" he says.

"The money you and Lesley think you're going to screw out of me."

Eddie lets it filter through for a moment or two.

"I'm sorry," he says, "I don't get it."

"That's true enough," I say, "you don't. But you understand what I mean. Don't you, Eddie?"

Eddie shakes his head, squeezes the bridge of his nose. "I'm not with you," he says. "You think Lesley and I are out to screw you out of some money?"

"Now you're with me, Eddie."

There's a short silence.

"Look," he says, "you're loaded. It's obvious. And when you lent me the money, well, I figured it was because you fancied Lesley, and I must admit, I hoped, when we got going, you might invest a little bit in us, I can't deny you. But I wasn't trying to screw you, honest. Neither of us was. I mean, it wasn't that way at all. You got it all wrong."

"You've blown it, Eddie," I say to him. "You may as well tell me all about it."

"All about what?"

I take the gun out of my pocket and lay the barrel against his cheek. Eddie tries to look at the gun without moving his head, his left eye almost popping out on to his cheek.

"Everything," I say.

Eddie's mouth works for a while before any sound comes out. When it does, he says, "What's going on?"

"That's my question."

"I don't know what you mean. Honest."

"Where does she live?"

"I told you. I don't know where she lives."

I take the gun from his face and shove the barrel into his ribs and give him time to get his breath back.

"Where?" I ask him again.

He shakes his head.

"I don't know. Honest."

"Listen, Eddie," I say to him. "You know who I am. You know what I could do. Don't you think you ought to tell me?"

"I don't know what you mean. 'Course I know who you are."

"Who am I, Eddie?"

"What you talking about? You're Mr. Carson, aren't you?"

He looks down at the gun that's still sticking into him.

"Honest, I'd tell you where she lived if I knew, I would, honest."

I get up and point the barrel at his forehead, laying the metal lightly against his skin.

"What are you doing?" he says.

"Waiting for you to tell me what I want to know."

He shakes his head and the gun vibrates slightly in my hand.

"I can't," he says, "I can't if I don't know."

I press the gun a little harder.

"Don't," he says. "I don't know what this is about. But don't, please."

I hold the gun there a moment longer, then let it drop to my side.

"All right, Eddie," I say. "I believe you."

Eddie stays the way he was, like a municipal statue.

"I apologise," I tell him. "I made a mistake."

He still doesn't move, not one muscle.

I slip the gun in my pocket.

With that, Eddie's off the seat, up the slope of the mound like a greyhound out of trap one.

I rush after him and it's not until he's almost at the top of the mound that I catch hold of him by his ankles, but even on his hands and knees he's still trying to make it to the top. I heave myself on top of him and flatten him beneath my weight and when he's given up I roll him over on to his back, keeping a grip on him by his collar.

"All right," I tell him. "I've told you. I made a mistake. You've nothing to worry about. All right?"

Eddie just stares at me.

I feel in my jacket pocket and withdraw my wallet. Eddie watches my every move, and even when he clocks that the wallet isn't the gun he still stares at it as though it is.

I let go of him and, still leaning on his chest, I sort two hundred quid out of the wallet and put the wallet back in my pocket.

"Look," I tell him, showing him the money, "this is for you. You can have some more, next week. On one condition. You don't talk to anyone about this. Anyone. Particularly the girl. Particularly her."

He looks at the money, then at me, then back at the money.

"Because I'll know," I said. "If you tell anybody. You can be certain of that."

He doesn't say anything. I waft the money in front of his nose.

"You want this, Eddie?"

He nods, very slightly.

"You want some more, next week."

He nods again.

I get up, and he gets up. I hand him the money. He takes it, and begins to back up to the top of the mound. I walk slowly up after him.

"There's nothing to worry about," I said. "I just made a mistake, all right?"

He nods, still backing away.

"I'll see you in the week, about the other," I tell him.

By now we've changed places in the sense that Eddie has reached the summit of the mound and is descending the side that faces the town, still backwards. I, on the other, now stand on the summit.

"Yeah," Eddie says. "I'll see you in the week."

Then he turns and begins to scamper down the mound, not too quickly at first, but gaining momentum the farther down he goes.

"Hope your hangover clears up," I call after him, but I doubt very much if he'll be able to hear me, the way the wind'll be roaring in his ears.

THE SMOKE

I TRUNDLED THE MOTOR along the track that led to the brickworks and parked next to the nearest of the disused kilns.

I put the shotgun across my knees and waited. The holdall was on the seat next to me.

The first car to appear was a Granada. It stopped about thirty yards away, on the other side of the open area, headlights floodlighting the middle of my motor.

The second car was the Mercedes. It parked up by the Granada, but not pointing at me, at a right-angle to the Granada, parallel to mine.

One of the Granada windows rolled down and a loud-hailer was stuck out into the night. I rolled down my own window.

"Bring out the money, Fowler," the voice cracked.

I shouted back, "Fuck off. First I see Jean."

There was a short silence. Then one of the Mercedes doors opened and the figure of Jean emerged into the darkness, sealskin coat, new hair-do. The door closed and the figure stayed where it was. The loud-hailer came back.

"All right, Fowler?"

"All right."

"Now fetch the money."

"You think I'm stupid. Send somebody."

"There's a shooter on her, Fowler. You want to see that?"

"You do that, and there's no money. If it's the money you want."

Silence.

"All right. Throw the bag out of the window."

I heave the bag out.

"The minute your man picks it up, Jean starts walking," I shouted.

Silence.

"Right," from the loud-hailer.

Nothing happened for a moment. Then one of the rear doors of the Granada opened and someone got out of it and began to walk towards me.

From the outline, as the figure approached my motor, back-lit by the Granada's headlights, I judged it to be Rich Shepherdson.

Maybe James had been right; they could have sent anybody out, if it was me and not the money they wanted.

Rich got as far as the holdall.

"Stop," I said.

Rich stopped.

"He's covered," I shouted. "Jean starts. Then he can pick up the bag."

Nothing happened for a few seconds. Then Jean began to walk forward.

"All right," I said to Rich. "Pick it up."

He picked up the bag and turned his back on me. It would have been so easy.

He began to walk away. Jean came closer. The minute they passed, Rich began to run, and the Granada's engine gunned up, started to reverse. I daren't shoot at Rich's flying figure, because in their headlights Jean was a perfect target for them. Rich dived into the Granada.

"Run," I shouted to her.

She stopped walking, looked back at the reversing Granada, as though she was confused.

"Run!" I shouted again.

She did. But in the opposite direction. Back towards the reversing Granada.

The Granada stopped reversing, shot forward, between me and the Mercedes. Jean was stark in its headlights.

"Jean!" I screamed at her, scrambling out of my motor.

The Granada swung across her path, broadside on. Another window rolled down.

The blast hurled her backwards and upwards, like a punch-bag when Frazier's hit it.

I screamed and fired. All the Granada's side windows shattered. Somebody else screamed, inside the Granada.

Then I became calm. Because I was now out of the headlights, I was no longer a good target. So while the driver was trying to sort out the gears I took out both the nearside tires. Doors began to open. I pumped shells into the chambers and fired at the figures emerging on my side of the Granada. They were no problem, those on this side of the Granada; it was those who'd got out on the opposite side, those that were making for the Mercedes.

I ran forward. The figures wrenched at the doors. I lay across the bonnet and fired and took out the one trying to get in on the passenger side. He was still hanging on to the handle when the other one set the Mercedes off and began to scream it off into the darkness. I blasted out the rear window, but that was all I could do.

The Mercedes disappeared into the night, leaving everything very quiet and very still.

I ran back to where Jean was and knelt down beside her and lifted her up in my arms and looked into her face and the wig slid off.

It wasn't Jean.

THE SEA

I CARRY THE CARDBOARD box back down into the basement and put back the ones I've already run through and re-fit the box with those I haven't.

When I've done that, I light a cigarette and stare at the racks.

The section devoted to Jean is at the far end, near the foot of the basement steps.

Three shelves full.

Some of the boxes even have her picture on the outside.

I continue smoking the cigarette, and looking at the shelves.

When I've finished the cigarette, I tread on it, pick up the refilled box and walk towards the foot of the stairs.

When I get to the bottom step, I put the box down on the fourth or fifth step and straighten up and look at the shelves containing Jean.

Neat rows of boxes and cans.

Videos. Eight-mill boxes. Sixteen-mill cans. With sound.

I extend an arm.

At random, I take one of the eight-mill boxes off a shelf. It doesn't have a picture of Jean on it. I put it in the cardboard box, on top of the others.

Then I pick up the box and walk up the steps and put the box down on the garage floor and close the trapdoor behind me.

When I'm back in the lounge, I pour myself a drink and look at the films as they lie in the box. They all sit neatly in there, except for the box with Jean in it. It makes an angled diamond on top of the straight lines of the other boxes.

It has to be done, some time.

But will I be able to bear it, after what happened to her?

To look at her again, the way she used to be.

Part of me is screaming for me to pick up the box. The rest of me is screaming, just as hard, not.

I reach forward, to pick up Jean's box.

There is a tapping on the window.

I look up.

Lesley is standing there, twinned by the double glazing, illuminated by the room's soft lighting.

There's nothing I can do. All the movie equipment's out. The cardboard box containing the films is in the middle of the floor.

And she's smiling at the scene, her icy smile.

The interesting thing is, she's come back.

I hadn't expected her to come back. I'd expected her to phone.

She's either very stupid or very cocky.

I go down the steps and operate the window. It slides open, she walks in, the window slides back. Cold night air hesitates at the edge of the room's warmth behind her.

"An evening at home," she says, surveying everything.

I walk back up the stairs.

"You really don't believe in doorbells, do you?" I say to her.

"I'm just not very lucky with them," she says. "I did try, but like the other time, it didn't seem to be functioning."

"Odd, that," I say.

"Isn't it?"

We look at each other.

"A drink?" I say.

She nods. I make her a drink and hand it to her.

"You're not in all your splendour," I say.

She shrugs her Afghan off and shakes out her long black hair, but the dark glasses stay on.

"I'm not working tonight," she says.

"Aren't you?" I ask her.

"I'm not with you?"

I smile and sit down.

"Funny," I say. "That's what Eddie said."

She sits down opposite me, indicates the movies.

"It's true what they say, then?" she says.

"What?"

"That too many off the wrist sends you barmy."

"I don't think it's me that's barmy."

She shrugs. I watch her as she sips her drink.

"Aren't you going to put one on then?" she says.

I don't say anything.

"A movie, I mean," she says. "I mean, don't let me spoil your evening for you."

I drink some of my drink.

"I didn't find you yet."

She looks blank, then looks at the gear. She laughs.

"You didn't think you would, did you?"

I stay quiet.

"Jesus," she says. "You believed me. You really believed me."

She continues laughing.

"What made you think I'd let you out alive?" I said.

She stops laughing.

"You what?"

"If you came back, what made you think I'd let you walk out again?"

She just looks at me.

"How much were you thinking of?" I say. "Just as a matter of interest."

She still doesn't answer.

"Money," I say. "How much money?"

Her expression changes to amused contempt.

"What," she says, "you mean to sleep with you?"

"Don't be fucking stupid."

"Well, I mean, I know you're a watcher, but I thought you might fancy a change. Silly of me."

"You're being very silly."

"Look," she says, "I know I'm thick, I must be to be in this dead-and-alive hole, but just what the fuck are you talking about?"

I stand up and refill my glass and when I've done that I turn to face her again.

"You know who I am. Somehow, some way. Whichever is unimportant, but you'll tell me, anyhow. You've known for quite some time. And as nothing's happened to me since you've known, I'm still walking about, my picture hasn't been all over the papers, I figure you'd like some money not to tell various people who I am."

She just looks at me, expressionless. Then she leans back in her seat.

"And you are?"

"I've told you," I said. "Stop being silly."

She inclines her head and takes her dark glasses off. Something familiar again. Her expression is now one of exaggerated incredulity, an expression that under different circumstances could appear to be registering pain.

Pain.

I look at her.

Pain.

The last time I saw a girl register pain.

The last time before Jean.

Remember the last time.

Remember.

THE SMOKE

IT HAD BEEN LUCKIER for her than it had looked. They'd only got her in the upper legs. Although she'd never dance with Nureyev, if that was her ambition.

"Who are you?" I said, holding her torso upright.

She tried to move her legs and screamed.

"Don't do that," I said. "It'll only hurt you. I'll call for an ambulance. Just tell me what happened."

She stared up into my face, like a rabbit in a snare.

"Tell me," I said. "Then I'll get you help."

"It hurts," she said. "Christ it hurts."

"I know," I said. "I'll help you. If you tell me what happened. All right?"

She bit back some pain and tried to speak. I waited until she tried again.

"They wanted me to give you something," she said. "They wanted me to dress up like this. In these clothes."

I undid the coat. The dress was Jean's, as well. I looked down her legs. And the boots.

"What did they want you to give me?"

"An envelope."

"Where is it?"

"I— Christ! I dropped it. It's over there."

"What's in it?"

"I don't know."

"You're lying."

"I'm not. Help me. Please."

"What did they tell you to do?"

"What I did. Walk to you. Give you the envelope. I was to—I was to tell you, 'This is from Jean.' And then when they started the car I was frightened. They hadn't said they were going to do that. They were going to wait."

"Where's Jean?"

"I don't know any Jean."

"You're wearing her clothes."

"Christ. They gave them to me. I don't know any Jean."

I laid her flat on her back and went over to where the envelope was and picked it up.

"Help me," the girl said.

The envelope was manuscript-size and sealed. I ripped open one end.

A spool of eight-millimetre film clattered down onto the ground.

I bent down and picked up the spool and looked at it.

Then I straightened up, put the spool in my pocket and walked past the girl and over to the Granada.

"Help me," the girl said.

Charlie and Rich lay beneath the Granada's open doors. I looked beyond the bonnet, to where the Mercedes had been. Jimmy had been the one who'd been trying to get into that. I walked over just to make sure he was dead, like the others.

When I'd done that I went back to the Granada and took Rich's handgun from its holster, and walked back to where the girl was, carrying the gun.

"Help me," she said.

THE SEA

I LOOK DOWN AT her, as she reclines there, the dark glasses dangling from the tips of her fingers.

Could be.

A reasonable motive.

Not necessarily involving money.

I'd not killed the girl in London, at the brickyard. I'd shot her, but she hadn't died.

Normally I would have shot her through the roof of her mouth. But I'd wanted her to look like one of the casualties, as random as possible. Using Rich's gun.

So instead of getting up close I'd stood back, and to one side, and shot her in the head, once, with Rich's .38 revolver.

Unreliable at the best of times. And in the dark.

But I'd had to do it. I couldn't send for the ambulance so that they could get her all well to give them a description.

After I'd shot her, I hadn't stayed to check.

She'd stopped whimpering.

I should have done. I should have stayed to check.

But all I was thinking about was Jean.

And getting to Walter, so that I could get to her.

But I hadn't got to Jean, and the girl had lived.

But she hadn't talked. They'd sat round her bed for weeks, but there'd been nothing they could do. She'd just told them she'd been hired to deliver a parcel and pick up a holdall.

Couldn't do her for that, could they? And she'd been injured. She hadn't seen a thing after she'd been injured.

No, she didn't know any of the people involved. No, she'd never seen them before.

They'd got her into court, sure, but they couldn't make her change her tune.

Not, for some odd reason, that they'd pressed her too hard.

At the time, as James hadn't been able to get to her, her being on the other team, I'd assumed Walter had seen her well set up; that was why she'd kept quiet.

But now she'd run across me, and Walter had gone.

There was more to life than money when it came to getting even. I know that more than anybody does.

She puts her dark glasses back on. The scar wouldn't show, not the way she did her hair, it'd be deep beneath the shiny black tresses. And on occasion, beneath a wig.

Perhaps, unseen, her optic nerves had been affected.

But the other wounds would show.

The ones on the legs.

"You're mad," she says. "I've never seen you in my life before."

"Stand up," I say to her.

"You what?"

"Stand up."

She stands up. I swallow some of my drink.

"Take your jeans off."

Faint amusement from behind the dark glasses.

"Oh, so that's what you want to pay me the money for. Just to look."

"Do it."

"When I was a kid I used to do it for sixpence," she says. "What's the going rate these days?"

I take the gun out. The amusement doesn't quite disappear.

"Do it."

"You know what they say about men who like guns," she says.

"Are you going to do it?"

"Sure," she says. "Why not?"

She undoes the broad buckle of her belt and unbuttons the metal button at the top of her fly and unzips herself and slides the jeans down her thighs.

I look at her thighs. Her knees.

"Turn round."

She turns round, full circle.

Not a mark. Not the trace of the smallest of scars. Not even a bramble-scratch.

I stand there, just staring at the sheerness of her.

"That it, then?" she says. "Only, it's getting a bit chilly."

Convulsions begin to surge up my body from the base of my stomach.

I turn away and run for the bathroom, knocking into the cardboard box as I go, tipping films out all over the floor.

THE SMOKE

I GOT INTO the car and slammed the door and sat there.

Where would he go?

I had to think. He was the only way I could get to Jean. However slim the chance that she was . . . however slim the chance.

But where would he go? He hadn't banked on all this going down. So there would have been no contingency plans, not with him. And now, he'd know there'd be nowhere public he could go. He'd have to go to ground. Eventually somebody would grass, but the grasses didn't even know what had gone down yet. And I didn't have time to wait for them.

I switched on the engine and negotiated the girl and the Granada and Jimmy's body and lurched the motor on to the track that led out of the brickyard.

What I hadn't banked on, with his three brothers lying dead back there, was their unavenged bodies being more important to Walter than the holdall containing the three hundred grand.

I only survived the first blast because the tire bounced off a rut in the track and I was lower than he'd expected me to be when he'd squeezed the trigger. But it was still good enough to take the windscreen out completely.

I threw myself across the passenger seat and lay there and managed to get my hands on my own shotgun.

But I didn't want to kill him. Not while there was a chance.

"Fowler?"

The voice came from a long low tile shed that ran alongside the track, a shed with empty tile shelves instead of walls.

"If you move you're dead. If you don't move you're dead. Have it whichever way you like."

He laughed, and fired another broadside into my motor. The car rocked.

Another blast. At the same time I slipped the lock on the passenger door and rolled out of the car on the opposite side to where Walter was under cover. Then I crawled to the rear of the motor and tried to peer beyond the darkness, into the deeper darkness of the shed.

Another blast and I ran across the track, quietly. I stopped at the shed's open end. The shelving wall stretched away from me, into blackness. But I knew where he was from the shot gun blasts. I moved forward, soundlessly.

"Fowler?" he shouted.

I moved closer.

"Fowler. You're a dead man. Like—"

I trod on an old tile. It snapped in two as if I'd hit it with a hammer.

I threw myself to the ground as Walter whirled round and blasted in my direction. I was completely without cover. The blast had lit up where I'd thrown myself. He knew where I was. I heard him pump two more up into the breech.

There was nothing else I could do.

I fired a second before he did. His shots finished up in the ceiling. Mine finished up in his chest and his neck.

When I got to him blood was pouring from a hole in his throat, like wine from a punctured goat-skin.

I looked down at him.

"Where is she?" I screamed at him.

But there was nothing, just the sound of the wind drifting through the empty tile racks.

I found the Mercedes parked up behind the tile shed. The

holdall with the money in it was lying on the passenger seat. And even though there was no longer any glass in the rear window, perfume still lingered in the Mercedes's interior.

But it wasn't Jean's perfume.

THE SEA

WHEN I GO BACK into the lounge from the bathroom, she's kneeling by the box, putting the films back.

"Does it really make you feel that bad?" she says.

I don't say anything.

"You really are a mess, aren't you? I mean, how do you manage to stand looking at the movies if what happened just now made you feel physically sick?" she says. "Still, maybe when it's on the screen, celluloid, not reality . . ."

I look at her legs. She is wearing her jeans again. She clocks me looking at her.

"I figured I could put them back on," she says. "No point in not, so to speak."

"Who are you?" I ask.

"I'm Lesley," she says. "Remember? I'm the one who's supposed to know who you are."

I pick up my glass and take it over to the drinks and almost fill it to the top and drink and then fill it up again.

I turn to face her.

"What do you want?" I ask her.

"I just came round to help you pass the time," she says. "To be pleasant I even took my jeans off for you. Now what could be nicer than that? And all you keep asking is, what do I want, who am I, and if I know who you are and pointing guns at me.

I mean, I came round for a drink. It's Sunday night. What else am I going to do on a Sunday night in Mablethorpe?"

I stare at her.

"I mean, I'll go if you want."

"No," I tell her. "No, don't do that."

"Looking at me like that, I'm not so sure I oughtn't. Can't you put that fucking gun down?"

I've forgotten I'm still carrying it. I put it down on the piano lid, where Jean's photograph used to stand.

"Why do you keep it?" she says. "Frightened of intruders?"

"You weren't frightened of it."

Faint amusement.

"Does that make me a guest then? And not an intruder?"

I nod.

"Yes. Yes, it does," I say. "It does make you a guest."

"In that case, am I entitled to another drink?"

I nod.

She stands up and picks up her glass and goes over to the drinks.

I shake my head, and my whole body seems to shake, too, like an enormous shiver.

I must have been mad; I'd made it all up. I'd had all the pieces as I've seen them and I'd had the time to make them fit, as I've seen fit, to conform to my preconceived pattern, the pattern caused by my present state of mind. And as they say in the play, that way lies madness.

I nearly blew it, because of a pattern I'd woven myself.

Jesus.

Nearly blew it with her, and with Eddie.

She's just what she appears to be.

A talented girl who knows a good thing when she sees it. That's why she hasn't let my antics send her off. She knows the kind of score I can add up to. She's not going to be frightened out of that kind of count.

As far as Eddie's concerned, I can square him properly tomorrow. Give him more than he expects, explain again.

As for Lesley, for the moment, I can smooth her by just behaving normally. For the moment.

"I'm sorry," I tell her. "For behaving like that."

She shrugs.

"Nobody can help the way they are," she says. "Although I could have done without the gun, even though you were only pissing about."

"Yes. Look—"

"I mean," she says, "that was a figure of speech, wasn't it? About me leaving here alive?"

"Of course. I mean—"

She stands in front of me and puts a hand on my shoulder. Faint amusement.

"I'm joking," she says. "You've got to understand. I'm joking."

I manage to smile.

"I bet you even believed me when I told you I was frigid," she says.

"Well, I—"

She sits down and looks up at me.

"Although, the way you are at the moment, I don't suppose it makes any difference whether I've even got one, or not, does it?"

"I—"

"What happens? Is it different if you've watched a movie? Does that help? Or do you just watch the movies and that's that?"

"No. It's nothing like that. It's—"

"I'm interested. If I put a movie on, could you make it with me?"

"I could make it with you regardless."

She gives me a long look from behind the glasses.

"I don't believe you," she says.

"Honestly—"

"Look," she says, "you don't have to prove anything to me. I understand."

"It's not that. Since my wife—since my wife left, I haven't made love. Not with anyone else. I haven't been interested."

"Oh, it's the old mental impotence bit, is it? Erection rejection."

"It's not that. It's—"

"I've told you. I don't mind. Things like that I understand."

It's no use arguing with her so I pour myself another drink. She slips out of her seat and on to the floor and picks a few boxes out of the stack in the cardboard box, sifts through a few of them, reading the titles, looking at those with pictures on the boxes.

She looks up at me.

"Do you want to put one on and see what happens?" she says.

She's so keen to keep me sweet for whatever she wants she's even prepared to go along with what she thinks I want her to go along with.

Which is the greatest irony of all. Because, since Jean, I've never had the faintest desire for another woman. And here's Lesley, thinking that I'm suffering from impotence, offering to run one of the Blues I brought here for mine and Jean's entertainment. And after my previous behaviour, I suppose I ought to go along with her.

I can always plead impotence. And the way I feel at the moment, maybe it won't be merely a plea.

"Yes, all right," I say.

"Any particular one?" she says.

"It's up to you."

She looks through the boxes.

"I thought you might have a particular favourite," she says, looking up briefly, exhibiting her faint amusement again.

I do, I think. And, Christ, how I need her.

I watch her as she keeps sifting through.

I drain my glass and go back to the drinks.

All right, I think. Let's play Russian Roulette. If she comes up with it, I'll run it.

I need her.

How it would affect me, I don't know.

In any case, it would be a forty-to-one chance, if she came up with Jean.

I fill my glass and drink, fill it again, with my back to her.

"All right," she says. "Let's go blind. How about this one?"

THE SMOKE

JAMES LOOKED SURPRISED WHEN he let me into the Penthouse. I wasn't surprised he looked surprised.

He got me a drink and himself a drink and sat me down and sat down opposite me.

I told him what had happened.

"Jesus Christ," he said, when I'd finished. "Jesus Christ."

He got up and took our glasses over to the drinks. While he was pouring, he said, "What a mess. What a ber-loody mess."

He brought the drinks back and handed me mine and sat down opposite me again. He drank some of his and said, "Anway, at least they're all cleared out. There'll be no more trouble from that quarter."

I didn't say anything.

"Look," James said, "about Jean. It doesn't necessarily follow that—"

"It follows, James," I said. "It follows."

"Not necessarily. Look—"

I held up the spool of film.

"Why do you think they went to all this trouble?" I said. "Just what do you think is on here?"

"Well, it could be—"

"It could be. It could be anything. But it isn't. They wanted me to see this. They didn't expect the girl would panic. They shot her, to be sure I'd see it."

James concentrated on his brandy, frowning.

I stood up.

"Wait here, will you," I said. "I'm going to run this."

"I'll come with you."

He began to get up.

"No," I said, stopping him. "Wait for me in here."

I went through into the projection booth and loaded the spool on to the eight-mill projector and when I'd done that I went and sat in the theatre, in the chair with the control panel on the arm.

The lights dimmed, and up on the screen grainy black-and-white leader began to scratch its way across the screen.

THE SEA

I TURN ROUND TO face her.

Still kneeling on the floor, she's holding out one of the boxes in my direction.

It's the one with the film of Jean inside.

I don't move.

"What's wrong?" Lesley says. "You look as though you've seen a ghost." If she only knew.

I still don't move. I'd gambled. While I'd been getting my drinks I'd said to myself, if she comes up with Jean, I'd run it. I'd made a bet against myself. A forty-to-one shot. And now it had come up.

I'd promised myself.

I take the plain box from her and look at the title. It's one of the early ones. Jean and two other girls. The first one she ever did, just with other women.

"All right," I say. "Why not?"

I walk over to the projector and slip the spool out of the box and fit it on to the projector's arm.

How am I going to feel?

I thread the leader on to the sprockets and press the automatic and the film glides through and takes up on the pick-up spool. White light blurts out onto the screen.

I switch off the projector. Lesley looks round, mild surprise.

"The lights," I tell her, going over to the panel. "There's no definition with the lights on."

I switch off the lights. The room is illuminated only by the flames flickering in the fireplace.

"Cosy," she says.

I go back over to the projector. What she doesn't know is that I've turned the lights out to veil any reaction I might not want her to see.

I switch on the projector and the white light glares out again, briefly, then is diluted by the grey monochrome of the exposed film.

The moment that happens, I close my eyes. For a while, I can't look. I'm like a man with a ghost at the foot of his bed, hiding under the blankets.

You've got to, I tell myself. It had to happen. You have to look. You've got to face it, some time.

I force open my eyes.

I stare at the screen. I don't understand.

I squeeze my eyes tight shut, to help me understand.

I open them again.

It's not imagination.

I haven't gone mad.

It isn't one of the early films.

It's a print of the final film that was made of Jean.

But not made by me.

And I'd destroyed the only print I'd had of that, the final one.

THE SMOKE

THE FIRST IMAGE WAS a close-up of Jean.

She was looking straight into the camera, frightened.

Her mouth was taped shut.

The camera zoomed back, shakily, to reveal Jean in the centre of a grubby basement. There was a chair and a table. On the table there was some rubber tubing and an axe and some other things.

Jean was sitting on the chair, naked, except for her jewellery. Her hands were behind her back.

Three men stood around the chair, hooded, but I could tell who they were. Jimmy must have been the one operating the camera.

One of the men, Charlie, reached out and grabbed Jean by the hair and struck her. Then all three of them lifted her out of the chair and pushed her over to and on to the table.

And then they started.

I watched, because there was nothing else I could do.

For almost twenty minutes I watched.

Watched what they did to her.

Then, twenty minutes later, the camera angle changed. Changed to a close-up of her feet, looking down, as they protruded over the edge of the table.

Her feet were very still.

The camera panned up her legs, up her bruised and lacerated

torso, arrived at her neck, hesitated slightly, then completed its movement, to reveal that now her neck didn't end with her head, just a bleeding stump that gushed black blood on to the table top.

CUT.

To the chair, a long shot.

The Shepherdsons, naked except for their hoods, stood round the chair, looking at the camera. On the chair seat, at a slight angle, was Jean's head.

THE SEA

I SCREAM.

At the point where the Shepherdsons manhandle Jean on to the table, I scream.

And, screaming, I realise the only way the film could have got to me, into this house.

But at my screaming, she is on her feet, already darting away into the darkness, and my dive at her through the projector's monochrome channel is already futile. I hit the piano stool and draw myself to my feet via the keyboard, giving silent-movie accompaniment to the events up on the screen. My hand finds the gun on the piano top and as Lesley flies down the steps into the room's lower depths I fire three shots after her, but in the room's semi-darkness she still appears to be moving towards the door. The dark rectangle at the room's lower corner opens and I fire three more shots.

The rectangle slams to and I run down the steps and pull open the door just as at the other end of the hall the front door crashes closed behind her. I fire two more shots at her rippling shape beyond the frosted panels, shattering one of them completely, and then she is gone.

I stand there for a moment.

Then I scream again. While I'm standing there, up on the screen, in the lounge, they're doing those things to Jean.

I've got to stop them.

Still screaming, I rush back into the lounge and up the steps, firing at the screen as I go. One of the Shepherdsons is beating her with a hose while the other two hold her down.

I reach the screen and tear it from the ceiling but the images keep on screaming from the projector, flowing all over me, sticking to me, like old blood.

I aim at the white-heat centre of the projector's lens and fire.

Everything stops. Only the echoes of the gunshots remain.

I sink to my knees and crawl to where the telephone is and pick up the receiver and dial and listen to the ringing tone.

You've got to be there. You have to be.

I clutch the receiver against my face.

You've got to be there. Answer.

At the other end of the line the receiver is lifted.

"Hello," James says, "James Morville speaking."

"James," I say. "You've got to help me."

James's tone changes.

"What's wrong?"

"Listen," I say, "they've got to me. They've—"

"Who? Who's got to you? Who could?"

"I don't know. But she—"

"She?"

"Lesley. She got the film to me. Into the house."

"Lesley? What film?"

"I don't know what's happening. Now I've seen the film, they're probably coming for me. Outside. I need help. James, you have to send help. I need help quickly."

There is silence at the other end of the line.

"James?"

I hear James breathing in, then out, like a man who's just surfaced for air.

"James?"

Again, his tone has altered slightly.

"Yes, I'm here," he says.

"You've got to help me."

"I will. I'll get some people together. In fact I'll come myself, if you want."

"Anything. Just hurry."

"Yes," he says. "Now. What's the address?"

I tell him the address and give him precise instructions how to find it when he gets close.

"Good," he says. "Good. I've got all that. Now, how long do you think it'll take us?"

"Four hours. No more than four hours."

"I don't know how long it'll take to collect people," James says. "People we can trust."

"Just hurry."

"I will. You were saying, about outside . . . there may be someone waiting."

"I don't know. I don't know what's happening. Just get here. I can keep anybody away till then."

"I'm leaving right away. We'll be careful. And George?"

"What?"

"You be careful, too," James says, and hangs up.

I put the phone down.

I stand up and look at the shattered projector.

Then I go over to it and take off both spools and kneel down in front of the fire and unwind the celluloid and tear it into short strips and throw the strips into the flames, piece by piece.

After I've done that I reload my Browning and go down into the basement and wait.

THE SMOKE

AFTER A WHILE, I was conscious of a tapping noise. It stopped. Then it started again. Stopped.

Then the door to the theatre opened.

"George?" James said.

I vomited, just once.

I sat there, perfectly still, and one single jet of vomit streaked towards the screen, descended on the seats in front of me.

James didn't move.

After I'd done that, I stood up and walked towards the door, where James was standing.

"James," I said. "I wonder if you'd do me a favour? I wonder if you'd take that reel off the projector for me?"

"Of course."

"Don't run it. Just bring it to me in the lounge."

I walked past him and through into the lounge and walked round the sunken area, to where the open freestanding brick fireplace was, square beneath its hood.

I put a match to the permanently set fire. By the time James came through it was blazing away quite nicely.

James gave me the reel, and I began to unwind the film, tearing off little bits of celluloid at a time, dropping them piece by piece into the flames.

"Jean's dead," I said.

For a while James was silent. Eventually, when he spoke, he said, "What will you do?"

I threw same more celluloid into the flames. Black smoke rushed up into the hood.

"You ought to go away for a while," James said. "I can take care of things. For a while you can be missing, presumed dead. I'll be able to square things in the long run. There's no evidence against you. Farlow won't feel like providing any, not with his support no longer around."

"Yes," I said.

"When everything's cooled down, they'll probably put you up for the Queen's medal when you come back. I mean, the entire Shepherdson family."

I didn't say anything.

"And don't you worry about me. I'll keep everything ticking over. Everything's very straightforward. I'll even be able to run rings round Parsons at the same time. But for the moment, I think it's safer, just in case Parsons does anything rash and out of character, like trying to fit you up."

I tore off another strip of celluloid.

"And it's better, as far as the Shepherdsons are concerned. There may be some young heroes on their books that would like to make a name by topping you."

"Yes," I said.

"Go to the place in Wales. You'll be safe there. You'll be able to keep in touch. I'll be able to come and see you and tell you what's happening."

"Yes."

"Nobody else knows about Wales?" he said. "Besides me?"

I shook my head.

"Good," he said. "You'll go to Wales, then?"

"Yes," I said. "I'll go to Wales."

But I didn't.
I went to Mablethorpe instead.
Where nobody, not even James, knew I had a place.

THE SEA

IT'S COLD IN THE basement.

I look at my watch. In an hour it'll be dawn.

What's keeping them?

Where are they?

I take the top off a fresh bottle of scotch and tumble some of it into the glass and drink.

I'm sitting at the far end of the basement, my back to the wall. Ahead of me, at the other end, are the steps, in full view.

Anybody wants to come and get me, they have to come down those steps.

There's been no activity from outside. Nobody trying to get in. I can't understand that. But at least when James gets here, he'll be able to talk to me, make suggestions, help in that way.

Where are they?

What's keeping them?

I take another drink, stop in mid-gulp.

Is that the sound of a car? Or is it my imagination?

I get up and go to the foot of the steps and listen.

It's the sound of a car. Getting nearer, slowing, as it bumps along the track between the trees.

I lift the trapdoor slightly.

Yes. It's the sound of a car.

The sound stops.

I push back the trapdoor and climb up into the garage.

Silence.

Then, beyond the garage door, the sound of a car door opening.

Nothing.

Then footsteps.

Cautiously walking to the flight of steps that leads to the bungalow's front door.

I go over to the switches and flip one. Whoever is outside will now be illuminated by the outside light.

"Christ," from outside, as whoever it is dashes back to the cover of the car.

Silence again.

I wait, by the switches.

Eventually a voice says, "George?"

I close my eyes and lean against the wall.

"George?" James says again.

I flip the switch that elevates the garage door and, still holding the Browning, I walk forward to the edge of the garage light.

A car door opens and James gets out.

"George," he says. "Are you all right?"

I just stand there, glad.

The faint dawn light begins to define and separate the trees behind James and the car.

Two more cars' doors open and two more figures get out and begin to walk towards the starker light of the garage. They're both carrying shotguns.

Well prepared.

Then I squint into the darkness as the taller of the two figures comes closer to the light.

The figure is familiar. It begins, slowly, to raise the shotgun it's carrying, taking hold in both hands, pointing the shotgun towards me.

The figure is one I know very well.

It's Ray Warren.

I hurl myself across the face of the garage and I'm rounding the corner of the house as the first blast shatters into the brickwork.

"Take it easy," I hear James call out. "Take your time. Don't make a pig's ear of it."

I run down the side of the house and turn the other corner and take off through the trees for the gorse, in the direction of the beach.

Once I'm out of the trees and into the gorse all I can do is to keep on running. I can hear them, crashing through the gorse behind me, not firing until they've got a target they're certain of hitting.

Ray Warren. I can't believe it. Ray's dead. Mickey topped him. Mickey topped Ray. And James. I—

A shotgun booms out behind me. One of them has tried a shot. I throw myself down into the gorse and roll over and over and then I reach the beginning of the sand dunes. Just one small dune and I'll be out of sight.

I scramble up the small hillock and roll over the top.

Another blast screams above my head. I get to my feet and run along the depression of the interlocking dunes until I reach the track that leads on to the beach.

I turn on to the track and suddenly, beside me, as if she's been waiting for me round the corner of one of the dunes, there's Lesley, running alongside me.

"Don't stop," she says. "Hurry. You'll be safe with me."

She takes my hand, still running, towards the gap that opens on to the broad beach.

"Hurry," she says, "it's getting light."

Now we're on the beach, running towards the tank, a just-discernible blot against the early-morning blueness of the sea and the sky.

"Hurry," she says, "you've got to hide. You know where to hide, don't you? You'll be safe there."

The tank is getting closer.

"Don't worry," she says. "I'll help you. You've got to hide first."

We reach the tank.

"Quickly," she says. "Inside. You'll be safe inside."

I clamber into the turret; she follows me down. There's just room for the two of us.

Silence.

I look at her.

She smiles at me, knees up against her chest.

"Don't worry," she says. "I won't leave you. Not now."

Outside, on the beach, there are sounds.

I look through the observation slit.

I can only see one of them.

I squeeze the Browning through the gap and fire but I'm a mile wide. The figure runs out of sight, to my blind side.

All I can do is to listen to them discussing what they're going to do. I can't hear the words, just the voices, soft, thoughtful.

Then, when they've come to a decision, I can hear some of the words.

"Right," Ray's voice says. "I'll wait here. If he sticks his nut out I'll take it off for him. But don't be long. It'll soon be daylight."

I look through the slit again. The other one is running back down the beach.

I loose off another shot but I can't get a proper aim.

"Leave it out, George," Ray calls. "That won't get you anywhere."

I look at Lesley.

But she's not there any more.

"Lesley!" I scream. "Don't leave me!"

Silence.

I look up at the sky through the turret top.

"Lesley!"

I stick my head through the gap. All I can see is Ray Warren, thirty feet away, levelling his shotgun.

I hit the bottom of the tank as the blast slams the turret with a sound of thunder.

Then there is another sound, a small scrambling. Lesley reappears through the hole in the turret, squats down opposite me.

She smiles.

I stare at her.

"Ssh," she says. "It won't be long now."

I open my mouth.

"Don't," she says. "I won't leave you."

The sound of a car at the gap that opens on to the beach. I look through the observation slit again.

Headlights made golden by the deep blue of dawn.

A door slams.

The other man comes running back along the beach.

Carrying something. Something flat, rectangular.

As the figure gets closer, the flat rectangular shape makes a swishing swilling sound.

As if there's liquid inside it.

"Hurry up," Ray calls to the running figure.

I look at Lesley.

She's still there.

Still smiling.

"Don't worry," she says. "You'll be all right with me."

She stretches out a hand and touches me on my wrist.

"Stay," she says. "You'll be safe here. Honestly."

There's somebody on the roof of the tank. Crawling. Something clanks against the blackened iron. Metal against metal.

Something swills.

Something is unscrewed, slowly.

I look at Lesley.

She smiles at me.

"Don't go," she says. "Not now."

She touches my wrist again.

“Don’t leave me now,” she says.

Suddenly, drifting in from outside, there is the smell of petrol.

Then it’s filling the inside of the tank, raining down on our heads in its liquid form, splashing all over us.

I scream.

Lesley smiles.

I look up at the turret. There is a great blossoming whooshing noise and beyond the turret lid the dawn blue sky turns orange, and then the inside of the tank turns the same colour and I can’t stop screaming; can’t stop looking at Lesley, a mirror image to myself, as her skin and her flesh burn brightly away, burning off her, beginning here and there to reveal the bone underneath. The dark glasses melt and fuse into her eyeless sockets and the last of her flesh falls away from her as she smiles her final smile at me.

THE SMOKE

STANDING IN FRONT OF the plate-glass window of the Penthouse, James raised his glass and said, "To your continuing good health."

"Cheers," Ray said. "Here's luck."

They both drank.

James smiled to himself.

Luck was right. A lot had depended on luck, on chance. But that was the way it had to be; informal, flexible. So as not to have tipped their hand. It had been a hand played with a lot of wild cards, of necessity. And playing them against Fowler, the risks had been extremely high.

But it had worked.

Not entirely as expected, but it had worked.

It had had to work. Fowler had had to be stopped; the Force could wear so much, but the torturings and the killings had been in danger of becoming too public. Justice would have to be seen to be done. And if that had happened, the Force itself would have come out of it extremely badly.

So, of course, James thought, would his good self.

The trouble was, his association with Fowler's organisation had been extremely valuable. Too valuable to terminate.

So. The association with Fowler had to be terminated. But not with his organisation.

Terminate Fowler. Not his organisation.

Otherwise the torturings and the killings would have continued and Fowler would have gone down and taken James with him. Fowler had enough on file to see to that. And Collins, and perhaps Farlow, if the Shepherdsons were involved.

Parsons had been particularly concerned about that. Parsons hadn't wanted any more Law in the headlines.

James smiled again.

"What's tickling you?" Ray said. "Got a feather in your Y-fronts?"

James shook his head and sat down at the glass-topped desk.

"I was just thinking about Parsons," James said.

"Yeah," Ray said. "How about him?"

"Amazing, really," James said. "When he first approached me, I'd expected dark warnings concerning the wages of sin."

"Yeah," Ray said, "instead of just wages."

"Well, now, be fair," James said. "His seat on the board isn't purely due to that particular kind of self-interest. After all, he's extremely well placed to make sure there isn't the kind of surface activity that would lead to the Force being brought into any further disrepute. He was very concerned about that."

"Like Collins and Farlow were concerned," Ray said.

"For totally different reasons," James said. "Be fair."

"The Filth's the Filth," Ray said.

James shrugged.

"They all helped, in their own ways. All three of them."

Which, to an extent, was true. But without Parsons, of course, the other two could never have been rowed in.

Together, he and Parsons had reached an agreement.

The agreement being, irrespective of method, remove the Fowlers. Continue the running of the business, so that its dissolution wouldn't lead the press into further pastures of police corruption.

A more stable figurehead, maintaining a lower profile.

And a seat on the board for Parsons, to ensure the maintaining of the organisation's low profile. Which would keep the Commissioner happy.

What he didn't know always kept the Commissioner happy.

"You have to remember," James said, "if it hadn't been for Farlow, we'd never have discovered your arrangements with the Shepherdsons before Fowler got to you."

"There is that, I suppose."

"Certainly there is. And your new status, as surrogate figurehead."

"I have to admit," Ray said. "It certainly worked out a treat."

A treat, James thought. Not only Fowler, but the Shepherdsons as well.

Parsons had been particularly pleased about that.

The trick had been that neither Fowler nor the Shepherdsons had known what was going on.

Fowler had had to think that Mickey had been involved with Ray; it had had to look as if he'd killed Ray before Fowler could get to him and make him talk. Killing Glenda had been a stroke of genius. It had made Mickey look more like the candidate they'd wanted him to seem, more as if the Sheps were trying to fit Fowler up.

And all the Shepherdsons had thought was that Fowler had tumbled to Ray. They genuinely hadn't understood about Glenda, and their supposed association with Mickey.

And Fowler had swallowed. To him, it looked as if Mickey and the Sheps were combining together in a takeover bid.

And when Collins had fed Fowler the pack of lies about what Johnny was supposed to have said, that had been the clincher.

Ironic—Collins's reward was the money for the lies. Paid for by Fowler.

Farlow's reward came from Parsons; not to point A10 in his direction.

When the inevitable explosion had arrived, James hadn't

counted on the way the Shepherdsons had retaliated for Johnny, with Jean.

But that couldn't have worked out better, either.

The only trouble had been, Fowler had got out alive.

And he hadn't gone to Wales, where James could have had him seen to.

But at least for the time being, he'd been out of the picture; business since the aftermath had been got under way.

It was going to take a miracle to find out where he'd gone to ground; Parsons hadn't wanted the Law to find him. He'd wanted the legend printed in the press to be preserved, missing believed dead.

And it had made a good press. O'Connell had been very helpful in that respect. The Law had come out of it looking as if they'd just been about to collar the lot of them before they topped each other.

But it was going to take a miracle to find him.

A miracle, apparently, had happened.

It had taken the shape of madness.

Hardly surprising, after what the Shepherdsons had done to Jean Fowler, brooding on it in his isolation.

Ray picked up the copy of the Grimsby *Evening Telegraph* and looked at the news item again. The headline read:

ACCIDENTAL DEATH OF MAN ON BOMBING RANGE:
TRAGEDY AS MAN TRIES TO AVOID MISSILES

The story went on to describe how the body of a Mr. Roy Carson, an occasional visitor to the area, had been discovered in a tank used as a target in RAF rocket manoeuvres on a beach near Mablethorpe. It was assumed Mr. Carson had ignored the red warning flag and had taken cover in the tank when the manœuvres had begun.

"Handy," Ray said, indicating the newspaper.

"Not if we hadn't cleared the house it wouldn't have been."

"No," Ray said.

He lit a cigarette.

"What I can't understand," he said, "was all that business at the end; all that screaming and shouting for some bloke called Lesley."

"It wasn't," James said.

"Beg pardon?"

"It wasn't a he. It was a she. On the phone, he kept saying she, Lesley. She's here. All that."

"At the time, Gerry and I thought he'd got some assistance who'd hopped it as soon as we turned up."

"No, it was definitely female, whoever he was referring to."

"Yeah, I know," Ray said. "But he was on his own when we done him. But it didn't stop him screeching his head off as if she was in the immediate vicinity."

James stood up and picked up his and Ray's glasses and took them over to where the drinks were.

"Maybe she was female company he'd got hold of. Could even have sent down for her," Ray said.

James shook his head.

"He wouldn't. Whoever she was, he'd picked her up up there. He wouldn't risk it."

Ray thought about it. With his track record, he knew a lot of the girls on Fowler's books.

"Lesley," he said. "Lesley."

James came back to the table and set the brandies down on the glass top.

Ray picked up his glass, shook his head.

"Lesley," he said.

He swilled the brandy round in his glass.

"No," he said. "No; the only Lesley I can think of who we ever had was a bird called Lesley Murray."

"Who was that?"

"Used to be a fair piece. A singer. Good, as I recall. Sang at the Moulin for a while."

"What happened to her?" James said.

"I remember Mickey pulled her out one time, told her to meet this particular bloke in a pub. Just pull him, get a lift home. Nothing else. 'Course, the fellow she was pulling was only Jean's old man, wasn't he? And she naturally didn't know the steering had been fixed, did she? Or she wouldn't have gone, would she? So, what happened to him, happened to her."

"I remember," James said. "A casualty, so to speak."

"Yeah," Ray said. "Anyway, that's the only Lesley I can call to mind, in my experience of the firm. I mean, he didn't even know her name. She was just somebody Mickey fixed up for him."

James took a sip of his brandy.

"Well," he said, "I'll say one thing for him."

"What's that?"

"He kept an extremely acceptable brandy."

"Yeah," Ray said, drinking. "Very nice. Very warming."

THE SEA

EDDIE WALKED INTO THE Dunes, holding the rolled-up newspaper, but this time there was no thigh-slapping, no three-chord mental harmony to add a spring to his step.

Howard had his pint ready, as usual, by the time he reached the bar.

Eddie put his change down, took a deep drink.

"Better?" Howard said.

Eddie took another drink, dropped the newspaper on the bar's surface.

"Seen this?" Eddie said.

"I've seen it."

Eddie shook his head.

"Lucky for some," Howard said.

All right, Eddie thought. Make your remarks, you stupid old puff. You don't have to think about the extra you're now no longer going to get.

"Still," Howard said. "Not surprising, really."

"How do you mean?"

Howard mimed tippling a glass.

"Yeah," said Eddie. "Well."

He took another drink.

"You haven't seen Lesley about, have you?"

"Not today."

"Only we're playing the Kings Arms at Tealby tonight. Haven't made the arrangements. About the time."

"Been in the South?"

"Yeah. No sign."

"Probably be in later on."

"Yeah."

Eddie drank the remains of his pint.

"Anyway," he said, "I'll go and have another look."

Leaving the newspaper on the counter, Eddie walked out of the Dunes and along the mini-promenade until he came to the row of bollards at the top of the ramp. The sky was clear and blue and the beach was almost golden in the morning sunshine.

The fellows on the funfair were testing the ferris wheel again. Eddie watched them for a few moments, the black shadows of the circle and the struts revolving over him like a spool from some giant film projector.

Then, after a few moments, he walked down the ramp, towards the street and the South, in search of Lesley.

Afterword

Derek Raymond on Ted Lewis

GBH IS A NOVEL as direct as it is stunning. The impact of the opening scene, in which a group of villains, led by its psychopathic leader, tortures another villain, suspected of grassing, to death—indeed the tracking down of grasses and inside traitors, whether inside the mob or inside the police—underlines the author's loathing of all denunciation; and the book as a whole, which never relaxes its grip for a paragraph, has as shattering an impact on the reader as did its famous predecessor, *Jack's Return Home* [also published as *Get Carter*].

Ted Lewis died of alcohol in 1982 while he was still in his forties; and his death was a major loss. For, as the contemporary black novel in Britain is concerned, he was the prototype, the first in the field of my generation anyway, of the rebirth of black writing, so much so that, in *GBH*, the hallucinating effect that his portrait of the killer, described in the first person, has on the reader is one that the latter is unlikely to forget for some time—if, indeed, he ever succeeds in forgetting it.

Another point that needs stressing here is that, if Lewis is not much better-known than he should be in his own country, it is because, in the days when he was writing (I hope, I think the situation has improved now) the better written, the blacker, and more direct a novel was, the more liable it was to upset the delicate sensibilities of squeamish publishers whose blind devotion to—and thus fear of alienating—middle-class taste (which, above all, dreads reality in literature and anything that cannot be mentioned in the drawing room) was true across far too wide a sample of British editors. The bowdlerizing attitude reduced the quality of most British fiction to the level of the simpering dare, and of course, also biased editorial views in their commercial judgment—a judgment which, by the way, was at times ridiculously, indeed, quite spectacularly wrong. To take a classic example, my own first publisher's reaction to Len Deighton's *The Ipcress File:* "Interesting, but of course sheer fantasy . . . could be of no interest to the general reader . . ."

Moreover, the result of this attitude was that even if an enterprising junior editor in a big firm went out on a limb and accepted such novels as Lewis's, the governors upstairs, by not lifting a finger to promote them, went subliminally out of their way to make sure they were sabotaged.

Yet you have only to read him to see that Lewis was one of the first British writers in the sixties to take Chandler literally—"The crime story tips violence out of its vase on the shelf and pours it back down into the street where it belongs"—and *Jack's Return Home* is a book that I and plenty of other people at the time considered to be a classic on these grounds, besides the sheer writing ability that it displays, and still do. But it, too, has doubtless become unavailable, out of print, pulped, thanks to the attitude—virtually amounting to disinformation—prevalent in that section of British publishers that I have just referred to, which seems unshakably convinced that as long as Agatha Christie and P.D. James are selling all right, then you've quite honestly covered the ground, as well as not spitting on the Union Jack.

What this means, as I have said, is that they have covered a good deal of startling and original work with ground—i.e. buried it.

And besides, how wrong can you be? The difference between what people want to read now, as opposed to what their parents read fifty years ago, has changed as utterly as the problems that confront society (social realities which literature ideally exists to reflect) and that is why more and more black work is being produced in the UK now which has no point of reference whatever with the two writers I have just named.

What a pity Ted Lewis didn't live to see it.

Reading *GBH* I am mindful that its author was from the north of England; he was born in Manchester and studied for four years at Hull Art School—very probably at the same time as Peter Everett, who wrote *Negatives*, another very black novel, grossly underrated in Britain, which Cape published (rather nervously, if the incomprehensible jacket is anything to go by) in 1964, and which was subsequently filmed by Claude Chabrol. This book, just like Lewis's work, put murder back in the street too, in the suffocating slum existence of Notting Hill; it, too, joined madness and sexual perversion to murder (none of the three ever travel apart, whatever the M'Naghten Rules may say) just as Lewis's novels did.

As for those decaying, economically dying and unprivileged northern towns—Newcastle, Liverpool, Hull and Manchester—I have known some of them; apart from London they are the most violent, the most despairing we have, and Lewis's grasp of their atmosphere of hopelessness, the dialogue hissing with internecine distrust, boiling with hatred even among members of the same family, or apparently lifelong friends, makes me wonder just how closely the sinister stories he tells were, if not autobiographical, linked to people close to him in real life, perhaps family even; I find it hard to see how, where or why he made such a close study of them otherwise.

I knew Ted Lewis—no, I didn't, I only sat next to him. Nobody I knew ever knew Ted Lewis—it was impossible to get to know him, even superficially. I only met him because

Jack's Return Home appeared in the same Hutchinson's list, New Authors (long since defunct), as my own first novel; Lewis therefore frequented the same pub downstairs from Hutchinson's offices, the Horse and Groom in Great Portland Street, as the rest of us did (including my editor, Graham Nicol, and his). And for the same reason—not just for the beer, but to see if we couldn't dig a few more quid out of their pocket against our advances (we none of us ever had a light, and I, anyway, had an expensive girlfriend!).

But Lewis invariably sat on his own at the far end of the bar, and I never saw him with a girl. He usually sat bent over in an attitude vaguely resembling prayer with his head on his arms; and none of us ever got to know him, because he was always totally drunk. He was blond, good-looking, had a face I liked—and I wouldn't at all have minded a long talk with him or even a short one, particularly after I had read *Jack's Return Home*.

I never managed it. You could say something to him, but he never talked back, and when you looked at him all you got in return was the mysterious kind of look you might expect from a stained-glass window. That would have been in 1962 or '3 I suppose. Then I went back to Spain and Tangier, and I never saw him again.

I don't know if any of us in The Horse ever really knew him (I never saw him anywhere else). But then what person is more secretive than the speechless drunk?

Don't think that any of the foregoing is a criticism of Lewis; it isn't. It is just the memory I retain of him—and that a 28-year-old one. Criticism? Far from criticism, Lewis makes me think rather of what I imagine David Goodis to have been like, and I could hardly be more complimentary than that.

But to return to my beginning, reading *GBH* certainly gave me an insight into why its author drank. As I say, I reckon he knew a good deal of what he was writing about from very close to—perhaps dangerously so. That leaps out of his work immediately. Whatever the truth, he got their dialogue correct, right down to the last cadence.

So all I can do now is pay my respects to his courage which enabled him to write the way he did for as long as he did, describing the horror around him in terms of his own interior horror, if necessary with the help of alcohol or any other weapon to keep him going. By preferring to look the street straight in the face instead of peeping at it from behind an upstairs curtain, he cleared a road straight through the black jungle; and that, for me, would have earned him a place in the top rank even if he had survived.

He is an example of how dangerous writing can really be when it is done properly, and Ted Lewis's writing proved that he never ran away from the page.

No—because with Ted Lewis, the page was the battle.

Derek Raymond, Le Peuch, August 5th, 1990.